I AM USHRIYA

BEVERLY YOUNG

BALBOA.PRESS

A DIVISION OF HAY HOUSE

Balboa Press books may be ordered through booksellers or by contacting:

Balboa Press
A Division of Hay House
1663 Liberty Drive
Bloomington, IN 47403
www.balboapress.com
844-682-1282

Print information available on the last page.

ISBN: 978-1-9822-7847-2 (sc)
ISBN: 978-1-9822-7845-8 (hc)
ISBN: 978-1-9822-7846-5 (e)

Library of Congress Control Number: 2022901030

Balboa Press rev. date: 02/04/2022

USHRIYA

U shree a

(הָיִרְשׁוּא)

Hebrew name meaning "blessed of
God" or "fortunate of God."

Dedication: To my darling husband, Mark Douglas Young, who encouraged, cajoled, and critiqued with love and patience. When you passed into the loving arms of God, I promised I would someday hold a book in my hand. Here it is, my love. This is for you.

My most sincere heartfelt thanks to the following for bringing a dream to reality:

To **Donna Adams Enbysk**, for reading revisions, long conversations, patience, encouragement, faith, biblical knowledge, love, and long friendship. To **Gail Culbertson**, for the unrelenting support, biblical knowledge, long conversations, love, and long friendship. To **Tammy Everall**, for the creative banter, love, and long friendship. To **Caitlin Rose**, for your beautiful face, talent, and willingness to make Ushriya come alive. To **Cindy Hookland**, for the research of ancient hairstyles, then styling Ushriya's hair perfectly. To **Meghan Ceallaigh**, for highlighting Caitlin's face with expertise and magical art. To **Chris Sloan**, for flawlessly capturing Ushriya with a brilliant photographic eye and bringing her to life. To **Sharon Bryson**, who line-edited my manuscript with the utmost care, meticulous eye, patience, and love. To **John Larison**, my instructor at Oregon State University, who without him, this novel would not exist. To **Leslie Wells,** my editor, who sent me back to the computer more than once to expand and write the story she knew was there. To **Dee Marley**, whose Historical Fiction Club connected me to authors of the world and whose graphic design excellence created a book cover beyond my wildest dreams. To **Pastor Ben Bryson**, who listened to an inkling of an idea, then patiently ignited an interest in the early Christians and encouraged the writing. To my family, for their love and support, **Tony Jones, Carrie Jones, Spencer Jones, Tatum Jones, Lucy Jones, Declan Jones, and all of Mark's family**.

CHARACTERS

Ushriya	Main protagonist Fiction
Ruth	Ushriya's domina (Matron, slave owner in Rome) Fiction
Eliezer ben Zacchai	Ruth's father, Jewish priest Fiction
Marcus Acacia	Ruth's husband Fiction
Lucius Rufus Acacia	Marcus' father, aedile in Roman government Fiction
Empress Agrippina	Ushriya's mother Historical
Emperor Claudius	Ushriya's father Historical
Narcissus	Claudius' formerly enslaved person (secretary) Historical
Emperor Nero	Agrippina's son (Ushriyra's half-brother, fictional) Historical

Caligula	Agrippina's brother, immediate past Emperor of Rome before Claudius Historical
Messalina	Claudius' wife before Agrippina, mother of Britannica Historical
Britannicus	Claudius' son of Messalina Historical
Hanoch	Bakery owner Fiction
Justine	Hanoch's wife, Ushriya's adopted mother Fiction
Priscilla	Owner/Madame (Lena) of the brothel, the Lupanare Fiction
Augusta	Mother of Priscilla and Alexis, matriarch of the Lupanare Fiction
Alexis	Male prostitute at the Lupanare, Ushriya's lover Fiction
Servius	Bakery slave, also a medicine slave, Ruth's lover Fiction

Centaurus	Bakery slave Fiction
Bacchus, Nigel	Slave traders Fiction
Quintus	Oldest slave child in the slave cargo Fiction
Cyrus	Oldest son of Hanoch and Justine Fiction
Julius	Youngest son of Hanoch and Justine Fiction
Camas	Bakery slave of Justine Fiction
Flavia	Bakery slave who befriends Ruth Fiction
Pauline	Famulus of the villa di Poppaea Sabina in Oplontis Fiction
Dominicus	Head guard of the villa di Poppaea Sabina Fiction
Emericus	Overseer of the slaves at the villa di Poppaea Sabina Fiction

Gustavus	Driver of the slaves at the villa di Poppaea Sabina
	Fiction
Timeus	Melita's boyfriend
	Fiction
Gaius Antonius	Ushriya and Alexis's baby boy
	Fiction

CONTENTS

Chapter 1 1

Chapter 2 9

Chapter 3 15

Chapter 4 21

Chapter 5 27

Chapter 6 33

Chapter 7 39

Chapter 8 47

Chapter 9 53

Chapter 10 59

Chapter 11 65

Chapter 12 71

Chapter 13 75

Chapter 14 83

Chapter 15 99

Chapter 16 105

Chapter 17 111

Chapter 18 119

Chapter 19 125

Chapter 20 131

Chapter 21 139

Chapter 22 145

Chapter 23 151

Chapter 24 157

Chapter 25 163

Chapter 26 169

Chapter 27 177
Chapter 28 183
Chapter 29 189
Chapter 30 195
Chapter 31 201
Chapter 32 207
Chapter 33 213
Chapter 34 219
Chapter 35 225
Chapter 36 231
Chapter 37 237
Chapter 38 243
Chapter 39 249
Chapter 40 255
Chapter 41 263
Chapter 42 271
Chapter 43 279
Chapter 44 285
Chapter 45 293
Chapter 46 301
Chapter 47 307
Chapter 48 315

CHAPTER 1

AUGUST 20, AD 48

A baby was not in the emperor's plans, and certainly not with his niece.

"Silence that woman!" Claudius' voice boomed through the palace. Agrippina's relentless screams echoed from the birthing chamber. Claudius trembled, nervously running his fingers through his thin gray hair. He was not looking forward to how this birth must end and now his age was beginning to betray him. He grew weaker with the passing years and not even his nobility could protect him from the birth of an unwelcomed baby. From the chambers, he heard doors slamming, slaves running back and forth to the culina carrying water, bringing fresh cloths to soothe Agrippina's angry labor. Slaves who practiced medicine were discreetly escorted to the chambers by the emperor's freedman.

This baby was ill-fated. Along with illegitimacy and the need for secrecy, Claudius worried about strengthening the perverted bloodline of Agrippina's brother, Caligula. The madness of his nephew, the immediate past emperor of Rome, assassinated only eight years earlier, was well-known for his feats of cruelty that terrorized the imperial city and branded the young man of twenty-nine years; a monster. Claudius had not wanted to give credence to his already tarnished family, but here it was.

The emperor's vulnerability to gorgeous women was legendary, and Agrippina's extraordinary intelligence enhanced his desire. He had not seen her since she was a child, so she captivated him when she entered the palace for a chance visit. Eyes wide on her face, a long suitable nose centered above her small feminine jaw, she wore her golden red hair in the braided fashion of the elites. She made no attempt to cover an eye-catching white streak in her hair just above the right side of her forehead. And her walk. She seemed to float above the ground as if levitating. She also had a double canine in her right upper jaw which, all Romans, especially Claudius, regarded as a measure of good luck.

Agrippina's visits to the palace became more frequent, and reasons for their regularity more transparent. Day by day, her erotic presence aroused Claudius to the point of neglecting his duties.

On a warm day in spring, when the green tender leaves burst on the lemon trees outside his window, Claudius nodded as the door opened from the tablinum. It was Narcissus, his longtime secretary freedman, whom he had not seen in a while.

"Agrippina would like your audience, my emperor."

The mere mention of her name stirred Claudius.

"I am delighted at your presence, Narcissus. I didn't know you were just now in residence. I had heard you were going to return. A pleasure. And yes, of course, please escort Agrippina in at once." With the niceties finished and relieved he hadn't stuttered, Claudius eagerly watched the door slowly open. A subdued purple toga hugged Agrippina's curves as she glided towards him. Narcissus bowed and walked backwards out of the door. Claudius was oblivious.

"My emperor, I have brought you the first lavender of the season." With a deep curtsy and a calculated feminine tilt of her golden-red braids, her long eyelashes fluttered. As he stood, his knees buckled, but found his balance.

"I am grateful for your gift." Claudius' stammer subsided. His trembling stopped. Stepping down from the throne dais as though magnetically pulled, his face softened as he approached her. She gradually looked up until her eyes met his. "May I kiss you?" he asked.

"I would be honored, my emperor." Agrippina closed her eyes and his lips met hers. Gently at first, then forcefully pulling her to him, his kisses became insistent. The lavender fell to the floor.

Aware that Agrippina had an appetite for powerful men, Claudius understood that a man of influence, regardless of his age, was merely a means to power for her. Even her own brother, Caligula, whom she had regularly bedded was a just another step to her goal. This complicated, notorious woman genuinely believed that an incestuous relationship could only make any child she bore much more sovereign, and the possibility thrilled her. Strengthening the family of Augusta also meant she had to win the hearts and loyalty of the people she led. He had watched her present herself in privileged company with style and majesty as she skillfully learned to manipulate the masses. Her charm and education espoused old elite Roman traditions, which impressed Claudius. He was pleased that all who witnessed Agrippina treated her as an empress. While Claudius had great lust for her, he also knew that she intended to maintain the rights and privileges afforded her position at all costs. And even though she had little to no conscience, and could breach rules of humanity at a whim, Claudius could not renounce her. He suspected that if she had found it necessary to kill her own brother, who had become an obstacle in her path, she would not see the immorality of it. Claudius had no doubt that she was, indeed, involved in his murder. Murder was a way of life in the family of Augustus. But unlike her brother, Claudius knew Agrippina's callous, murderous, qualities were well-disguised, unknown to her admirers and covertly wrought.

This baby, as it entered the world, would be a concentrated blend of the might and flaws of all facets of the imperial lineage. In an ideal situation, if born a male, he could be one of the most powerful heirs ever to ascend to Roman sovereignty. Pacing feebly back and forth through the halls of the palace, Claudius heard Agrippina's cries intensify.

"Tiberius Claudius Drusus Nero Germanicus, I loathe your existence!" With each push, Agrippina exhaled profanities.

Gazing up at the palace's crimson walls bordered in gold, Claudius rolled his eyes. A knock at the door interrupted his thoughts.

"Emperor, may I have a word?" The gigantic wooden door creaked open. Narcissus stepped in.

"Please enter, Narcissus. I need d-d-d-distraction from the constant screaming and profanity of that woman. W-w-w-hat have you?" The diversion relieved Claudius but wrinkled his face when he stammered. "Another p-p-plot to end my life? Or are the Jews causing disorder once again?"

"No, my emperor. You will live a long life. But there have been requests for your presence at houses of the ill and there are many who have requested to resume sacrificial rituals. And, yes, the Jews are gathering, some are encouraging the ideas of a new teacher." Narcissus' voice was cautious.

"No to the requests of my presence out of the palace. I will not give another assassin with a knife a chance at me! I would sooner abdicate my r-r-r-oyal duties than present myself as a t-t-t-target." Claudius' temper flared with panic. "As for the Jews, must I expel them if they cannot adhere to the law?"

As the emperor of Rome and after the assassination in year AD 41 of his malicious grand-nephew and stepson Caligula, Claudius ruled with suspicion and anxiety. He was afraid of most things. Before he entered any premises, guards went before him to search for danger. Any prepared food was thrown out if not witnessed by one of his entourage. Unexpected visitors were not permitted entrance to the palace. Assassination plot rumors relentlessly tyrannized his frail, sickly constitution to the point of ordering freedman to observe him while he slept.

With increasing trust in his ever-present guards, he became more confident as emperor. Though not slender, with a full neck, he was tall and had a commanding presence when seated. But as he walked, he wavered: his legs occasionally collapsing beneath him during stressful times. He stuttered when he spoke, especially if he was worried or angry, at which time saliva foamed at his mouth and his nose ran. His head shook frequently, causing him to appear dull and stupid, especially when he dealt with matters of the Roman Empire. His maladies made him impatient and angry, but the frequent loss of his temper could work to his favor. Those around him saw this as a sign that he was a strong leader.

Frequent large banquets of meat and alcohol contributed to another condition: stomach ailments. So much so, he often thought he wanted to die. Gluttony and intoxication led to the emperor falling asleep with his mouth agape. It was a ghastly and dishonorable sight for an emperor, but one all too familiar. One story had it that his servants tickled his throat with a feather so he would vomit. But with all his disgusting ailments, Agrippina saw abundant opportunity in Claudius.

"Your royal Emperor. I will reject the inquirer's requests." Narcissus knew he rarely left the palace but was prepared to use his position as the royal secretary to communicate to the military that the emperor would require added protection, in the event Claudius changed his mind.

The ruler returned to his chair by his favorite window where he found a scroll on the table, along with a quill and ink bottle. He tried to concentrate on his projects of public works but instead toyed with the quill. Agrippina's shrill cries were incessant.

All Claudius could do at this moment was sit, wait, and yearn for Agrippina to finally deliver a girl. A female child would make his decision to expose his own baby, though royal, uncomplicated. No questions asked. He did not have to be responsible for an illegitimate female child who could not be his heir. Abandonment meant certain death of an ill-timed, female infant. Claudius had the authority of life and death over all his children, so it would be socially acceptable amongst the elites to expose the child or let it die and not have the responsibility of an ample dowry for a girl.

When Agrippina informed him she was with child, his anger erupted.

"The gods will condemn you, Agrippina! You told me a baby was not possible! You have betrayed me. We are not yet betrothed. You are the daughter of my brother; this baby is illegitimate. We both have sons. I will not allow it!"

"Emperor, calm yourself. This baby could very well be a girl... and I will stay hidden within the palace so no one will see me," Agrippina placated him.

Claudius dismissed her from the room.

He desired a wife, but neither he nor Agrippina welcomed another child. They didn't need another heir. They both had sons. Claudius had Britannicus, and Agrippina had Nero. Both understood secretly that Agrippina would be Claudius' next wife. There were other women outside the palace, but none compared to Agrippina's wealth, beauty, and pedigree. Claudius pondered the challenge of bringing Nero, Agrippina's son, into the royal line as his stepson. Nero was four years older than Britannicus, Claudius' son with his third wife, Messalina. By aristocratic traditions, Britannicus was heir to the throne, but Claudius feared Agrippina would favor Nero as the heir. When lust subsided and he regained his senses, Claudius was fully aware Agrippina lived for purposes of the aristocracy and was manipulating the union of Nero to his daughter Octavia. Claudius was mindful that this whole situation put Britannicus in harm's way since Agrippina's goal was that one day her only son would be the future emperor of Rome. Another child would complicate the circumstances. Yet, right now, at the birth of this baby, for once, he could appreciate Agrippina's ruthless character. He was confident his conniving niece, mistress, and future Empress was capable of killing this inconvenient child, no matter the sex.

At last, the staccato cries of a newborn reverberated through the palace. Claudius took a deep breath. Agrippina's screams quieted. Narcissus emerged from the birthing chamber and approached Claudius with head bowed.

"Agrippina is sleeping. You have a healthy, beautiful daughter, your majesty. She carries the white streak in her red hair; the same as her mother and her brother, Nero."

Claudius scowled.

"Prepare it before Agrippina awakens. Bring it to the atrium vestae."

CHAPTER 2

Grave disapproval came from the Roman people and elites when they learned of Claudius and Agrippina's affair. An affair and marriage between an uncle and a niece were prohibited under Roman law, notwithstanding an illegitimate child. Senators rushed to spread gossip of the illicit relationship to all who would listen. Word of mouth ruled communication in Rome. News of the birth of this child would only add to the already shaky confidence of Claudius' governance. Never having exposed a child, especially one he knew to be his royal bloodline, the concept was entirely different when it was right in front of him. What if he allowed it to live? What would its life be like? Would Agrippina kill it, even if he didn't? He feared so. But he had no choice.

"At your request, the baby has been taken to the House of the Vestal Virgins, the atrium vestae, Emperor," Narcissus informed him. "Would you like me to accompany you?" Narcissus watched as Claudius' trembling, stuttering, and muscle weakness returned as he strained to conceal his emotions.

"Yes, N-n-narcissus." Claudius stammered. "Your assistance would be greatly appreciated." He rose from his satin chair like a man much older than his fifty-nine years. Narcissus rushed to the emperor's side and gently helped Claudius to his feet. Faltering,

Claudius stepped on his toga, causing a cascade of Tyrian purple to fall away from his shoulders.

"Let me rearrange your toga to ease your path, Emperor," Narcissus said, trying to save Claudius' dignity. "Will you be needing your royal staff or scepter? Or would you appreciate the small cart? The house slaves may bring it to you promptly."

"Ah Narcissus. It is always y-y-you who has been here for m-m-me in times of d-difficulty. No, I do not need a cart. Walking will clear my head. Let's go to the a-a-atrium." Claudius was pleased his most favored freedman was with him.

Beams of sunlight brightened their path as Claudius and Narcissus made their way from Claudius' tablinum through the colonnade. Crimson columns with rings of azure at the tops and bottoms lined the hallway of the spectacularly crafted, bronzed marble floors. Large paintings with pictures of royal battles hung on both sides of the long passage. High-arched tray ceilings, lined in ornate gold molding, towered above them. At the end of the grand hallway, Rome's namesake, the baby Romulus, suckled at the breast of his adopted mother wolf with his brother Remus. Preoccupied with the diminished strength in his legs, Claudius resolved to make it to the atrium, conserving energy with his silence. Narcissus stayed close as they turned right around a corner passing the royal gardens. Claudius slowed his steps. The beautifully manicured gardens were in full bloom. Ordinarily, he would stop to admire the grounds which the palace slaves toiled all year to maintain, but this day he kept going. Planted with hedges in perfect geometric shapes, walking paths strategically wove through the flower beds of vivid reds, yellows, oranges, and purples. Planned carefully to sequentially replace each flowering plant when it had finished its season, the gardens burst with color throughout the entirety of summer. Roses of every hue surrounded the whole area. Never wasted, the flowers were used in perfumes and decor at the palace. Trees of apples, cherries, and pears provided fresh fruit at the emperor's feasts. Claudius' favorite lemon trees planted especially for him grew beside the windows of the tablinum.

Unmindful of his surroundings, Claudius was elsewhere in his thoughts. He slowed his stride to regain control of his legs. Passing through the eastern edge of the Forum, they grew nearer to the House of the Vestals.

"Narcissus, do you have children?" Claudius inquired.

"No, Emperor. I have never married." Narcissus was surprised by the question. "My life's work has been in the service of Rome. My work is all I have known," he replied with a hint of melancholy.

Claudius brought his hand to his chin, "Have you had a special woman?"

In all the years Narcissus had known Claudius, he had never asked about his personal life, but Narcissus indulged him.

"Yes. She was quite lovely. I met her at Circus Maximus. Sadly, my love died in childbirth before we could marry. It was then I listened to the gods. They knew that having a family was not my fate. That was long ago, before I came to your service."

"Ah, Narcissus. There are the up s-s-sides and the downsides of both. While women are impossible to understand and very demanding, they are so damn irresistible! My l-l-l-loins have never been able to resist a lovely woman. I find the most b-b-b-beautiful come with a high emotional price, paid with s-s-sanity and wealth. I know, I have paid both. I have never had the fortune of luck with the love of a good woman. I f-f-fear I am about to continue the tradition. One of the h-h-h-highest prices I will have ever paid is what I am about to do. No baby deserves what I am bound to w-w-wield." Claudius dropped his head and sighed. "I have deeply considered what e-e-e-lites would do when they come upon this same situation. Many have relegated undesirable daughters to the H-house of the Vestal Virgins to live out their lives. I have put g-g-great thought and consideration into the idea. Admittance isn't permitted until the age of six. Where would she stay until then? And then after her admission, as she becomes known--and she will, because of the mark she carries from her mother--she will be chastised or even murdered. It is best that I, as her father, spare her that fate. I can't allow myself to ponder the whole rotten situation any further. I will do the only thing I can to honor her, by taking her into the House of the Vestals. She will be in the hands of the gods."

Baby gurgles echoed against the cavernous walls of the long, opulent atrium vestae as Claudius and Narcissus entered. Three stories tall, totaling fifty rooms, it looked out on the atrium courtyard. Two large fountains gushed torrents of water towering above ponds lined with roses surrounded by dazzling colorful tiles and brilliant sunlit pools. Imported red and silk chairs graced the colonnades for the convenience of guests. Marble statues honoring past vestals lined the great atrium.

Claudius stood motionless. A female nurse slave, with braided black hair, sat cross-legged with the baby cradled in her arms at the furthest end of the pool, singing softly. She didn't notice Claudius and Narcissus approach.

"E-hmmm." Narcissus alerted her to their presence. She stood and bowed her head. Narcissus turned to his Emperor. "Would you like to hold her?"

"My Emperor, I was just...." The nurse slave stammered. Narcissus nodded, motioning her to put the baby down on the sapphire blue mosaic floor. She obeyed and backed away. "Shall I stay?" she asked.

"Yes." Narcissus answered. "But behind the corridor, out of sight." Claudius fell forward. Narcissus quickly assisted him.

"Ah, ye gods! What have I done?" Claudius raised his hands to the sky as he spoke. "This innocent baby has no say in her fate. She is my daughter. She is my blood. She is my legacy. But she is not an heir, she is illegitimate and bears the mark of her mother. What kind of life would she have? I cannot allow her to live. I have no satisfaction in choosing to expose her." He dropped his arms by his side and arose with Narcissus' help. "When Agrippina awakens, tell her the baby did not live." Claudius turned to exit. "I will walk back to the tablinum alone."

When he was out of the atrium, Narcissus went to the nurse slave.

Tears trickled down Claudius' face as he made his way.

"Please stay with the baby until she has left this earth. When she has passed, take her to the infants' site." Narcissus turned to follow Claudius in case he needed help.

The young woman cradled and rocked, knowing the baby was healthy and it would be hours before she passed. Shaking, then crying, then wailing, the baby began to cry along with her.

CHAPTER 3

AUGUST 21, AD 48

Hanoch and Justine were well-known for their sweet, nutty bread made with flour from spelt grain. Grown in small plots throughout the Roman Empire, spelt grain was far easier to chew than the coarse flour used in most Roman diets. Hanoch held tightly the secret recipe he'd learned from his father. The bakery thrived and supported his family for generations.

As they made their way toward the exit of the palace grounds, Hanoch reflected on the last two summers since Emperor Claudius had visited Pompeii. A need for fresh bread had sent a palace kitchen slave onto the streets in search of a bakery. She'd found Hanoch and Justine between one of the great houses and the main thoroughfare of the Via dell'Abbodanza. Along with their two sons, the couple lived in the upstairs of a two-story building operating their bakery downstairs. After this chance encounter, Claudius was so impressed by the tasty bread, he requested Hanoch, and Justine bring as much bread as would stay fresh whenever they made trips to Rome. Hanoch smiled as he remembered his modest cart of bread on their first visit. On one particularly grand occasion of another festival, the same kitchen slave suggested to the emperor that he invite them to stay in Rome

---

and make bread at the palace, so it would be fresh for the festival. Honored by the request, Hanoch immediately found a spelt farmer slightly outside of Rome who could supply flour, making it easy to stop by the farm on his way to the palace. The palace opened their culina, creating a special section especially for Hanoch's breadmaking. Several times, Hanoch brought Servius, his most favored slave, to assist. Association with the royal Emperor was such a colossal success that trips to Rome became more frequent, and subsequently word spread in Pompeii. Soon everyone in Pompeii wanted a loaf of the "royal spelt" bread.

"Do you hear a baby? I do. That's a baby crying!" Justine exclaimed to her husband as he maneuvered the donkeys around the outside of the atrium. Ears down, the noises of horns on the grounds of the palace always made them anxious. A loud crack sounded from the back wheel, and Hanoch slowed the edgy animals to a halt. He jumped down, motioning for Justine to take the reins. The cart tilted back. "Hanoch, I can still hear a baby. Why is there a baby in the House of the Vestal Virgins?" Justine knew of the virgins; this was a sacred place where two young virgins guarded the fire of Vesta, the Goddess of the Hearth. The women weren't allowed relations with men, so childbirth was forbidden. A baby should not be here. A vestal could be burnt alive if it were found she lost her sacred virginity to rid the disgrace of a child born out of wedlock.

"Silence, Justine! Mind the reins! Get the donkeys to rock back and forth so we can get out of this rut. Hmmmpf, -- a rut in a palace road!" Disgusted, Hanoch shook his long auburn hair and heaved a sigh. Justine halfheartedly obeyed. The donkeys stepped back and then pitched forward, pulling the cart free.

"What luck the back wheel didn't split." Justine fretted, looking in the direction of the baby's cries.

"Hanoch! Do you hear that baby? I'm getting down off this cart to see." Not waiting for his reply, she moved her toga aside to step down and made her way to the open arch on the side of the atrium vestae. "Come with me." Justine motioned behind her.

"You know men are not allowed in the House of the Vestals. I'll wait here." Hanoch reluctantly tied the donkeys to a nearby post. His wife's stubborn streak made him wary of what was to come. "Be careful!" He called.

As Justine drew closer to the baby, she heard sobbing. The structure of the Templum Vestae echoed cries throughout its vast spaces. Disoriented, she rounded a tall column and saw the shadow of a woman rocking a baby. When the woman became aware of Justine, she immediately lay the baby down and dashed out of the atrium. Justine rushed towards her, but she vanished in an instant.

"Why would you leave your baby? Are you a vestal?" Justine called, hurrying into the atrium, darting right, then left. She caught a glimpse of the young woman, but then she disappeared hastily around a corner. "Have you had a baby you can't keep?" Justine's shouts echoed as she dropped to her knees beside the squalling infant. The vestals wore white togas, but the young woman left before Justine could discern if her clothing was white. Justine decided. She scooped up the child and returned to her husband, who was pacing frantically at the entrance of the atrium. Justine hurried towards him, holding on tightly to the baby. "This baby has been left to exposure. The mother left it to die." Hanoch's brows deepened. She pulled back the bunting around the infant's legs and shouted, "A girl! It's a baby girl! Oh! We must save this baby!" Hanoch stayed silent briefly, and then with a deep sigh, found his voice.

"Justine. We have two sons of our own to raise. We do not need another child. We will try to find a home for her." But Hanoch's attempts to reason with his wife were futile. Justine had longed for a daughter but had been barren since their last son. In her soul, motherhood stood above all.

"And we are too old!" Hanoch added.

"We are not too old." Justine smiled down at the baby, then gently opened the blanket. "Look, Hanoch." Her voice was soft. "She has red hair just like you but look at this patch of white hair. How unusual!" Justine examined the baby's umbilical cord. "Just hours old! What a blessing. She must be in God's plan for us. We shall name her Ushriya. I have always loved that name. My sister's husband had a sister named Ushriya. It means blessing from God. She will be our Ushriya." Justine smiled at Hanoch as she stood rocking the baby.

Hanoch relented. She was happy, and that made him happy. "Well, she does have my hair color." He grinned.

"Thank you, my love." Justine wrinkled her nose at the odor rising from the baby. "This child is in desperate need of a change. We must stop at the Forum for some goat's milk until I can bring my milk in." Justine had produced ample milk for her own babies, and she had wet-nursed her sister's baby, so she had no doubt she would have enough milk for this baby. Pushing her toga down, she positioned the hungry infant at her breast to let her body know she was nursing again. Gently, she made her way back to the cart. Hanoch helped his wife up, then went to the opposite side and pulled himself into the seat. With a slap of the reins, he nudged the donkeys back on the road towards the exit off the royal grounds of Palatine Hill. Glancing sideways, Hanoch heaved another big sigh and smiled as Justine gazed lovingly at their new daughter.

CHAPTER 4

SEPTEMBER 3, AD 48

Hanoch and Justine furnished a small utility room upstairs, where the family lived, for Ushriya. A small wooden box once used for olive oil shipments served as her bed, and Justine found cloth in the storage downstairs for the baby's clothing. Justine calmed once her breasts filled with milk and was finally able to nurse little Ushriya, now two weeks old. As Justine gazed into the infant's tiny, shining eyes, she could sense an impatient energy. Although Ushriya was ready to get on with life, Justine couldn't have been more content with her baby girl in this moment.

Her thoughts wandered as she rocked Ushriya in the same rocking chair she had rocked both her sons. Justine knew the likelihood of this precious baby surviving infancy was minimal. Without knowing her natural parents, she had no idea of possible inherited maladies. Justine and Hanoch's two boys had grown up and now contributed to the family bakery. At ten, Cyrus, the eldest, held sway over his younger brother, Julius who was five. Both boys learned a strong work ethic and knew every job in the bakery from milling to selling while rambling about the bakery. Cyrus' tireless strength made loading grain sacks from the cart to the upstairs storage easy. Julius' talents came with his ability to converse with all the patrons, elite or not, at the sales counter. He was a sickly baby bothered with wheezing and coughing in both spring and winter which stunted his normal growth and constantly worried his parents. Most days, he stood on a stool his father made for him and sold bread. A protective mother, Justine was vigilant of both of her sons' whereabouts because of the constant threat of slave traders who roamed the streets looking to add to their bounty. But for now, she focused on her new daughter. Ushriya kicked her legs as she nursed at her mother's breast.

"Ushriya, my sweet little seraph," Justine whispered softly. "You will grow to be a strong, beautiful woman. Your father will provide a dowry so that one day you may marry and have children of your own." Ushriya wriggled under the new bunting. Justine curled the baby's silvery lock of hair around her finger, hugging her cherubic cheek tightly to her own.

JUNE 11, AD 50

"Ushriya! What mischief have you made? It didn't take you long to find trouble!" Justine came around the milling stone and found her little girl sitting in the middle of a torn flour sack. Ushriya was swishing her hands on the floor making arches in the dust, then gleefully grabbing handfuls of flour, and throwing the tan powder into the air. Tiny particles fell all around, covering her in a thin layer of soft spelt dust; she looked like a tiny bear cub. Her emerald eyes peeked out from behind the coating of flour.

"Why?" Ushriya laughed at the new experience, and from sheer joy. "Why?"

Justine stood with her hands on her hips, smiling down at her precocious ball of energy, not yet two years, "Why" was Ushriya's first word. Both question and statement, it was the word she knew was sure to get a response, and one that showed her growing wonder of the world.

"Why does the flour stick to you? Or why is it brown. Or why are you such a happy girl?" Justine could not resist. She sat down on the floor with Ushriya as her baby girl climbed into her lap. Thinking nothing of how much work it would be to clean, flour coated her woolen toga. Ushriya hurled a flurry up into the air, the tan dust cascading all around. They collapsed in giggles.

"Why Moo-ma!" Ushriya shrieked as the flour came down on them like snow.

"You said it! Ushriya, you said 'Moma'!" Justine clutched her daughter to her breast, twisting from her waist in abundant hugs, not the least bit bothered that now they were both covered in flour.

"And what trouble have you two made?" Hanoch stood smiling above them. Murmurs of muffled laughter came from all corners of the bakery.

SEPTEMBER 14, AD 52

"Hanoch, a basket of bread is missing that was set out to be delivered this afternoon. The oven slaves have told me how many loaves came from the ovens this morning. Have you any idea where it is?" Justine wiped her hands on her toga.

"I have not been near the counting table. Have you checked with your sons? They are like growing trees, and sometimes their appetites get the better of them, especially Cyrus."

"But a whole basket? Sometimes they sneak a loaf between them, but this is too many." Justine went to look for the boys.

"Cyrus, Julius, I need to know if you…." Justine stopped in the middle of her sentence and looked down at her sons, squirming in their chairs. They kept their eyes down at the game they were playing on the table avoiding her gaze. "So, it was you who took the bread? You know we need those loaves for our deliveries!" Her voice raised along with her hand.

"It was Ushriya! We saw her!" Both boys shouted at once. Justine dropped her hand. They hesitated because Ushriya had their mother's favor, and they weren't sure she would believe them. But she did. Justine turned and marched towards the room where her four-year old daughter spent most of her time. She pushed the door open, but Ushriya was not there. Justine peeked around the back of the door. Not there.

"Ushriya? Where are you?" Frightened, Justine's thoughts went straight to her worst nightmare. Although she had taken great pains to teach Ushriya of the dangers of the streets, this was not a child they could teach to be afraid of anything. Talking to strangers and embarking on new adventures did not intimidate her and this thought sent shivers of terror through Justine.

"Ushriya! Where are you, my daughter? Hanoch!! Ushriya is missing!" Not waiting for his answer, she went from the flour room to the mixing table, to the kneading table to the mill stones, bumping into slaves as she turned and twisted her way through the bakery. "Has anyone seen Ushriya?" Met with silence and heads turning no, Justine was both angry and terrified. A four-year-old girl would be a target of slave traders-especially one with an unusual marking. Slave traders were efficient and fast, leaving town once they had a full bounty. "Someone has to have seen her! Did she leave the bakery? Did she leave on a cart with deliveries?"

Looking over her shoulder, Justine saw that the delivery carts were back. Justine yelled, "Ushriya! Where are you?" She charged out of the back door of the bakery, calling as loud as she could. Looking into the faces of every child, she hurried through the streets of Pompeii. Reaching the house of Ushriya's friend, Mariana, she saw Mariana's mother who shook her head no when asked if she had seen her daughter. Now she searched Ushriya's favorite places: the stables, other friends, the old man on the corner, the painters repairing walls, and anybody within the sound of her voice on the streets. Just when Justine was running out of breath, Hanoch and the boys charged up beside her in the cart. Justine climbed in. Every block, Hanoch and the boys jumped out together, then divided and searched. Justine kept the reins, all the while hollering Ushriya's name.

"Ushriya! Where are you! Ushriya!" All three called until their throats were dry. Dogs barked; chickens scurried from the urgency of the cart.

They searched the Forum, the baths, every shop where the bakery delivered bread, and the synagogue. They ran through the Basilica, not caring if they were offending or interrupting the elites who loitered by the podium. Recognizing their favorite baker as he ran by, they called out.

"What has happened, Hanoch?"

"I fear my daughter, Ushriya, has been taken by the slave traders! Have you seen her?" Hanoch yelled, now running backwards as fast as his age would allow.

"How long has she been missing? they inquired.

"Just this afternoon," Hanoch answered, then paused for a breath. Leaning over, hands on his knees, he sobbed. "Ushriya!" he cried. "Where are you?"

Distraught with exhaustion, they searched until the sun set. Hysterical now, Justine cried out, "Oh, Ushriya, my baby girl, where are you? Where are you?"

When word spread that little Ushriya was missing, friends and neighbors, knowing full well what fate might have allowed, gathered at the bakery, taking over the search with lanterns and candles. They returned to the bakery to refresh themselves, then began searching anew, working in shifts of volunteers throughout the night, checking and re-checking with everyone they knew. As night turned to dawn, the search expanded further and further away from the bakery. There was no need to describe Ushriya as the little one with the golden red curls and the white streak in her hair. Everyone knew of the curious tiny girl with green sparkling eyes. Hanoch slumped on the steps in front of the bakery the next morning, realizing that his daughter was long gone by now.

CHAPTER 5

"Hello there, little pretty one." Startled, Ushriya stopped splashing in the gargoyle fountain. She picked up her basket of bread, her toga dripping wet, and backed away. A tall man with shoulder-length black hair seemed to appear out of nowhere. "Funny little creatures, aren't they?" he said, pointing to the gargoyle. "Scary, even though they collect the liquid of life." He smiled shrewdly down at Ushriya. "Can I help you? Are you lost?" the man asked.

"No!" Ushriya said what her mother had told her to say to strangers on the streets.

"Don't worry, I mean you no harm. I just happened along and thought you were lost. Are you hungry? Would you like something to eat?" the man insisted, edging closer to her.

"I don't know you!" Ushriya dropped her basket.

"I don't know you, either. But I'd like to. There is a thermopolium around the corner. They have lots of fruit. Do you like grapes?" Ushriya relaxed. She adored the sweet fruits of summer, and something to eat besides bread sounded good. This man seemed nice enough, so she decided to follow him. His voice softened, he slowed his gait and grinned, waiting for her to catch up. He offered his hand, and she took it. "I'm sure it's just around this corner." Disoriented, Ushriya trusted this man knew where he was going. Riding along with her father on many bread deliveries, as well as with many of the delivery slaves, she knew most thermopolia, but didn't remember one at this corner by the gargoyle fountain. She knew of the thermopolium close to the street of Via del Teatri because the painter always waved to her. She knew of another further down, because the donkeys led the cart returning to the bakery straight to the hay bin. But if this nice grownup told her there was a thermopolium here, it must be true.

When she finally realized his direction was towards the Porta Marina exit, she knew there were no thermopoliums there. The man had lied to her.

"This is the way my apa takes me with him when he goes to the big house a long time away!" Ushriya jerked her hand, but the man clamped on tighter. Another man jumped from behind a column and grabbed her. Ushriya squealed like a piglet, wriggling, and twisting, screaming as loud and long as she could. A big fleshy hand solidly clamped over her mouth, at once silencing her.

"Is she dead?" Ushriya heard a child's voice somewhere in her daze. Straining to open her eyes, she wiped dried crusty blood from one eye, then the other. A circle of children surrounding her came into focus. A shackle around her ankle rattled chains as she sat up. Awareness crept into her consciousness. She was inside a cramped cold stable with straw on the floor. One small window leaked sunlight.

"Am I dead? What is dead?" Ushriya groggily asked no one in particular. Then she boldly stated. "No, I'm not!"

"I guess not, if you're talking." A boy with an older voice stepped forward. "You've been asleep for a long time, but now you're awake, so you'll probably recover." The boy who seemed to be in charge called over his shoulder, "Someone bring her some water."

Ushriya whimpered, struggling to sit, grasping that she was not only bloody, but her almost naked body peeked through her torn tunic. She tried to cover herself.

"Don't worry. We all come to this place looking just like you." He cupped his hand, dipped in the small bucket of water, and splashed cool water on her face. It felt good. Ushriya straightened up and glanced down. "I am Quintus." Tilting his head, with knitted brow, he sat back on his heels. "Hmmm, I recognize you. You ride with the bakers. I've seen you on the baker's cart."

Ushriya ignored him. "Where am I? I want my moma and apa!" All at once the putrid smell of feces and urine hit her. She gagged and began to cry.

"They bring pots every day along with some bread. When the pots fill, we have no choice. And I don't know where your mother and father are, but you probably won't see them again," Quintus said, "because I've overheard that we are leaving for Rome tonight."

Ushriya sobbed. "Who are they, and what is a 'Rome'? What do you mean? Leaving for Rome?"

"The slave traders..." Quintus began.

"What will they do with me!" Ushriya shrieked. She knew the words 'slave traders' meant danger. The children backed away. The bolt rattled from outside the door. Children scampered like mice into the corners of the stone floored stable.

"Why do I have these on my feet? Moma and apa will look for me. I want to go home!" Ushriya shouted as the door opened.

"What is happening in here?" Ushriya recognized the voice as one of the men who brought her here. He approached Ushriya. "Ah, the feisty one with the white streak. Causing a disturbance, are you?" He drew his hand back.

Ushriya recognized the man she had met at the fountain. He reached for the other man's shoulder. "Bacchus, don't bruise her! She will bring a high value."

"Where are my moma and apa?" Again, Ushriya demanded. "I want to go home now!"

Bacchus dropped his hand and laughed.

"You tell her," the other man said.

"I will tell her." Bacchus turned coldly to Ushriya. "They're dead."

Ushriya stood up, wrapping herself in her torn tunic. This was the second time she had heard the word 'dead.' Thrusting her chin towards the drunken pair, her despair turned bold. "What? Moma, apa?"

"We killed them. Yes, we did. Your whole family. Left them where they lay," Bacchus proclaimed. "We burned your house down, too. You can never go home again."

Ushriya understood the word 'kill'. It meant they had left the earth. It meant she would never see them again. It meant she was alone. It meant 'dead', the word she had just learned and would never forget. A shrill, earsplitting tantrum erupted. The children put their hands over their ears.

"This one will be hard to handle. Gods! She has to go first." The men turned and left the stable, bolting the door behind them.

An ominous darkness fell over the stable as sunlight faded. Children huddled together, sniffling and whimpering until most were asleep. In the silence, mice scampered in the hay searching for the leftover crumbs of bread.

Murmuring people gathering nearby broke the silence. Ushriya strained to hear the voices. "I want my moma and apa! I want to go home! Now!" Ushriya called. Kicking at her chains over and over to no avail, she collapsed in tears.

"Quiet! They can't hear you. Even if they could, they wouldn't come." Quintus' voice spoke out of the gloom. "You will be the one who gets us beaten if we aren't quiet at night. People gather to hear about a man they call the Wonder Maker."

"What is a Wonder Maker?" Ushriya asked.

"I think he must be a criminal because they gather in secret." Quintus motioned towards the voices.

"Why won't they come if we yell?" Ushriya's childish voice was desperate. "Don't they care?"

"You're too young to understand, but we're children. They don't care about children," Quintus explained. "Anyway, why do we want them to come? The traders could easily recapture us and bring us back. Don't you see? We *want* to be slaves. Slaves are fed, clothed, and sheltered. Better than we have it now, children on the streets begging for crumbs. After we're sold, if we don't cause problems, we'll have a place to be. How can that be bad? You, you've had a good life. We haven't. Now, without your father and mother, you are one of us. Just be quiet and go to sleep." Quintus exhaled heavily and shook his head.

Ushriya slumped down, chains pulling at her feet, the stone wall scratching her bare back. Afraid and cold, she fell into a restless sleep.

"Time to get up, all of you!" Bacchus' partner's silhouette bounced off the door as he kicked it open. He lifted Ushriya's full weight up by her arm. Standing, she yowled. "Hurry. Daylight is breaking."

"Nigel, I told you to be careful with that one!" Bacchus said to his partner as he came through the door with keys to unlock the shackles. The two slave traders pushed Quintus by the shoulder and roused the six others. "Hurry, get them in the cart."

"That's all we can take," Bacchus said, as he pushed eight children, including Ushriya, out the door to a waiting cart on the side of the stable. One by one, Nigel heaved the children into the back of the cart. "I loaded it last night with provisions." he said.

"You were so filled with wine; I'm surprised you could load provisions." Bacchus quipped.

Both men climbed into the cart and whipped the reins. The four donkeys tugged on the load, gaining momentum as they rolled towards Rome.

CHAPTER 6

Long stretches of hot sun burned their tender backs. The wooden wheels jarred the children along the rough cobblestones of the Via Appia. Most were naked, but some had scraps of cloth to cover themselves from the searing heat. Quintus' arm bumped against Ushriya's sunburned face, but it didn't hurt; his touch comforted her. She scooted closer to him. He was about the same age as Cyrus, who protected her from the world, then played long and hard with her, lifting her on his shoulders, swooping her down grasping one arm and one leg and swinging her in circles around him. To Ushriya, her big brother was one of the strongest people in the world. She could not comprehend what had happened to him or her family.

Monotonous sounds of the clip clop of the donkeys, passing carts, people talking, shouting, some crying, some stopping for a break along the road, were familiar. The redundancy of the surroundings relaxed her. Her mind wandered as she watched the people move about their business. Her curiosity to know them, to know their stories, to understand how they found themselves on this road at this time crossed her mind in childish wonder. She realized that she had traveled this road many times with her apa when he bought wheat or spelt grain or when he was delivering bread for the emperor. His voice rang out over the cart. "We have to get to the palace before this bread gets old." he would say. They covered as many miles as possible during daylight while apa told stories and sang songs, turning the trip into special time with him. Laughing as her little body bobbed up and down on the seat, he yelled, "Hold on, little one! The road smooths out after Caslinum." Ushriya giggled, adoring her apa's chuckle as he held the reins with one arm and put his other around her tiny shoulders. Barely two suns had passed since she had seen him; she longed for her apa's arm around her again.

The cart came to a sudden halt, pitching the children forward. "Better give 'em something to eat, or we might not have anything to sell." Bacchus pulled a basket from under the seat and threw wheels of bread into the cart as if he were feeding chickens. All the children except Ushriya lunged at the bread catching it before it landed. Not realizing this was mealtime, she watched as the older children caught the most, so she held back. Most of the children were six to ten years and were accustomed to street life and hunger. It was all they had ever known.

"Better get some." Quintus leaned over to Ushriya whispering through a mouthful of bread. "Might not eat again today." Ushriya looked away, recognizing the bread from her family bakery. The way it was cut, the size. Her eyes filled with tears. Bacchus hurled a pail of water that splashed over the side of the cart and tossed a cup alongside. Parched with thirst, the children emptied the bucket, and Nigel refilled it until the children drank their fill. When they finished, the donkeys were able to rest and drink from the refilled bucket.

The men knew better than to let either children or donkeys go without water or food. Deprived, it was certain death for their cargo or their animals. The two had learned this lesson the hard way since losing three slaves and their only ox on their first trip. Drunk most of the way, they'd paid no attention to anything but their next drink. Consequently, the ox died just before they reached Rome, so they had to walk with the four remaining captives until another passing slave cart took pity on them and allowed passage, but only if they paid him half of their earnings at the auction. With no money, no food or water and severely weakened slaves, they had no choice.

At the auction, the deprived slaves brought a pittance. After they paid their passage to the trader, they promptly found a tavern and drank away the remainder of the money.

Bacchus and Nigel urinated alongside the road. The children used the latrine pot in the cart. Returning to the cart, Bacchus reached under the seat for the wine he'd stashed and threw a glance at Nigel. Nigel grinned and nodded. When the two men finished the wine, they heaved themselves into the cart. Nigel shook the reins. Bacchus gazed off in the distance.

"What are you thinking about? Not like you were never there before. It's the place we usually make the most coins. If we can keep 'em healthy, they should bring fifty to sixty sequesters each, I think. Do you remember the name of the dominus that wanted a young girl around five or younger? That little one in the back with the streak should fit, I would think." Nigel said.

"Are they talking about me?" Ushriya whispered to Quintus. Quintus nodded.

"Dominus Acacias is his name, and he is an aedile magistrate elected to oversee buildings and festivals. His son, Marcus has a new wife and wants a young girl child to train as famulus," Bacchus replied.

"What is a famulus?" Ushriya wanted to know.

Quintus put his finger to his lips. "Don't let them hear you," he said. "A famulus is the head slave in a house."

"I don't want to be a slave," Ushriya whispered. Quintus smiled.

"I don't think you will have any choice," he stated. "Now stay quiet." Tears spilled down Ushriya's cheeks.

"Elites enjoy novelty. She was a good find. I knew it as soon as I saw her playing by herself in the fountain." Nigel yanked the reins to barely miss a sizeable rock in the road. The lead donkeys flung their heads throwing the cart sideways.

"The gods will damn you. That donkey knows to go around a rock!" Bacchus snatched the reins, pulling the cart to a halt. "I'll get us there from here, you drunken maggot!"

"I've been up since before the sun, and I've done my share of goading this team on. The reins are yours." Nigel tossed them over to Bacchus. "Get us there, then. Only a short while until we lose daylight. Remember that grove of olive trees right before Caslinum where we stopped last trip? There is a creek beside the road. It will be a good place to stop for the night, if it is not overrun with travelers."

As they approached the olive grove, a bulky man sprang from the shadows. Another stepped out from behind a large boulder. Grabbing iron bladed swords from the back of their seats, Bacchus jumped down while Nigel stayed at an advantage in the cart above the two men. As one of the bandits struggled to climb the wheel into the cart, with both hands wrapped around the handle, Nigel thrust the sharp tip of his sword into the throat of the offender, causing blood to shoot upwards, dropping him instantly. He pulled his pugio from his underarm sheath and leapt down from the cart. From behind, Nigel sank his dagger into the other bandit's back while Bacchus' sword impaled him from the front. Blood poured from the fatal wound. The robber fell at their feet. Looking across the body at the other, chests heaving, Bacchus and Nigel glared at each other, then roared with laughter.

"Ah, my friend. We have not lost our talents! The army taught us well!" Bacchus proclaimed.

"And just a short while ago, you were calling me a drunken maggot," Nigel retorted.

"You are until I need you to help me in battle and then you are quite the master. Now you are a drunken Venalitti." Bacchus smirked, grabbed Nigel around the neck and shook him in jest, rubbing his calloused knuckles in Nigel's grimy brown hair. "You are indeed a fighter." They ambled over to the cart arm in arm.

Frightened, but relieved, Ushriya huddled with the other children in the cart, now peeking over the sides. Peasants from neighboring carts and wagons gathered to cheer Bacchus and Nigel for killing the bandits, who were known to threaten and murder travelers on the Via Appia. Strutting like roosters, they took their accolades.

As the sun began to descend, the men built a fire. Feeling generous after their victory, they gave the children an extra meal of bread with raisins and some coverings to sleep under the cart. One by one they climbed down, crawling behind the wheels.

"Is that what makes people dead?" Ushriya asked Quintus once again.

"Yes, and we're grateful they won, or we might have been left to find our way to Rome." Quintus was visibly upset.

"You would've taken us there and I know this road leads to Rome." Ushriya said with pride. "My apa took me down this road with our bread. It goes to the big house with the man who has a crown on his head."

Quintus shook his head slightly as the other children gathered around layering themselves on top of him.

Not used to the constant agitation and emotion, Ushriya gave into sheer exhaustion. The warmth of the fire flowed under the cart, soothing her.

Without vigilance to further danger, Nigel and Bacchus drank wine by the fire until they fell into a woozy slumber.

CHAPTER 7

At twilight of the third sun, their cart reached the Vicus Iugarius, the road that led to the slave auctions in Rome. Nigel guided the donkeys to the Graecostadium tucked behind the Basilica Julia in the Forum. Though the reputation of the Venalitti was tainted by the unscrupulous service they performed, the elites looked the other way when the slave carts loaded with human cargo rolled in. Relieved they had arrived before dawn, Bacchus and Nigel would be ready when the auction started. Wealthy elites from all over the Roman Empire entered the Forum early to appraise the slaves. The two drove the donkeys hastily down the road to prepare for potential buyers. Washing and feeding the slaves for presentation was vital. No clothing of any type was allowed because the buyer would assume the trader was trying to hide defects.

"Some nice goods we have in this cart. The best we've brought in a while," Bacchus remarked, sizing up the slave cargo of traders from other countries.

"But the one we have with the white spot in her hair is the prize," Nigel chuckled. "Lucius Rufus Acacias will think she is something special. Rich old fool. Little does he know she is quite a handful."

Weary and parched, the children were quiet. Bewildered, they dismounted from the cart. They entered the bath, dipping their sun-burned bodies in cool water. Quintus splashed Ushriya.

His dark skin glistened in the rising sun as she returned the favor. The children stayed close to Quintus. In the calm, Ushriya remembered several of these children as she had passed in the streets of Pompeii on her apa's cart. Now she was one of them.

"Where are we going?" Ushriya asked sheepishly, scooting closer to the child next to her.

"We will go to the auction. Do you even know what an auction is?" Quintus asked. "I have seen them in Pompeii. They will put us in cages first, then on a stand and the people will look us over. We will all go to separate places to do different things. Since you are so pretty and well fed, you'll probably go to a rich domus." Quintus winked.

"I don't want to go to a domush. I wanna go home." Ushriya sobbed. "I want my moma." Quintus sighed.

The children half-heartedly continued to splash each other. Enjoying the respite and feeling a bit refreshed, they plunged their heads in the water, shaking the water off like little dogs. Ushriya's tears stopped, then she paddled around in the bath. The water felt good; she could see the children relax, so she took their lead. Here she was, far away from home, with seven other children. She had been to the baths in Rome, but not the slave baths. She wrinkled her nose. No one was smiling or laughing. Some slaves were old. Some were strong, some frail. All were quiet.

"Get out of the water. You're clean enough," Bacchus commanded. "Go over in the sun, so you can dry off. There is bread and water in the cart." The man Ushriya thought friendly enough to follow in Pompeii had turned into an ugly monster; mean and greedy. She got out of the water with the younger children. They went over to several benches at the edge of the bath. The rising summer sun dried them quickly. After returning to the cart, they devoured the leftover bread and quenched their thirst.

"Here is the chalk, Nigel." Bacchus threw white chalk to Nigel so he could whiten one foot of each imported slave to signal they were from a Roman province, as was the custom at auctions.

"We have no imports from abroad. Some of them might look like it, though," Nigel responded.

"Whiten the ones that look like it. They will appear rare and bring more value. I'll take care of the tituli and hang them around their necks." Bacchus took a piece of charcoal, went to the cart, grabbed a pile of wooden placards with a piece of rope through a hole at each side of the top, and sat down in front of the smallest slave. "This one's eyes squint. So, Serica. That's probably where one of its relatives are from." He scrawled on the placard. "Boy." Lifting the young boy's upper, then lower lip, Nigel continued. "Teeth are good. Probably five years." Turning the boy around by his shoulders, he looked up and down at his body. "Good health. Strong legs. Will be a big man. Too young to know good and bad habits. Trainable. There! First one done." Bacchus hung the placard around the little boy's neck and went to the next slave.

"What about his name?" Ushriya whispered to Quintus. "Don't they want to know his name?"

"No. He will probably be given a new name once he's sold." Quintus lowered his head. "You will get a new name as well."

"No! I. Won't!" Ushriya got up and began to run. Nigel took two strides to her one and grabbed a fistful of her long red hair. She yelped and skidded to a halt on her bare feet, twisting and flailing her limbs.

"Let me go!" She shrieked.

"You are full of trouble, but worth far too much to escape. Bacchus, throw me the ropes from the cart. I need to tie her up," he yelled.

Climbing into the cart, Bacchus found the rope and threw it over the side. "Don't give her rope burns. Acacia will not want a bruised slave."

While Nigel bound Ushriya's feet and hands, Bacchus returned to creating the description of each slave for the placards. Quintus was dark-skinned, so the two guessed he was from Africa terra. "About twelve years. Good health. Starting to show muscle for a good field slave. And he is a hard worker." Bacchus laughed to himself.

When he got close to Ushriya, she spit in his face. A hard slap to her jaw sent her head sideways.

"Damn ye gods, Bacchus! You just said we didn't want this one bruised. You're too strong, now look what you've done." Nigel swore.

"Aren't no slave going to spit in my face no matter her size, valuable as she may be." Bacchus backed up. He took the last placard and began listing Ushriya's qualities. "From Pompeii, since we killed her parents, we know that." Bacchus winked at Nigel. He chuckled. "Girl." He continued. "About four years old. I'm not going to lift her lips, she might bite me, so good on the teeth." Ushriya hissed at him coiling her knees up to her chin. "Good health. Will make a good head house slave, nurse or kitchen slave...and she... is... one of a kind." He snickered. "Though a bit head strong. Come here, Nigel. You lift her in the cart. We have to get back to the auction cages." Ushriya took a big breath. All she could think of were the ropes burning her sore wrists and ankles.

After all the children were in the cart, Nigel took the reins and steered the donkeys back to the Graecostadium, where the Forum slaves had placed the auction slave cages around the yard. The auction stand was in place. Maneuvering the donkeys beside the cages, Bacchus herded their cargo into them. He lifted Ushriya from the back as she screamed and kicked at him.

"I want my moma and apa! I want to go home!" Two other men came to help Nigel and Bacchus take Ushriya to a private viewing room known as the arcana tabulate catastae. Reserved for slaves of perceived rarity or exceptional beauty, they dropped her onto a table and began untying the ropes. Ushriya squirmed until she fell off the table, landing on the stone floor. Bacchus and Nigel lifted her and sat her down hard on the table. Ushriya submitted to their strength.

"You WILL calm yourself or the whip will find your backside." Ushriya hushed. A door in the side of the room opened and a tall man wearing a white toga entered. Standing at attention, Bacchus and Nigel nodded to the man as he walked past them.

"This is the girl you promised me?" He sounded a bit irritated. "She is young."

"Yes, dominus. She is a spirited one, which is why she is bound; she will be quite beautiful with a rare bit of white streak in her hair. She is almost five years, and quite healthy," Nigel offered.

"Do you know of her heritage?" Acacia circled Ushriya. He touched her white streak and she jerked away. Bacchus scowled at her.

"No, dominus. But we know she lived in Pompeii."

"My Moma and Apa made bread," Ushriya cried.

"Of what does she speak?" Acacia looked at the two.

"Ah, she is a storyteller, this one," Nigel quipped. "She is orphaned since her parents died in an accident."

"Quite extraordinary," Acacia circled her again. "Stand her up." Bacchus pulled Ushriya up by the ropes around her hands. "Since she is so young, I suppose you will want top price for her."

"Why yes, dominus. We would not sell her for less than twenty thousand sestertii."

"Quite proud of her, are you? I'll give you ten."

"The white streak is a sign of great intelligence," Nigel added. "And we know there are others that are interested…"

"She does have clear smooth skin, a small nose. Her red hair… quite extraordinary and attractive. Well taken care of, looks healthy. Where did you say you gathered her?"

"In Pompeii, roaming the streets," Bacchus said.

"Fifteen thousand sestertii. Final offer," Acacia said. Nigel and Bacchus side glanced at each other, then nodded, tipping their heads in respect.

"Leave her bound and put her in my cart. My driver is just outside, the one with the white horses." Bacchus lifted Ushriya, now limp with exhaustion, and took her to the waiting cart. Nigel collected the fee from Acacia, and the two disappeared out the front door without another word.

Ushriya slept the short distance to Acacia's domus. When the cart came to a standstill, she awoke from her deep sleep. A young woman with dark hair peeked over the side of the cart. She had the hair style of the elites and wore expensive jewelry.

"Is this the new slave child Acacia bought for Marcus and me?

She is so young and small. Look at the pretty white streak in her hair," the young woman said to the driver, nevertheless sounding pleased.

"Yes, domina. Your father-in-law instructed me to bring her to you," the driver said.

"I will call her Sarah, after the strong woman of legend," the kind lady said to no one in particular.

Instantly appalled, Ushriya declared. "I am Ushriya. I can hear and I understand you. I want to go home. I want my moma and apa!"

"Ushriya is an odd name. What does it mean?" the woman asked, ignoring Ushriya's plea.

"My moma told me it means I'm a blessing from God," Ushriya stated indignantly.

"Oh, how lovely. You can keep your name, then. I am called Ruth, and I am your domina." The young woman turned to the driver. "Please bring Ushriya to the culina. Untie her...and please be careful."

Ushriya heard kindness in this new voice and found herself relaxing for the first time since her capture. The driver drove around the domus to the culina entry, carefully lifted Ushriya out of the cart and placed her into the culina where Ruth was waiting.

Ushriya wondered what a *domina* was.

CHAPTER 8

JUNE 5, AD 57

When Ruth was sixteen years, she had wed Marcus in a traditional Roman ceremony. Considered the month with the most luck, their wedding was in June. Calista, her closest friend, had shared the day as matron of the bride. She'd helped with Ruth's hair, made sure she had her yellow shoes and white veil over a white robe, characteristic of Roman ritual. Her mother had helped dress her, and that evening, three sons of close friends had accompanied her to Marcus' home. There, she received the keys to his house. Then, Marcus had held her hand as they'd stood before a priest and recited the lucky chant, "When and where you are Gaius, I then and there am Gaia."

A feast of lamb, hare, cheese, pig, mounds of bread, beef, goat, and chicken had graced tables around the home of Marcus' parents. Ruth's mother and father had sat in the vestibule as lilting notes of the cithara drifted through the celebration. Guests had enjoyed nuts, fruits, and spiced wine set on ornate, marble pedestals. Vines had draped the pedestals with early summer flowers, brightening the day.

Marcus' warm breath had brushed against Ruth's ear. She had trembled knowing that this was the best day of her young life. He had embraced his beaming bride, dancing late into the evening until at last, he took her arm, along with her mother, and walked to their new home under cascades of nuts. When they'd arrived, Marcus had scooped Ruth up and stepped over the threshold of their new home.

"I will always protect you and love you as long as I have breath," he whispered. Ruth shivered.

Like his father, Lucius Rufus Acacia, Marcus was destined to become a soldier, marry well, and create an heir continuing the heritage of the Acacia line. Though Marcus' family was not Jewish, his mother had acquaintance with Ruth's mother, and both were intrigued with the potential union of the son of a warrior and the daughter of a Jewish priest. Marcus was seven years on this earth when both mothers approached their husbands to discuss the betrothal of their children. The promise of a tall, statuesque physique with potential strength and power appealed to Ruth's mother and a large dowry appealed to Marcus' mother. Eliezer ben Zacchai's initial hesitation at the idea of his daughter marrying a Gentile soldier subsided as Lucius became aedile within the Roman elite and gained considerable power. Their mothers relished consent and anticipated formidable grandchildren. When Marcus became a soldier, he would attain all the *virtus, gloria y fama* following in the footsteps of his father. Granting the betrothal, both Eliezer ben Zacchai and Lucius Rufus Acacias were pleased.

With the blood of a soldier coursing through his veins, Marcus' chiseled good looks and aggressive ways effortlessly drew the veneration of the same and opposite sexes. His wife was to head the household and satisfy his desires, nothing more. Since a betrothal to Ruth was inevitable because of the wishes of their families, though not his first choice, her strange beauty fascinated him, and he deemed the commitment to his liking. There would be other women, but she would be the mother of his heir.

After their betrothal, young and enamored, Ruth frolicked with Marcus in the baths most nights. His black curls flung the water around him as his handsome broad smile enticed Ruth to swim towards him, her long dark hair trailing. He disappeared beneath the water, drawing her under with him.

As rains swept through Rome, at the onset of her first winter with Marcus and Ruth, Ushriya began learning the responsibilities of the head household slave, the *famulus*. Though still only nine years, giving direction and overseeing less capable slaves came naturally to Ushriya. Regina, whom Ruth inherited as head house slave after marrying Marcus, was becoming frail with declining health. Ushriya stayed by her side until the culina was familiar and she could scoot a stool to the table to help with meals. Once Ushriya could manage the large task of famulus, Regina would be there until she went to be with God, a planned and smooth transition.

"I have done this many times." Ushriya said. She knew the culina so well that other slaves in the house began depending on her.

"Ushriya, how will I know the best lemons?" a new slave asked as she left to market. Ushriya told her to sniff the end of the lemon, that its smell would hint at its ripeness.

"And how will I know how long to bake the bread?" asked another younger kitchen slave. Surprised at her own considerable expertise in the culina along with her easy manner in directing others, Ushriya was learning that knowledge was power.

"Bake it in the oven for the same amount of time it takes to cut vegetables for cena. If we both cut vegetables at the same time, we can arrange the platters. We'll remove the bread when we finish. But we must check to make sure the oven is not too hot." The slave nodded and obeyed.

"If you stand in a line facing me, I will give each of you a piece of bread." Ruth heard Ushriya's voice as she turned the corner. She backed away so the children couldn't see her. Dressed in rags, dirty and hungry, they all were about the same age as Ushriya. The children fell into line as promptly as soldiers in an army. Ruth stayed still, spellbound.

"Good job. Now I will give you some bread." After Ushriya had given a piece of bread to each child, she motioned to them to get back in line. They devoured the bread and took their places. "Now, please, if you would like another piece of bread, stand on one foot." All the children stood on one foot and Ushriya doled out another piece of bread. Once again, she motioned for the children to get into line. "Now, please if you will, raise your arms above your heads." When the bread was gone, Ushriya swung the empty basket. "I will be back tomorrow." Every child came forward and hugged Ushriya, then quietly scampered away. Ushriya smiled to herself.

"Ushriya!" Ruth called.

Ushriya's head swiveled. "Domina!"

"Where did you get the bread you are giving away?" Ruth demanded. Without waiting for an answer, she grabbed Ushriya's arm. "I don't doubt the bread you just gave away was for meals at the domus!"

"Those children have no parents. They live on the streets and beg for food or steal. Sometimes they volunteer to the slave traders when they search the streets for children. I wait until the bread is days old and will be given to the chickens." Ruth let go of Ushriya's arm.

"Why were you making them stand on a foot or raise their arms?" Ruth asked.

"I wasn't making them, I was asking. They don't know it, but they need to feel like they are earning their bread. It's like the coins at the bakery. People give coins and they get bread. They have coins to give. These children do not have anything to give, so I made up something they could give. They know everyone will get bread if they stay in line and do what I ask them to do. Did you notice how kind they were after the bread was gone? They can also give hugs. They think I will be back tomorrow with more, so they don't want to hurt me."

"You should have asked." Ruth said. Ushriya said nothing, just held her head high.

"Where did you learn this lesson?" Ruth asked.

"I'm not sure, but I think I learned it from where I lived before, I came to you. Now that I have been a slave, I know more than ever that when people get what they need or want and they have something to trade in return, they are happier. If they have nothing to give in return, they become angry and steal. These children needed to feel like they had something to give in return for the bread.' Ushriya looked up at Ruth. "I'm sorry I didn't ask, but can you see why I took the bread?"

Ruth's arms circled Ushriya's shoulders.

"Domina?" Ushriya whispered.

"Yes," Ruth answered softly.

"I've been taking bread to the children for a while now."

"Hmmm, then maybe we should save enough bread for two extra baskets next time." Ruth stroked Ushriya's forehead, catching silvery hair in her fingers.

CHAPTER 9

JUNE 15 AD 61

When Ushriya entered her thirteenth year, things changed. The sight of a baby lamb brought tears. A misinterpreted laugh from a friend made her cry. Full of joy one day and gloomy the next, Ushriya's body felt strange. She wanted to be a woman one moment yet remain a child the next. It was all so confusing.

"I think it is time to visit Juno Soraria at the Temple of Jupiter." Ruth whispered to Ushriya. Ruth smiled at the thought of taking Ushriya to see the statue which would be an honorable rite of passage into womanhood, and not something she ordinarily did for slaves. Ruth remembered her own pilgrimage to the statue and how her mother explained that, even though they were Jewish, women should take advantage of all the protection available. She was pleased that Roman women believed in Juno, the goddess of marriage and childbirth, who watched over and protected the women of Rome, even if she was a pagan goddess. As a girl, Ruth had cried when she placed her favorite doll at the feet of the statue as part of the ritual.

Ruth gently touched Ushriya's shoulder. The girl abruptly stood up, withdrew, knitted her brows, and stomped out of the culina, slamming the door behind her. An amphora of garum toppled over, sending foul fish sauce across the absorbent stone floor.

"Ushriya! How could you? Come back and clean up this mess!" Ruth screamed.

"I hate this place! I hate you!" Ushriya called behind her, grabbing cloths from the pile beside the door as she ran out of the house to the streets of Rome. She knew she had insulted her domina. Ruth could have her killed if she wanted, but she knew that Ruth cared for her, although right now, it didn't matter. She was at this instant a disobedient slave, and it didn't matter what happened to her. She wouldn't live to see the consequences or become a woman, anyhow. Because she was dying. The red blood running down her legs was without a doubt a sign the end was near. For the last several months, two lumps had appeared on her chest, and a foggy malaise overcast her otherwise sunny nature. Not paying attention to where she was on the street, tears streamed down her cheeks, causing her vision to fog. She found herself alongside a fountain with a lion's head spewing cold water. Quickly glancing around to make sure no one noticed, she washed the blood from between her legs. With new cloths placed as secure as she could under her tunic, she knew she would have to walk like a wooden soldier. The bleeding had started yesterday and her whole body ached. Her abdomen felt bloated, and the lumps under her nipples grew bigger and more tender. Yes, she was sure of it. She was dying and had no idea how long she would live. Perched on the edge of the fountain, tears streamed down her cheeks. *What have I done?* She asked herself.

Ushriya sensed someone looming behind her. Pushing off the side of the fountain, she ran, dropping bloody cloths from between her legs. A burly arm firmly clutched her shoulder rendering her helpless with the force of his weight.

"You're not going anywhere." She could hear the whistle in his rotten toothless smile.

"You will not do this to me again!" Ushriya twisted, ripping her tunic, spitting, kicking with the disgust of reminiscent memories.

"Do what again? We are here for some..." The man hesitated, spotting the blood-soaked cloths behind her. "Aeiiii, this one has the curse of the black witch! Not worth the monster that she will make."

Another foul-smelling man stinking of wine stepped from behind him. "It don't matter," he slurred. "We'll never see 'er again. Let me have a try. You hold 'er still." He lifted his tunic. Biting and scratching, Ushriya flipped her body sideways, spraying droplets of blood into the assailant's face, at once tamping his lust. "You are full of the black witch!" Ushriya's knee came up squarely into his jaw. Annoyed, he fell backwards dropping his tunic. Then he stumbled and kicked at her.

"Let me go! Help me!" Ushriya shrieked, but no one came. Now both men were on her; one jumped onto her shoulders, the other stayed at her feet, ripping an already tattered tunic to reveal her pubescent body. Laughing, one of the men slapped her, silencing her.

"You little wench! I'll show you." The man at her feet stood up, lifted his toga, and urinated on her torso. Gagging at the stench, Ushriya's head lurched forward. Avoiding her vomit, the other man hastily pulled himself up from the ground. Ushriya struggled to rise but fell backwards.

"She's no fun. Let's find us one who don't got the black witch." Drunkenly kicking at Ushriya, the pair turned and disappeared, stumbling around a corner. Ushriya's bruised body shivered on the abrasive stone as she stood up. Still gagging, convulsing sobs wracked her until she heard raucous jabber from another group of men ambling down the street. Determined to avoid them, she summoned the strength to hide behind the fountain. Once she was confident that they had turned in another direction, she rounded to the front of the fountain. Still gagging, she washed her face, her hands, her hair, her whole body, splashing harder and faster.

"Ushriya!" Spinning around, she saw Ruth running towards her. "What has happened to you?" Ushriya dropped her wet hands, sobbing as Ruth embraced her. But she knew. "Curse those cowards!" She wrinkled her nose. "Let's get you into a bath." Ruth checked Ushriya from top to bottom as a mother would, turning her, running her hands through her hair, and tucking her tunic to cover her body.

Ushriya's breathing slowed and she calmed as they walked slowly away from the fountain. "I'm so sorry I said those terrible things to you. I hope you know I didn't mean them."

"Of course, I forgive you." Ruth caressed Ushriya's hair. Ushriya leaned into Ruth and hugged her.

"Who is the black witch?" Ushriya asked.

"Why do you ask?" Ruth wanted to know.

"Because those men said I was full of the black witch and if he did what he wanted to, I would make a monster, so whoever it is-the black witch saved me." Ushriya supposed.

"It is what men call women's monthly loss of blood. That's what is happening to you and has been coming for a while now. It happens to every girl when she becomes a woman. It is God's way of telling a young lady she is able to bear children," Ruth explained.

"But I don't want to have children. If it is from God, why do they call it the black witch and why do I have to learn of it by filthy drunken men? Men who threw me on the ground and ripped my tunic?" Ushriya's tears began, then stopped. She had more questions. "Why do we need to lose blood every month to have children? Doesn't a child need the blood to grow? If I don't want to have a child, then I won't need to lose blood every month, am I right?"

"Not exactly. It is your body's way of getting ready for a child. If the child within you has no father, it will not be ready to enter the world and you will continue to lose blood every month." Ruth clarified.

"How does the child find a father and what does the father lose?" Ushriya rationalized.

"He doesn't lose anything." Ruth skipped key details. "He gains an heir, hopefully."

"What is an heir?" Ushriya asked.

"A son. A male to carry on his bloodline," Ruth said.

"What if the child is a girl? Like you and me?" Ushriya asked.

"Then he has more children until he has an heir. If he does not have an heir, most times he will find a new wife." Ruth was a bit shocked at her own candor.

"So, a woman is worth nothing if she does not bear a male heir? I will beg your forgiveness, domina, but I have no interest in bearing children and spending all my days weaving." Ushriya stopped herself. "I'm sorry. You weave beautiful things. I know I am just a slave…but my soul searches further."

"Somehow, I've known that." Ruth hugged Ushriya as they made their way back to the domus.

CHAPTER 10

Different as the sun and the moon, their nine years difference in age encouraged a maternal bond budding with each passing year. While Ruth had raven hair that framed a distinctive Roman nose and kind brown eyes that matched her inherent soft-spoken nature, Ushriya's red golden hair curled around her oval face emphasizing her emerald green eyes that twinkled with insatiable curiosity.

Ushriya leaned over and kissed David on top of his head.

Catching dangling white hairs between his tiny fingers, he asked, "Why do you have this?" He asked with a five-year-old's curiosity. "I don't have it," he said swiping his hand through his hair.

"It's because I am blessed-at least I think so. Or at least I prefer to think so." Ushriya winked, recalling a vague memory.

Ruth was with child two times before David. Shortly after her and Marcus' wedding, following an extremely difficult pregnancy, she gave birth to a girl child much sooner than expected. Born with a gray pallor, the baby's breath did not come easily. Before presenting her to Marcus, the infant quickly went to be with God. The next child, a son, came within the Ides and could not breathe because the string of life swathed his neck. Ruth's midwife worked feverishly to find life, but they both knew Marcus would not pick up a son who may be weak and unprepared for this world, so Ruth closed her eyes and prayed until his spirit left. When she was with child the third time, David came into the world red-faced and making water. Pleased, Marcus picked him up immediately, smiled and raised him to God. He had a healthy heir. Finally. The Acacia blood would continue.

Wandering into the culina, Ruth dropped David's hand and helped herself to a fig from the fruit counter. David wrapped his little arms around Ushriya's legs.

"How are you, little one?" Ushriya asked, smiling down at him. He answered with a tighter hug.

One of the kitchen slaves had just arrived from the daily marketing. Several slaves were cutting wood for the open fireplace, and another for the warming oven to the right. Still another watered sprouts of thyme, bay leaf and rosemary in a deeply inlaid window, then continued to water more sun-drenched maturing basil, hyssop, and rue in another window. A warm orange room, red clay pots and ginger stucco walls lined carrot-colored tile floors. A long table, stretching the length of a man, held bowls of nuts, olives, and condiments, surrounded by five tables conveniently arranged for separate phases of meal preparation. One was for bread cutting, another for carving meat. One held a large wash basin, and still another had shelves underneath for storage. Large amphorae full of garum and dried goods lined the floor walls, while cooking utensils hung from above. Immediately beside the cooking oven was a latrine. Standing back silently, Ruth observed her favorite slave cut vegetables. Impressed by Ushriya's composure, her ability to adapt and problem solve, Ruth sensed an extraordinary force in this girl. She wondered where it came from; an exceptional aura with a unique presence, Ushriya had a gift of intuition, yet here she was, in Ruth's culina, a slave peeling turnips.

"Ushriya, are you truly from Pompeii, like you told me in the cart when you first arrived? Did you know your parents?" Ruth broke the silence.

"I don't remember telling you that, but maybe I am the daughter of bakers." She hesitated, looking away from the table. "At least I think I am. I remember being in a bakery, playing in flour. I do remember hearing Emperor Claudius' name. And there were boys who teased me." Ushriya finished chopping turnips and wiped her hands on a cloth. She shrugged her shoulders. "But it all seems so distant."

"Where are they now?" Ruth asked.

"I don't know and obviously I was stolen by slave traders because here I am." A sadness came over her face. "They told me they killed my family, but I was so young, I hardly knew what that meant. As I have become older, their story has become more believable. I remember it was a long trip from...where I came from--and you and dominus were kind." Tears flooded Ushriya's eyes as she grabbed the knife to cut more vegetables. "I try to remember how the people I lived with looked, their voices... but the memories are fading. Sometimes I will see something familiar, and bits of memory come back, but nothing for sure." She wiped her eyes.

"The daughter of bakers. Yet, you have a strong nature, along with a never-ending thirst for knowledge. I've learned a lot from you; mysteries that are kept from me otherwise. Your wisdom is far above your years. Where does this come from? Do you know how to read words?" Ruth asked.

"I know boys learn to read!" Ushriya exclaimed. "I've always known there are great thinkers and I know the earth is far grander than what we see in Rome. And I want to understand the way God thinks! I know the great teachers did, too." Ushriya looked to the heavens. Her enthusiasm was contagious as she twirled around the culina. David caught her excitement, grabbing her toga and spinning in delight. Roman law prohibited slaves, especially women, to read and learn, much less speak of great teachers. If she divulged this secret in any other domus, it could have cost Ushriya her life. Nevertheless, respect had grown between the two. Ruth's possessions of worldly things, a stately home, a young son and notably, her freedom, didn't make her happy. She was a woman and would always be a slave to her husband, but she too, dreamt of learning the ways of the great thinkers. Marcus raised his hand when she spoke of such yearnings and reminded her, "You are a woman. Put those things out of your head."

"Where did your visions and ambitions come from?" Ruth remarked. "I'm envious."

"I have no idea. I dream. They are only dreams." Ushriya reached for David's hand. "Time for your afternoon rest, little one." He willingly took her hand, and they started out of the culina.

"Ushriya?" Ruth asked after her. "Before you take David to rest, I want to ask something else. Do you know of a man, a teacher some people call the Wonder Maker who was followed by a Jewish woman named Mary?"

"I have heard of her. The woman named Mary provided for the Wonder Maker so he could be a teacher of good things and a good message," Ushriya answered. "She was a strong woman… the other followers envied, because the Wonder Maker had told her things they didn't hear from him. Because of that, they said she was a liar and because she was a woman, a woman that has known him, I am curious and would like to hear her teach."

"Wait, provided for…what did she provide? Did she…? Was she a prostitute?

"I've heard Mary was a repentant prostitute. Although some believe she came from wealth. I've also heard that she might still be teaching," Ushriya added.

"Marcus has told me of this man, has attended gatherings to hear his teachings, but doesn't allow me to come with him. When I ask questions, his answers are vague. Marcus is so secretive. He knows I am a Jew. He knows my father is a Jewish priest. If the Wonder Maker were a Jew and Mary was a Jew, why would he think I wouldn't want to hear the message of a Jewish teacher?" Ruth looked away musing to herself. "Of course, unless Marcus thinks he's the messiah, but my father has said the messiah has not yet walked the earth."

Under her breath, Ushriya whispered, "Maybe that's why." She led David out to rest.

CHAPTER 11

APRIL 16, AD 64

"To whom do you owe your fine hair and new stola?" Ruth asked Calista admiringly.

Incense greeted Ruth as she entered the splendid atrium. Grand, even for a soldier's wife, it was an uncommon luxury decorated in feminine motif and built especially for Calista. Her husband, Nikon, had imported chairs from Gaul made of oak, accented them with pillows of red silk, and had the walls adorned with magnificent frescos of their children. Black and white marble floors surrounded an oval turquoise pool with a trickling waterfall pouring from a vessel held by a cherub. The warm Mediterranean spring permitted Ruth and Calista to relish the open skylight over the pool as they watched fluffy clouds drift through the blue Roman sky. Occasionally a spontaneous cloudburst added water from the skylight, but mostly they were safe from sun and rain. The two friends made themselves comfortable while Calista's slaves served plates of fresh bread, sliced fruit, and grape wine. Quite a delicacy, the wine was from last year's crop that had just come to age.

"I saw this style on our Empress, Poppaea Sabina." Calista turned her head from side to side. "Can you see the small circles around my head? It took three of my slaves to arrange and plait it," she boasted.

"Ah, I do see it. It is arranged the same as her!" Ruth laughed, snatched an olive, and sank further into the luxury of Calista's domus. "Of course, I adore it! And your stola? Yellow and indigo haven't been your choices in the past."

"Something different, something new." Calista shrugged her shoulders. "Weaving becomes boring. Nikon is gone most evenings. He tells me he is busy with the business of the military, not to worry myself. Or as he says, 'my lovely little head.'" She rolled her eyes. "Well, he's right about that. I do have a lovely little head." She giggled.

"Does he come to you?" Ruth's head tilted; a bit concerned she would offend her friend.

"No, not lately, but I know he has many women." A shadow of melancholy overcame Calista and she gazed away.

"Why do you think he has withdrawn?" Ruth was convinced Calista knew more than she was sharing. It was apparent Marcus' absences were not military duties, either.

Calista went on. "He tells me it's his work, yet, he has mentioned a man who has a new message." Ruth sat up. "I don't know anything about him, except he was Jewish. He is gone from this earth now. I do know that. But people are gathering to hear his teachings and learn of his miracles. Nikon admitted he had been to some of the gatherings." Calista waved her bread. "I'm not the least bit interested in another man that performs miracles. Too many to count in Rome."

"Who was he and what miracles are you talking about? I'm hearing of a man who stood above the many miracle workers in

Rome. Why was this one so special?" Ruth took a sip of grape juice.

"I don't know why he was so special, other than he performed miracles. But don't they all? And because Emperor Nero is threatened by the gatherings, he has begun seeking them out and punishing those who attend. Ruth, I am frightened of what Nikon is involved in."

Ruth slipped on her sandals and paced the room.

"I wasn't aware Emperor Nero was displeased by the gatherings. Nikon and Marcus have been friends for many years, as we have. Marcus could easily be persuaded by a trusted friend or the reverse." Ruth's voice raised. "This is concerning. Curse them if they are putting our families in danger."

"My heart tells me it is too late." Calista sighed deeply.

APRIL 21, AD 64

Marcus insisted his belief in God was strong, but other duties were preoccupying his time, so he wouldn't accompany Ruth to the temple. *What could be more important than worshipping God?* She thought. Returning from the baths, Marcus didn't wear his military toga, which he had always worn with considerable pride. He no longer wanted to drink substantial amounts of spiced wine in the evening. On this day, Ruth coaxed him to their atrium to enjoy the warmth of the sun as it set. Reaching to caress him, he pulled away, dropping down onto a lounge. He fell against a pillow gazing up to the soft darkening blue sky. Right beside her, yet so far away.

"I know you are worried...and I'm fine. We're fine," Marcus began.

Ruth sighed. "Then why are you spending so much time with Nikon...and your mother? You dread talking with her most of the time, and now you are with her more time than me!" Ruth took a breath and continued without waiting for his answer. "I visited Calista today. Nikon has told her of a man he has begun following. Are you following him, too? Who is he? Why is he more important than the others? What does he do? Is he the reason you are so lost in your thoughts?" The questions fell out of Ruth.

Marcus abruptly sat up.

"If you will listen, truly listen, I will tell you." His angry eyes looked deeply into hers.

Ruth nodded.

His voice softened. "Mother told me of a teacher and orator who is known as Paul of Tarsus. At first, I refused her invitations. But she was relentless, so I finally consented when I heard through another soldier that Emperor Nero was hostile to these gatherings. I wondered why. This orator, Paul, spoke of a man named Jesus of Nazareth who was alive more than thirty years past, and who spoke with a powerful message of peace. Mother told me she had been following him and organizing gatherings of people for some time. I had no idea she was involved in such things, but knew she was putting herself in danger. I went as her protector, but as I listened, I became intrigued. There is another way to live; without debauchery, killing, always looking over your shoulder for enemies. As I get older and wiser, I realize that a soldier's life is full of discontent; that war and the pursuit of riches leaves me empty. After I heard Paul, I wanted to hear more of the message of this Jesus. Do you wonder if there will ever be someone who can deliver messages from God? I mean messages with lessons that will guide us to a more righteous life. Someone who can ease our burdens? Someone who will show us the way?"

"The way to where?" Ruth interrupted.

"The pathway to heaven, to a feeling of peace. The way to righteousness." Marcus continued, "Do you ever wonder if God will answer the prayers of the Jews and send his messenger? I wonder if this person Paul teaches about is the One, the messenger the Jews have prophesied would come. Nero's madness is getting worse and will destroy Rome...and the world. We all know it." Marcus spoke in earnest. "We can't follow such a tyrant."

"But what about your son and me? Are we not a part of your grand decision? And no, I have not wondered about anyone other than God guiding us. He is the only One." Ruth was emphatic.

"Ruth, I know I am a soldier," Marcus calmly replied. "And you don't have to remind me of my responsibilities to my family along with my obligation to the orders of the emperor. But what if I have decided there is a better way, and that even though Nero is our leader, he is immoral? I have begun to doubt that killing a man just because he has uttered a wrong word against Nero isn't justified by any means. Simply attending the gatherings to learn of the man many call the Wonder Maker might be my demise. Don't you think I haven't had sleepless nights worrying about you and David, knowing that I couldn't bear either of you losing your life because of my convictions. Suddenly, my destiny seems confusing. There are people who knew him, who have heard him teach. One of them is a woman named Mary, who was a close follower. She knew him. She believes that he had been in the presence of God. All I know is that when I hear his message, I feel my heart changing," Marcus pushed up from the lounge and looked down at her. "I ask that you be patient."

Marcus held his hand up to silence Ruth before she spoke, gave her a stifling frown, and left the atrium. Ruth wondered if the Mary that Marcus described was the same Mary that Ushriya spoke of. She had heard of many so-called saviors, but her father had not acknowledged any of them. And why was Nero against the gatherings? She feared for her husband's life.

CHAPTER 12

THE GREAT FIRE OF ROME. JULY 18, AD 64

Crawling over cobblestones through dense smoke, her head struck a lifeless foot. Ruth followed a smoldering leg up through the thick haze and squinted into the milky vacant eyes of a corpse. It was Marcus. She clutched the dangling foot between both hands and pressed it to her lips.

"Mama!" Ruth's head snapped up. Maternal instinct overpowered her grief, forcing her to leave the opaque stare of her husband's impaled body. The monstrous fire all around her picked up momentum; Ruth choked as the firestorm devoured the wooden frame of their home, the flames licking from recessed windows like serpent tongues. Searing currents of wind scorched her lungs and hot steam scalded her skin. Gray floury ash fell all around her, making it hard to breathe. She gagged, cleared her throat, then found her voice.

"David! Stay where you are! Sing to me. Sing the mountain song. I'll come to you!" Yanking her stola up over her nose and mouth, ripping a patch of cloth from the bottom, Ruth dipped it into a nearby water trough and inched towards David's voice. She brushed away hot embers and fought to keep her stola from igniting. Her hand touched a body, a woman, face-down, arms outstretched in her path. She turned the limp body over with gasp. White hair fell from a youthful face. Ushriya!

"Ushreeeaaa!" Ruth shook her, then leaned over to see if she was breathing. Her chest rose, then fell in fast shallow attempts to breathe. Ruth scooped her arm under Ushriya's shoulders, but her closed eyes were unresponsive. Ruth struggled for air. I can't help her, she thought. She quickly tore another piece of cloth from her stola, tied it loosely around Ushriya's mouth and nose, continuing towards David. The muffled voice of a small child trying to sing sounded again.

"Mama! I'm over here!" Five-year old David's voice rang through the smoke. She heard him cough.

"Sing our mountain song." David coughed again. Ruth frantically searched in the direction of the cough.

"Sing!" Ruth repeated.

"There is a mountain high above my head. I can see it from my bed!" David's voice levitated above the smoke. Suddenly, he emerged from the darkness and collapsed into his mother's arms. Ruth's head shot up to the whoosh of fire spiraling up a wooden column. She tied the cloth over his mouth and pushed David in front of her just as she heard the snap of a falling beam crashing to the cobblestone road. Cinders sparked, then exploded, igniting more fires in all directions.

"Mama! I'm on fire!" Ruth grabbed David and rolled him over to extinguish the flames spreading up his tunic. Squatting down, she drew him to her and pressed the torn wet cloth to his face, the other hand guiding him ahead. Disoriented, Ruth fell forward, eyes stinging as she searched for a hint of light through the dark smoke. Ducking David's head down, she created a tent with her stola as the heat singed her and forced them onward.

A dog howled pitifully in the distance. Ruth recognized the

whine of Korax, the guard dog of the House of Decimus in the east section of Rome. There! A direction at last. She listened intently as poor Korax's howl became more frantic, no doubt straining at his tethers trying to escape. Stay alive, dear Korax, so that you may guide us! She heard a man fall beside them. He gurgled and slumped to the ground. Can't help. Go! Move! She sidestepped through throngs of confused, bewildered people now mobbing the streets. Passing the baths, she could hear people shouting, trying to get into the water instead of leaving the inferno. Dazed residents of a two-story house threw their belongings out of windows, expecting to claim them on the streets. The fire took the fuel. Horses and mules crazed with fear reared up on their hindquarters, became asphyxiated, and fell to their deaths. An exhausted woman carrying her child collapsed ahead of them. Ruth focused. Staying ahead of the blistering fire was like running from an angry dragon inhaling everything in its path. The beast gained strength from the rising wind; Ruth remembered her father explaining that the best chance for survival was below a fire's smoke. Kneeling, she inched along the narrow streets on her belly, pulling David alongside. There were charred bodies lying on top of one another. If we're to survive, it will be by the hand of God, Ruth thought. With each intake of poisonous fumes, David coughed.

Just ahead, an abandoned cart came into focus. A horse still harnessed to it laid on its side, dead.

"Halt!" A voice boomed from the darkness. In the vastness and commotion of the fiery smoke, the sound of metal clinked then crashed together. Through the smoke, Ruth strained to see the faint shadow of a man running towards them. She crouched down and drew David behind the cart's wheels.

"Ruth! David! It is your Avunculus Solomon! Where are you?" His voice boomed. "Marcus sent me to save you."

Marcus could not have sent him. Marcus was dead. She thought.

Suspicion surged through her. Ruth edged David cautiously to the other side of the cart and continued in the opposite direction of Solomon's voice. Rounding a corner, Ruth again pushed David ahead.

"Run!" She whispered loudly. A gray pallor overtook David's terrified face as he ran as fast as his legs could carry him, then he collapsed in a fit of coughing. Ruth prayed her uncle wouldn't find them. The air became thinner. Unsure of where they were, Ruth lost the direction of Korax's howl, but glimpsed the stairs going up to the back door of the temple. She dragged David underneath the stairs, stopping to catch their breath. Drunken soldiers passed them, hurling torches, igniting the dead. The sickly odor of burning flesh filled the air.

"Burn Rome and impale the followers!" they shouted in their drunken stupor. "By the orders of Emperor Nero!"

"Where is my apa? And Ushriya?" David whimpered.

"Tomorrow we will see if …" With a thunderous crunch, the temple roof caved in beside them, embers lighting more fires. Startled, Ruth grabbed David's hand, scooped him up and ran. Her heart skipped a beat when she tripped over a sign, almost dropping David. It marked the Via Aurelius, a well-known exit out of the city. Marcus was dead. She prayed for Ushriya. A gush of resolve came over her as they headed out of Rome.

CHAPTER 13

THE DAY AFTER THE GREAT FIRE. JULY 19, AD 64

Ruth heaved David into the back of the first cart they encountered outside the entrance to Rome. Clacking wheels jostled them awake. Prickly spelt wheat scratched Ruth's burnt face as she struggled to see through the sheaves. She motioned David to stay silent. Covering her nose at the stench of urine and feces rising in the heat along the road, she peeked over the edge of the cart. There were hordes of disoriented people stumbling over cobblestones who had no idea where they were going any more than she did. But she did know her father had unknowingly helped them stay alive. He had shown her the way out of Rome as a small child, especially the exit that led them to the Via Appia. He had shared legends of the road famously built as a reliable stone military passage which allowed legions of Roman soldiers to swiftly navigate the countryside, even in winter. Ruth's father had taken great patience to share the traditional stories of men who toiled on Via Appia in the hot sun; how they unloaded and positioned every stone. He explained how they had labored long days with little food or water, causing countless to die. Generations later, her father had known some of their great-grandsons and knew many Roman families, even some elites, who began their legacies in slavery. Many of their deceased were entombed in extravagant family mausoleums along the road with detailed inscriptions. Now Ruth understood why her father shared their stories. They were the foundation of Rome. She sensed the presence of their spirits all around. The fire behind them added to their numbers by the hundreds.

David coughed. Ruth instantly put her hand over his mouth. He puffed air against her hand and coughed again. Too late, they had been discovered. The cart jerked to a halt, and the cloth covering them was abruptly yanked off.

"Who are you?" said a man peering at them from the driver's seat. His once auburn hair fell to the bottom of his neck, joining his graying beard. He had a straight nose with heavy eyebrows that connected as he stared at them. His small mouth was at odds with his demeanor. "Did you get on my cart when I stopped at the last water trough?"

Ruth held her head high. "I am Ruth. This is my son, David. We saw a cart as we ran. I know you did not see us climb in the back as you waited for the donkeys to drink. You were headed away from the fire; we had no choice." David buried his face in his mother's shoulder, digging his fingers deep into her stola.

"Where is your husband?" The man noticed David and the quality in her clothing, though her stola had holes where several patches were torn away. It was disheveled and smoky; her hair fell into her face, nonetheless, a style worn by the wealthy. A closer look gave pause.

Ruth sensed this man was a father. "We haven't seen him since the fire." Ruth's eyes dropped to David. She sat up straight and maneuvered so David was behind her. "He said he was attending a gathering, and we haven't seen him since," Ruth lied.

The man's eyebrows raised. "What is your faith?"

"We are of the Star of David...we are Jews." With a slight nod, the driver tightened the reins and clicked his tongue. The donkeys struggled against the weight of the cart edging forward.

The driver leaned back. "And where will you go--" Then he interrupted himself. "You wear the fine clothes of the elites."

Ruth sighed. "We will go where your cart takes us. We have no home. Our home has been destroyed."

"Very well, then. Pompeii is where this cart will take you." The driver shook the reins and the two gray donkeys pressed on under the harsh sun. Stopping occasionally for water when they could find it, they passed multitudes of people too dazed to know they even needed water. Thousands fell on the stones. Singed and starving, they died. With a somber expression, the driver stopped the cart to move the dead, as if he had seen this all before. Heat from the hot sun quickened the rotting of the corpses, and the stench of death overwhelmed Ruth. She gagged, battling tears and repulsion, but now, again she felt their souls.

"Who is your husband?" The driver asked after stepping back into his seat. An elite Roman woman with a child would be the wife of an influential man.

A moment passed before she could reply. "My husband is in the Roman Army."

"His name?"

"Marcus."

"Marcus Acacia?" A knowing look settled in the wrinkles around the driver's mouth; his lips tightened.

"Yes. Marcus Acacia. Do you know him?" The wheat stabbed through her stola. Ruth shuffled, swatting at the wheat. David coughed.

"I have heard of Marcus Acacia, the consul." The man raised his hand. "There is bread and water in the flasks beside you. Eat. Drink." He turned, grabbing the reins. "We will be there in three suns."

Not used to being dismissed, Ruth raised her tone of voice. "Pompeii? I have traveled to Pompeii, as a young girl with my father and mother. A slave of mine seemed to think she had lived there as a small child."

"Hmmph. Makes sense. Pompeii is a town that serves the elites," the man said.

"Since Rome is destroyed, I haven't any reason to believe my status still exists and even if it did, Rome will need to be rebuilt. It's my son with whom I am concerned. He'll need food and a place to rest. We'll return to Marcus when we can," Ruth added for David's ears.

Ruth tore the bread; deep in thought, she gave a piece to David. She thought of Calista's last visit, how they had discussed their husband's new interests; how they were frightened. The last conversation she'd had with Marcus, he'd told her he was changing, that he might be killed because of it. Damn this Wonder Maker! Of what wonder was he, when the Emperor of Rome saw fit to kill all who followed him! She thought of Ushriya and allowed the tears to come. For all of them. For David. For her life left behind. For the life ahead.

Hours later, long shadows signaled twilight. The driver finally found a small creek to water the donkeys. If donkeys could smile, they did right then and waded in, flipping water over their noses. Once calmed, both animals went down to their knees and rolled in the shallow edge. David smiled and pointed at them. He playfully scampered to the creek; Ruth caught up with him, grabbing his hand. Then noticing the water was shallow, decided to let him go. Down into the creek he went, splashing with the donkeys. He climbed over the rocks, shaking his dark curls, then made his way back to the cart. Smiling, he looked up at Ruth. She sighed, wrapping him with the cloth in the cart. After the driver shared more bread, he situated the cart under an olive grove, gathered some blankets from under the seat, and gave Ruth and David the largest so they could sleep in the wheat, while he crawled under the cart.

JULY 21, AD 64

Daylight came quickly. Recalling the Via Appia would turn to the ocean near Napoli, Ruth's heart quickened. For an instant, the thought of fresh salty air lifted her wounded spirit. Uneven ruts from the wheels of countless carts before, lurched and jolted them onward. But the sea was not to be. Ruth could tell this man was familiar with the road as he eased the donkeys inland, north to the town of Capua. Time passed slowly; the wheels clicked eternally on a road of monotony.

Occasionally Ruth glanced up as they settled in the bristly wheat and saw a few wispy clouds floating by. She could see the driver's shoulders relax. She wondered what he had encountered in Rome and why he was there, but nonetheless she found herself trusting him. At this point, she had no choice. His body caught the rhythm of the jarring side to side as he guided the donkeys. Wearing his age, this was a man who toiled for many years, but now, he seemed peaceful. He casually began to talk about his family. He had a son who oversaw the family business while he left to buy spelt wheat in Rome and was twenty years on this earth. Cyrus was now the sole eldest son betrothed to the daughter of a planter. He would eventually become the paterfamilias of a large villa. His youngest son, Julius, had not survived ten years.

"The planter and I have remained friends since childhood. Although he has become an elite and I am a merchant, we kept our promise to one another that our children would be betrothed. Cyrus will be a fine husband and will bring good fortune to his betrothed. Her father knows I taught my son well." He smiled with pride.

"You have not told me your name." Ruth stated.

"It is Hanoch," the man replied.

"Hello, Hanoch. And what is your family business?" Ruth asked. "Do you have daughters?" Ruth yawned, stretching her arms long above her head.

"We are bakers." Ruth could hear pain in his voice. "I had a daughter we accepted into our household many years past, but she is gone."

"What was her name?" Ruth closed her eyes and pulled David to her. The cadence of the wagon, the warm sun and partially full belly gave way to exhaustion. Hanoch's muffled voice faded in the distance. Groggily wrapping her smoky stola around David, she leaned her head on top of his, and they both fell into a deep sleep.

JULY 23, AD 64

When the sun rose on the fourth day, Ruth felt revitalized. David was still asleep when drunken voices bellowed in front of the cart. The driver stood up, bringing the donkeys to an abrupt halt. A man waving a long silvery sword pitched forward, catching himself from falling headlong into the rock. Ruth recognized the ornate garments of the Roman army on the inebriated soldier as other carts whipped their reins and hurried past.

No one stopped to help. Fire survivors kept their heads down using the strength they had reserved to hurry around them.

"Stop!" Ruth yelled, turning side to side, not knowing what else to do. "Help us!"

"Get down!" the man with the sword demanded. "Now!" He staggered, stumbling on the cobblestones. Hanoch whipped the donkeys and snapped the reins to ward off the bandit, but he couldn't dodge the drunken soldier's sword tearing deep into the flesh of his beloved donkey's throat. As dark crimson blood gushed from the wound, the animal collapsed. The cart tilted, cracking dangerously, causing the other donkey to rear up on its back legs. Angry, Hanoch reached for a wooden club, climbed to the top of the cart, lunged at the thief, fiercely swinging the club. Behind Hanoch, Ruth pushed David's head under the wheat. She climbed out of the rear of the cart, circling around behind the bandit, but it was too late as his sword wildly plunged into Hanoch's side. The bandit stumbled, stepping on the motionless body, pulled his sword out, turned and seized upon Ruth. He grabbed and ripped her stola, but she managed to pull free and climb up the side of the cart. She twisted, held on firmly and kicked the drunken thug in the face with her heel, using as much strength as she could muster. His bulky body, stinking of alcohol, fell backwards. Arms flailing, his head smashed onto the rocks and cracked open like a broken egg. She exhaled.

"Mama!" Ruth scaled the top of the cart, climbed back into the wheat and hugged David to her tightly. Rocking him back and forth, tears for a man she'd only just met spilled down her cheeks.

CHAPTER 14

JULY 28, AD 64

Ushriya pitied the oxen straining in the sweltering heat pulling heavy loads of fish up a steep incline to the bigger arch of the entrance to Pompeii. Fighting flies, they twitched their ears, and tossed their heads from side to side. Angry peasants shook their fists at the top of the ramp when they were told the streets of the town were closed during the day for pedestrian traffic. Ushriya could see large gates below her opening into warehouses storing fishermen's wares, salt, and clay containers. The fishy smell of carts coming from the sea grew stronger as the temperature rose. Two high arches stretching to the height of four men framed the gates with a sign designating the entrance of Porta Marina. Ancient stones arched over the entrance to a tunnel which had been used to fortify Pompeii long ago. To her right was a small niche with the statue of Minerva, the goddess of wisdom and strategic warfare, to protect the town. The bustling community awoke hours ago, greeting Ushriya when she climbed out of the merchant's wine cart. She doubted he even knew she was gone.

Ushriya picked up a stray twig and doodled in the sand between the rocks beside the steps. A small army of ants caught her attention, trailing behind her foot over the rocks in a perfect line. One ant dropped a kernel-sized nugget, and the others gathered around to help regain the load. It seemed to Ushriya that every living thing in this town carried loads. She glanced up from the dirt, startled to see the sign of the fish on a short column along the steps.

Shielding her eyes from the bright sun, she studied the two entrance arches. *Nothing compared to Rome*, she thought. Resting on a step in the shade, wrapping her arms around her knees, she lethargically watched foot travelers climb the stairs of the small arch closest to her. Her head dropped to watch the ants, then she caught a scent of her unbathed body. It had been many suns since her last bath, but now a full bladder sent her in search of a place to relieve herself. After making her way up the stairs through the entrance following the foot travelers, she found a bush of pink flowers. *This plant has been used before,* she thought, wrinkling her nose.

"Just arriving from Rome?" A striking older woman appeared out of nowhere.

Ushriya hastily pulled her undergarments up under her stained tunic, ran her fingers through tangled red golden hair and averted her eyes. "I have been walking for most of the day until..."

"Hundreds of people have descended on Pompeii. How did you get here?" the lady asked.

"A merchant bringing wine from Rome allowed my passage on his cart. I slept between the casks."

"And why did he give you passage and no one else?" The woman asked.

Ushriya shrugged, touching an amulet on her waist with her hand.

"You wear the sign of the fish. How brave of you given the times in Rome. I have seen the sign, and there are those in our small town...your garments are those of a slave. What is your name?" Her conversation wandered.

"I am Ushriya, domina."

"I'm not your domina. My name is Priscilla." A hand on her chin and the other on her elbow, the woman circled. Her azure tunic swished when she walked. Braids of black hair tinged with gray rose above her face, spilling down onto her high forehead into her wide brown eyes.

"You smell like soot and burnt swine. Odd name, Ushriya. Though you are quite lovely, certainly young enough. Exquisite long red flaxen hair. Men do take pleasure in that, for some reason. The white streak in your hair is...hmm, touched, are you? Nice emerald green eyes. Turn, let me see your back side," the woman said.

"I will not show you my back side! Who are you? What do you want with me? I am not 'touched'. And my name means, oh it doesn't matter..." Ushriya stopped herself and averted her eyes, embarrassed at her outburst. "Please accept my apologies. I have been forward."

"Such spirit for a slave. I like that. It is quite evident you need food and a bath." Priscilla touched her nose, gesturing Ushriya to walk beside with her.

Ushriya hesitated, then relented. Slaves were not permitted to walk beside the person who owned them. With domina Ruth, she kept her place and stayed two steps back. Priscilla was silent, so with a sigh, tipping her face to the sky, Ushriya savored the warmth. Echoes of David's terrified cries in the distance through the hazy smoke of the fire in Rome jolted her respite. She thanked God her life was spared from the fire. A peasant carrying a heavy bucket of water had tripped on a burning beam and had drenched her awake. Ushriya could not recall anything about the peasant's clothing, or even if her angel had been a boy or girl. But as soon as she had sufficiently recovered, she searched for any cart headed out of Rome to escape the fire.

Now, traversing the roads of Pompeii, Ushriya side stepped the blistering cobblestones. Many days without enough water lured her to a communal stone fountain trickling fresh water out of the mouth of a gray gargoyle. Priscilla watched Ushriya drink her fill, then splash water on her scorched arms, rubbing as much dirt off her grimy face as she could. When she finished, Ushriya stepped up on the side of the street, feeling less parched.

"New girl, eh Priscilla? With a bath, she will be a fine one!" a bureaucrat called from the street. A woman walking behind him heaved a sigh.

"Pay no attention. Animals. They are like wolves to blood," Priscilla whispered under her breath.

Ushriya accepted Priscilla's hand as she reached back to guide her on the high stones across the road built to avoid the reeking waste. She slapped at the tenacious swarms of flies diving and humming, arising from excrement thrown out into the roads. Bands of children scampered in front of them, laughing, running, and colliding into each other. Another group of children huddled in an alley. Orphaned street children flashed in her thoughts.

Ushriya felt the shade of the statue of the goddess Venus eclipse her face. Venus, the Goddess of Love and Fertility. After the shadow moved, she saw scarlet-and lime-colored mosaics that accented fine granite walls on municipal buildings.

"You have never been here?" Priscilla asked.

"Well, maybe..." Her thoughts trailed off.

"Slave traders continually prowl the streets looking for the vulnerable. Any man, woman or child can fall prey." Priscilla quickly changed the subject. "So! Plans are to restore the temple in our small town to make it more impressive than it was. The gods of Vesuvius became angry two years past and caused considerable damage. Many walls cracked and the timbers weakened." Amazed this woman would speak to her so informally, Ushriya relaxed. Priscilla pointed to a crevasse a painter was attempting to repair with plaster. "We are not a patient people, but eventually Pompeii will once again be restored to her former splendor."

They passed five grand doorways into the next building. Ushriya presumed it was the Basilica. *Not so grand as Rome*, she thought once again. Peeking into the entrance, she saw ornate marble columns lining the portico. A tiny dark-haired girl bumped into them, fell on her bare knees against the abrasive rock, and cried out in pain. Blood seeped through her tiny tunic and ran down her legs. Ushriya reached to help her up, but the little girl caught sight of her mother across the road. Scooping her up, the mother threw a scowl their way and faded into the crowd. Priscilla shrugged. "I am acquainted with most men in Pompeii. The women tend to avoid me." She laughed. Ushriya recalled Priscilla's statements about her backside and men appreciating the color of her hair. She shuddered at the obvious.

Further on, Priscilla stopped to greet an elderly woman who used a cane. "Used to be one of the best," Priscilla remarked. They passed another temple, the Temple of Apollo. Ushriya walked toward the sundial and saw a fish etched in the stone on the frame of the foundation. She ran her fingers over the coarse grooves.

"The fish. There it is. Told you." Priscilla motioned her onward until they rounded the corner to the left. A marker designating the street of the Via del Foro faced the stately façade of the Forum. Many times, dominus Marcus had sent her to deliver papyrus to the Forum in Rome. Because slaves are not allowed in the Forum unless they were serving their dominus, she rushed through the ornate portico of regal statues and marble floors. Ushriya envied the responsibilities of the bureaucrats because something told her that their duties couldn't be that difficult; that she could perform their tasks. Her leadership among the slaves, and even with domina Ruth, prompted the gift of solving problems. She had been told often enough she had wisdom beyond her years, but sometimes an opinion would burst forth at an inappropriate time. Domina Ruth never whipped her, but there were occasions when Ushriya knew she had overstepped. She recalled dodging through the commotion in the Forum in Rome to locate dominus Marcus, purposefully leaning in close, grazing against the clusters of senators to eavesdrop. Though just fifteen years, discussions of Emperor Nero's mental health, and the man, Paul of Tarsus, who witnessed the Wonder Maker after his death, dominated their conversations and fascinated Ushriya.

Now that she had witnessed the sign of the fish, she knew it meant that the followers were here. When domina Ruth left to visit her sister in Herculaneum four years past, dominus Marcus did not tell her he'd invited a gathering of the followers to their domus. While serving them wine, cheese, and bread, she heard Marcus tell of the arrival of Paul of Tarsus in Rome, which had led to a serious conflict with the Jews and was now to be put on trial.

"We will learn a new way from Paul of Tarsus, the teachings

of a man who appeared to Paul days after his death." Dominus Marcus smiled and looked to the sky. Ushriya could not stop thinking about this man who captivated even the slaves. They were excited about his teachings of equality and love for men, women, slaves, and elites, alike. Yet Ushriya did not seek out a gathering. She did not fall victim to rumors, but the change in dominus Marcus' demeanor over time caused curiosity. Everyone, both masters and slaves, began etching the symbol of the fish on meeting sites. The symbol of the fish arose from stories of the miracle the Wonder Maker performed by feeding throngs of people with a few fish and several loaves of bread. For the first time in her life, she felt a connection. This man who Marcus revered taught that everyone's life had meaning, that everyone was equal, so she proudly wore the symbol of the fish on an amulet made from clay by her friend, Lorena.

Another tremendous temple beyond the Forum blocked the sunlight. She appreciated the enormous letters announcing the Temple of Jupiter on the massive white slab of granite towering above their heads. Crumbling statues beneath it still waited for repair. Two porticos reaching through two levels: the great courtyard was comparable to the Basilica in Rome, where thousands of patrons came and went. It seemed Priscilla knew everyone.

The public baths were in sight. Priscilla read Ushriya's mind, reassuring her of a bath soon. *Why was this woman being so kind?* A young man wearing a white tunic cinched by a gold belt handed a coin to each patron on the steps to the entrance. He smiled and called, "Ah, Priscilla." She respectfully nodded.

"He is your age, yet it's quite obvious he has not missed many meals," Priscilla sneered.

"Why does he give a coin to everyone who enters?" Ushriya asked.

Priscilla kept her pace until she was sure the man could not hear her, then leaned in close and whispered, "He pays their fees to the baths because he wants the people to elect him Tribune. You have seen this in Rome, I am certain. A Tribune of the People is the leader of the plebs, and a part of the aristocracy. He has the power to veto any law the people he represents do not like...and he is one of our patrons, so we will support him."

"Patrons? What is your trade?" Ushriya was curious.

"I thought you had guessed by now. I own the Lupanare and am proud to have serviced most of the men in Pompeii...at one time or another." Priscilla winked.

"You are..." Ushriya's suspicions were realized.

"Used to be one of the best. One of the most beautiful lupas in Pompeii." Priscilla flipped her hair. "Now I *own* the best." Priscilla waved at another man, this one dressed not so formally. "Since you have no other options, come spend a night with us."

Ushriya hesitated, but this woman was right. She had no options.

"How does one become a Tribune?" Ushriya continued.

"He had at least ten years in the infantry or five years in the calvary, and wants to be a Senator...why do you ask?"

Ushriya felt once again that she had overstepped, but it became apparent it didn't matter. "We will take a most unpleasant short cut, be prepared!" Priscilla warned. Turning behind the Forum, they passed the latrines. Avoiding the sight of men with splayed togas sitting over the holes along the back walls of the baths, Ushriya gagged. Simultaneously discharging stomach gas and relieving their bowels, they argued their opinions.

"Are you in need of a latrine?" Priscilla's wry smile teased Ushriya as she wrinkled her nose.

The scenery changed as they quickly approached the Macellum and were greeted by drifting waves of freshly baked bread. Fragrant lilies mingling with the aroma of powerful peppers flooded Ushriya's senses. She fondly thought of recent market trips in Rome, buying lilies for the atrium and adding an extra dulcia in her basket for David.

Within the vendor shops, mosaics of cobalt and indigo frescos picturing fish, sheep and pigs decorated the walls behind the meat vendor. Daily fresh fish for the evening cena was a preferred delicacy in the House of Acacia. Blacksmiths, wine shops, locksmiths, hot food vendors, banks and hairdressers lined the streets, plying their trades. On the side of the potter's shop lodged in the stone, a massive beam softly groaned beneath the substantial weight of the roof.

"We have grown accustomed to Vesuvius' tantrums," Priscilla said.

After the Macellum, they approached the entrance of one of the grand houses lining the streets. Drawn by the reminder of dominus Marcus and domina Ruth's house, Ushriya cautiously peeked into the small passageway to the vestibulum, the corridor that led to the main entry of the domus. Just ahead, Priscilla turned at the street of Viccolo de Lupanare.

"We are here." She shoved the door open with her shoulder, forcing it over the uneven threshold. Ushriya tripped on an engraved stone at her feet. An odd, shaped arrow pointed towards the entryway. It looked like a phallus. She stepped over it.

As they entered, a drunken man backed into Ushriya, but Priscilla used her body to shield them through the entryway, sending her sideways into the wall. Ushriya recovered quickly to glimpse yet another statue of Venus, the goddess of love, looming ahead. Stairs led up to five doors along the balcony, designed in a square. It overlooked a little courtyard with a bench in need of cleaning and unkempt foliage. Turned over titulus on each closed door conveyed the status of the room: *occupata*. The titulus on the open doors were not turned over, but had names written in large letters with numbers of coins under them. Ushriya shrank at the sight of a red and gold fresco of a woman admiring a man with a phallus as large as a horse.

"It is the reason we eat so well," Priscilla uttered coyly.

A young girl with light brown tresses leaned over the portico, flipped her blue toga, and caught the eye of a boorish fat man at the foot of the stairs. His lecherous smile repulsed Ushriya. Hair but a distant memory, thinned to wisps, he bore the pompous air of the upper class. Wrestling with his stiff white toga, he grunted and groaned to climb the stairs. Ushriya's stomach curdled at the thought of the pompous, stinking man on top of such a slightly built girl.

"Elites of the government are not seen here regularly, but that snobbish drunk has a favorite," Priscilla said.

"Must you service me at the top of the stairs? Can you not lay with me down here? It will be my coins that buy your fine togas, will it not?" The man reeled as he attempted the stairs.

Looking down, the young girl teased him. "Yes, m'lord, but

you must climb the stairs. It is here I will make your loins tremble with the wrath of Vesuvius." Lust forced his girth up the stairs. She sighed, elbows apathetically leaning on the portico. Catching Priscilla's eye, she quipped, "This won't take long." Turning slowly to her room, she cupped her hand along his elbow and smiled sweetly at the sweaty aristocrat who had made it to the top of the stairs.

Priscilla directed Ushriya toward the back of the house to the culina. Too early for cena, though ravenous, Ushriya knew a trip to the markets was needed for the evening meal. Leftover food from the last meal would probably be scarce with the number of people living here.

"Augusta, this is Ushriya. Please see that she gets food and a bath," Priscilla directed an older lady.

"We will have the first meal together in the morning after you have a night of sleep. Augusta, put her in the guest room behind Emilia." Priscilla left.

Surprised at the change in Priscilla's attitude and that she had been left so tersely, Ushriya wondered how she would address this woman.

"You will be joining our girls?" Augusta said without looking at Ushriya. She pushed her short plump body up on her toes to pull bowls from the upper shelves. Then she grabbed a loaf of bread from one of the baskets under a heavy table in the middle of the small yellow room. Without invitation, Ushriya used her height advantage to help Augusta. Too hungry to think through the question, she pointed to a plate of bread.

"May I have a piece of that bread?"

"Why, yes." Augusta tore a piece and handed it to Ushriya, then pushed the entire plate to her.

A tall, dark-skinned young man dressed in a tunic burst through the side door, sandals sliding on the floor. He raised his dark eyebrows, wrinkling his distinctly Roman nose in disgust. "Must Priscilla rescue every waif on the street?" He winked at Ushriya.

"Alexis!" Augusta reprimanded.

He half-nodded a greeting, turning his attention to the food. "Am I to starve?" He turned to Ushriya, "I am Alexis, brother of Priscilla."

Ushriya felt her face turn red. "I am Ushriya."

Augusta waved him away and sat plates of spicy, boiled chicken and fish, vegetables, and dense wheat bread on the table. "Eat your fill, my dear." Ushriya scooted a chair to the table and began eating. She wished this handsome man would leave, so she would feel comfortable gorging herself.

"Now, my son, what's so important that you must fall through the door?" Augusta asked.

"And this is our mother," he said to Ushriya, then turned back to his mother, simultaneously helping himself to a bowl of dates and walnuts. "Rumors are spreading that Emperor Nero is to make a royal visit. It would be grand to see him as he passes in his chariot."

"Hmmppfff. He is a murderer and a ruffian. You know he has begun persecuting the people who gather to hear..." Augusta frowned. "Why do you want to see such a man?"

Alexis shrugged and grabbed an olive. "Who are you talking about?" Not waiting for an answer, he disappeared through the washroom door.

Alexis didn't say goodbye, but Ushriya didn't care. She

continued eating, a bit faster now. "I'm ever grateful for the food and the invitation to stay the night."

"I will find a clean tunic before we take you to the baths." Augusta hung a wet cloth on the hook beside the clay oven. She sat down at the table in the middle of the culina and leaned on her elbows watching Ushriya eat. "Tell me about yourself."

"There is nothing to tell. You can see I am a slave," Ushriya said.

"I can see you are not an average slave. You speak well and are dressed in the finest tunic a slave may wear. Tell me." Augusta cocked her head in curiosity.

Ushriya relented. "I was the famulus in the house of Marcus Acacia in Rome, a consul of the Roman Army. The house burnt in the fire, and I presume my domina is no longer..."

"Ah! A head house slave, the most coveted job of a slave! You have not carried many heavy burdens." Augusta sat back, holding her elbows.

"Yet I am a slave, a human being in bondage for another. I do not know if dominus Marcus or his family survived the fire, but I am desperate to know. I have no husband or children; their son David is my charge. I adore him as my own." Ushriya stopped eating unable to hold back her tears.

"Perhaps they are alive. How did you leave Rome?" Augusta asked.

"The Via Appia. They may have been there; dead bodies were everywhere, rotting in the sun. I did not look at their faces." Ushriya succumbed to her grief.

Augusta put her ample arm around Ushriya's shoulders, guiding her from the table to a high-backed wooden chair. Her eyes narrowed as Ushriya dropped down in the chair. "It's not without sorrow that I hear your story. I, too, was a slave, but you have the opportunity to rise above that destiny now, here... if you can lay with the beasts."

"I'll not lay with an animal!" Defiantly, she met Augusta's gaze.

"I mean men that can't control their lust."

Ushriya turned her head away.

"You are young, my dear, and probably never had earnings of your own. Think of it. The sign of the fish on the tie around your waist tells me you know another way. He would not begrudge you a better life," Augusta explained.

"But a common lupa, a whore!" Ushriya exclaimed. "I am not as acquainted with the Wonder Maker as it seems you are, but I do know that laying under a man for money is not what he would want me to do."

"Look at me." Augusta took Ushriya's face into her hands. "We do not suggest you become a common lupa, but a meretrix. Do you want to remain a slave your entire life? No one knows you are a slave and neither Priscilla nor I, care. I advise you to simply close your eyes, let the men do their bidding and take the coins. You can use your beauty to become quite wealthy." Augusta backed away, allowing the idea to soak in.

Ushriya crossed her arms, tilting her head. "Meretrix?"

"The highest status, the girls who command the most pay," Augusta said.

Ushriya thought for a moment. In her entire life, she had never had coins of her own. "And the sum?"

"Depending on the beauty of the girl and her talents, two to twenty aeses. Our lena, that is Priscilla, gets a portion for room and food and the girl keeps what is left. Though there are slaves in the lower rooms…." Augusta didn't finish her sentence and got up, clanking clay plates together as she bustled around the culina. Stowing away bread and fruit in the baskets under the table, she turned to Ushriya.

"As a young maiden, I was a meretrix. Men called me Meretrix Lupa, the she-wolf!" Augusta's eyes twinkled. "Those were quite the days." She patted her middle. "Ah, too much fine living. I stay here because Priscilla is my daughter. She is the lena of the Lupanare and I must see to her. When she was growing inside me, my days as a meretrix were numbered, and then rich food made me fat. Men don't like a woman with child or one who has grown old and fat. I don't know who the father of Priscilla is, but it doesn't matter. I am a mother to all the girls who live here. And they need me. Where else would I go?" Augusta went into the cleaning room and returned with a fresh soft blue tunic draped over her arm. Ushriya followed her to the door.

"You will have your bath now. You have much to think about." Augusta fell silent. They made their way to the baths. Ushriya realized that this could be the first time in her life when she might have some control over her future.

CHAPTER 15

Ruth's shoulders ached from the constant pull of the reins. Both she and the lone donkey were numb with exhaustion, but she forced herself to stay awake for David's sake. Ruth had not been paying attention to the landscape until now, when at last, the entrance to a city was in sight. Through her fatigue, she admired the small town ahead in the shadows of the great mountain, Vesuvius. Her father had told her stories of its fury; she felt fortunate to have been in Rome at the time of the mountain's last tantrum. The donkey's head was down, ears back, dried white lines of salty sweat covered its back and neck. Even so, the weary animal plodded diligently forward. Ruth thanked God for the animal's tenacity.

"Look, there's a town right there. I can see it." David stood up on the wheat and pointed over her shoulder. "Can you see it, Mama?"

"I do see it." Ruth heaved a big sigh as the donkey picked up its pace trudging onward. She was leery of what lay ahead, yet she felt relief.

When they arrived outside the gate, the donkey slowed, inching the cart through the archway of the herculean entry into Pompeii. Ruth saw a marker; "Porta Ercolano". Other carts laden with market produce passed her swiftly, cutting in line to be first when the gates opened at twilight for merchants. Foot travelers walked in procession through the small archways on either side.

"Woman! Get out of our way!" The merchants had no patience for a smoky, battered cart driven by a female.

Rowdy and unruly, the fast-moving carts all around her made the street hard to navigate. Ruth tried to steer the cart over to the side of the road, but the donkey refused and kept going forward. Since Ruth had no idea where she was or where she was going, and lacking the strength to control the animal, she had no choice but to allow the donkey its head. Finally, they passed through the entry.

"Curse you, woman! The gates do not open until dark. Get to the back of the line!" The merchants yelled at her, but the donkey's head was down. The animal persisted with instinct and direction, drawn to an unknown destination.

The streets were marked; this one was the Via Consalare. Since they were past the irate merchants and this remarkable animal was guiding the way, Ruth relaxed a little and scrutinized modest houses patched together to make wealthy residences. The donkey veered left onto Via Della Terme next to a huge house covering an entire block. Turning again onto Via Della Fortuna Augusta, the donkey took them past the baths.

How I covet a bath! Ruth imagined how she might gain entrance, but the donkey made no indication of stopping, and picked up its momentum. They passed houses of the privileged, adorned with columns and fountains, one after another. The donkey turned onto another street, Via Distabia, where construction of a yet one more new building was evident. After several more turns, the donkey slowed, and trotted into a small stable as if it had arrived home. David sat straight on the seat beside his mother looking all around at the hay bales stacked alongside the wall that led to a door. He watched a brown donkey eat at the hay feeder beside the water trough and saw another soft gray one settled into a bed of hay. The animals rose and nickered as the cart pulled into the stable.

"Where are we? Mama?" David whispered. "I smell bread. I'm hungry."

At once, a door swung open, and a smiling woman burst out.

"Ah, husband! You are ho…!" The woman stopped short and glared at Ruth.

"Where is my husband?" she demanded "Why are you in our cart?"

Ruth could say nothing, crumpling forward, overwhelmed by exhaustion. David sniffled.

The woman circled the cart. "Where is Hamor, the other donkey? Who are you?"

David wrapped his arms around his mother. Ruth sat up and put her arm around David.

Glancing down at the donkey, she remembered the man, Hanoch, telling her of his wife and of their bakery in Pompeii. The donkey knew its way. "H-hhe is no longer of this earth," she stammered.

Stunned, the woman's mouth dropped open. She staggered back. "What?" she gasped.

The story fell out of Ruth. "I am Ruth. This is my son, David. We found respite in this cart outside Rome the night we escaped from the fire. He kindly let us stay and gave us water and bread. Along the Via Appia, we were attacked by a drunken bandit who killed one of the donkeys. When your husband drew his club, the bandit stabbed him with his sword. I climbed over the side of the cart and kicked the bandit backwards as he tried to attack me and he fell to his death. That is what happened. I am so sorry." Ruth looked down at her hands as David snuggled closer to his mother.

"But where is his body?" The woman asked. Her lips trembled.

"I was unable to lift him onto the cart and there were bandits all around ready to overtake the cart, which was the only way we could escape. I had no choice but to leave him." David turned his head into Ruth's neck.

Grasping what had occurred, the woman collapsed to her knees in the hay, wailing.

Ruth gingerly climbed down from the cart and reached back to help David. He hesitated, but Ruth nodded reassurance, and gently lifted him down. Ruth went to the woman's side with David and sat silently. All three sat on the stable floor, taking in the immensity of what had happened to each of them. Ruth could shed no more tears, so she tried to comfort a woman she did not know.

After a while, the woman used her toga to dry her eyes. "I am Justine, wife of Hanoch. If he granted you passage, you knew him in his last hours. You are welcome in our home and our bakery for as long as you wish. Come." Ruth nodded gratefully and grasped Justine's hand.

Ruth detected an odor as she guided David behind Justine into the culina. She turned to her son.

"I'm so sorry but is there…." Justine pointed left to a latrine in a corner of the culina.

"You will find a pot of water there. Use the small clean tunic on the hook. One of our bakers leaves it there in case of accidents with her son." Ruth ushered David to the latrine and removed his soiled clothes, rinsing them in the clay pot. She dumped the water and left the pot outside.

When they finished, the scent of hot cakes and baked bread cooling on the thick wide windowsills tantalized them. Reminding Ruth of her own culina, the fresco scenes of different feasts, in red and orange, contrasted against soft brown and gray mortar. Shelves over-crowded with skillets, pans and large stirring spoons hung from the walls. Garum in terracotta pots sat in neat lines on the floor, along with baskets of grapes, pears, and roasted chestnuts. A large gray cat lounged under the mammoth wooden table in the middle of the room. For a fleeting moment, Ruth wondered if David's cat, Brutus, had survived the fire. Marcus had brought Brutus home as a kitten for David. She was not sure she wanted a cat in her home, but David loved him, and the mice population decreased, so she relented. Ruth saw her favorite sausages on the second shelf above the red fresco amongst more clay pots and jars of olives, beans, and broccoli. Following her hungry gaze, Justine invited them to eat. They devoured everything she put in front of them. The warmth of the bricks beneath the mortar of the cooking fire became intolerable on the sultry mid-summer day, so Justine encouraged them to wander out to the fresh air of the vestibule and dip their toes in a blue pool of clear, refreshing water. Ruth felt like she had gone from hell to heaven.

Waking on a couch with serpent's feet, David was asleep beside her. Ruth gently moved the covering and tip-toed to the culina where Justine was busily cutting bread and fruit.

"You have slept a long time; you must be so exhausted from the last days. Starting over will be challenging. The sun is high, and I am preparing prandium." Justine wiped her brow.

Ruth touched her arm. Justine sighed and stopped chopping. "What will you do without Hanoch?" Ruth asked, temporarily forgetting that she faced the same future.

"He would want us to go on. Many depend on the bakery."

"As we will without Marcus, my husband." Ruth heaved a heavy sigh, "In the short time I knew Hanoch, I knew he was a man of God."

"You have lost a husband, as well. We will begin new lives. And yes, Hanoch was man of God." Justine's shoulders sagged with sorrow. With a deep sigh, she straightened. "What is your faith?"

"I am a Jew. My father is a Jewish priest," Ruth said proudly.

"We are Jews, as well," Justine said.

"Hanoch told me about your son who is betrothed to a planter's daughter. You will be planning a wedding soon."

"Yes, and hopefully they will raise wheat for the bakery. Then long trips to Rome will not be necessary." A tear escaped and ran down her cheeks. "Oh, the loss of Cyrus' father will devastate his young life. He loved his father so much. They were more than father and son; they were friends. He will want to talk with you and hear about his last hours." Justine paused. "Now the loss of his father, along with a brother and sister, although long ago, will be a burden for his soul. I was awake long into the night, and I figured a way to manage the bakery," she said, thinking out loud.

The gravity of Ruth's new situation was beginning to settle in. She watched David play with the cat under the table.

CHAPTER 16

Dazzling sun radiated across the sill of the thick stucco window overlooking Vicolo del Lupanare. Ushriya had no idea what time or what day it was, and she didn't care. She propped herself up on a soft bag of cloth and rearranged the warm coverings on the hard bed, squirming to get comfortable. Never had she slept in a room alone. Euphoria came over her; dare she dream this was what it is like to be free? After talking with Augusta in the culina, a hint of independence kindled her excitement making sleep elusive until almost dawn. *I advise you to simply close your eyes, let them do their bidding and take the coins. You can use your beauty to become quite wealthy*, Augusta had said. Ushriya smiled, stretched her legs and flexed her toes, grimacing when she glanced down at her burnt feet. Surveying the room, she saw that there was a large latrine pot in the farthest corner beside a chair painted green. Another ornately decorated clay bowl with green leaves on white flowers sat on a small table holding water with a dark blue cloth beside it. Nothing fancy, but nicer than anything she had in the room she shared with three other house slaves at the House of Acacia. Augusta told her this room was reserved for the Priscilla's elite customers. She shuddered at the thought that she might be pressed into service right away. But a new confidence arose prompting a fresh perspective of the oversized phalluses of frescos on every wall. Now she understood the significance of the erotism; they were selling the wares! Even so, the best part of this moment was that no one was at the door prodding her to work. No one was yelling orders. No expectations. Lavender scents from the oils of last night's bath lingered in her golden red hair. She yawned, then dozed off once again.

A clamoring from downstairs jolted her awake. For an instant, she was in Rome with Ruth and David; what time was it; were they in need of anything? The lights needed to be lit: the marketing needed to be done. When reality returned, she sighed and wondered if they had survived. If they had, where could they be? Memories of dancing and singing in the culina while preparing garum as David played on the floor brought a smile. The recollection of miniature soldiers under tables and behind baskets reminded her of a time when she was kneading dough; her hand found what she thought was a stone. David giggled at her surprise when she pulled his toy soldier from the dough. David was all boy, rolling himself into a tight little ball and tumbling like a rolling stone into everyone or everything in his path. When David was born, Marcus had announced his son would become a great commander; he would follow in the footsteps of the Acacia dynasty. Ushriya had seen Ruth's envy of Marcus' unconditional love for their son in her sad eyes. She wanted him to love her like that.

Blisters on her feet bumped against the stone bed, a stinging reminder of the long journey from Rome. She winced as she swung her legs over the side. Bubbles of fluid on her skin, singed by the fire, ruptured as she rubbed her arms. Her stomach rumbled. It was apparent last afternoon's meal had worn off. As her hand reached for the lever, Priscilla pulled the door open from the other side.

"Oh, sorry to surprise you. Are you well?" Priscilla greeted her warmly. Ushriya admired her azure toga belted with a soft gray cloth. Her black hair was meticulously styled. Azure stones set in silver with a matching necklace completed a look of elegance and sophistication.

"I'm still very tired, sore and burnt with heat. Thank you for asking, domina." Ushriya looked down.

"Look at me." Ushriya lifted her head. "Please call me Priscilla. I am the lena of the Lupanare. When you talk to me, look into my eyes."

Ushriya gazed into Priscilla's face. *I will learn the ways of the world from this woman.*

"I see great things in your eyes." Priscilla smiled.

"But you have only known me a few short hours. You know nothing of me," Ushriya said.

"But I'm a good judge of potential. It's my job. If not, I wouldn't lead the life I do. I was born of a meretrix mother…"

"Augusta told me she is your mother, and Alexis' mother and that she was a great meretrix."

Priscilla nodded with a smile, "she tells everyone what a great meretrix she was. Have you yet laid with a man?"

"I was a slave, the famulus, in a great house where the domina protected me. Although, I have been dishonored as a woman, I have not been…" Ushriya declared.

"Defiled? Here, you will have the opportunity to buy your freedom, even though you have not been a slave of the Lupanare. Have you laid with a man who is gentle and knows how to please a woman?" Priscilla asked.

"Well, no. I have never thought of the idea of being pleased by a man. We are the creators of children. I thought they were to be pleased, not us. When men want to lay with me, they look at me like an animal to prey, tearing at my clothes and ..." Ushriya wrinkled her nose in disgust.

Priscilla placed her hands on Ushriya's shoulders. "You will lay with my brother Alexis. He will teach you that a man can harness his lust to please a woman."

Ushriya became nauseous at the thought of another man on top of her. Then she thought of Alexis, his mass of wavy dark locks, chiseled face, and muscular body.

"Will he pay me to lay with him?" Ushriya asked.

"Alexis will not. I will. I want you to know what it is to be with a man who knows how to satisfy a woman. Alexis is a male meretrix. He services the wealthiest matrons and patrons in Pompeii. He is eighteen years, and hasn't many years left to reap the large sums he commands," Priscilla said.

Ushriya nodded, feeling a twinge of curiosity and followed her downstairs.

After a feast of bread, fruit, and fish, Ushriya made her way back to the room where she had slept. With nowhere else to go and no one demanding her services, she wanted to rest. Stretching out on her bed, she heard the door creak open and hastily sat up. Alexis raised his finger to his lips, quietly crossed the room and sat beside her. She stiffened.

"Why are you...?" Ushriya asked.

He curled her hair around his forefinger and pulled his gaze back to look at her with flirtatious desire. Ushriya just had the conversation with Priscilla about Alexis and here he was. Nonetheless, her eyes followed him, then looked coyly away. He gently lifted her chin with two fingers while his other hand moved down the small of her back. Ushriya looked straight ahead and did not move. He scooted closer, his warm breath against her ear. She quivered. Tingling waves of anticipation spread throughout her body as Alexis' lips brushed against her cheek. Her will to discourage him gone, his hand found her breast. He gently lowered her backwards onto the bed. With a racing heart, Ushriya closed her eyes. As his lips met hers, Alexis released her, and stood up.

"And that, my sweet puella, is how it is done," Alexis proclaimed.

Ushriya sat up.

"You didn't want me to stop, did you? Seduction is power, my dear, and as you can see, it is quite intoxicating. Many people will pay large sums for the feeling you just had." Alexis reached for the door. "You are quite captivating. I will be your tutor anytime." And he was gone.

She wanted to scream, to kick something. Ushriya collapsed back on the bed. Her frustration turned to giggles, then laughter, as the realization of what Alexis had taught her sank in; that she did, indeed, have the power. Why, she could do what he did to any man or woman. What a revelation! Falling into a deep sleep, the shadows were long when she heard a knock at the door.

"Ushriya?" Priscilla did not completely open the door and eased in sideways.

"Yes?" Ushriya said.

Priscilla sat down on the bed. She reached into her belt and dropped a small bag of coins on the bed. "Here is the payment for Alexis' tutorial. Next time, it will be you who drops the coins on my table." Priscilla said, "Money is seductive. A woman can overlook a bit of inconvenience when she is gaining wealth."

"I am beginning to understand."

"People pay high prices to be a with a beautiful woman. You are beautiful. They will pay. Think about it," Priscilla's tone was soothing, yet firm. "I will expect to see you when you have freshened up." She rose and left.

As the door closed, Ushriya's thoughts raced. This was a new path from slavery, one she had never imagined. Alexis' words echoed: Seduction is power. Now she remembered the children in the streets of Rome.

CHAPTER 17

David stared at the ceiling as Ruth rolled over. Daylight peeked through the slits in the wooden shutters.

"My son, you are awake." Her arm encircled David pulling him to her. Dark curls were matted against his forehead. Ruth lovingly ran her fingers through his hair. Touching her finger to her tongue, her maternal spit pinned a stubborn curl to the side of his face.

"Mama, I want to know where my apa and Ushriya are. Where are we, and when are we going home?" David cuddled closer.

"We are in Pompeii. Since the man with the cart who brought us here is now with God, his wife has allowed us to sleep here. Maybe apa and Ushriya are with God, too. If they are, He will take care of them," Ruth explained.

"Will God give apa his spiced wine and Ushriya her dates?" David asked.

"Yes, He will, and we will see them again."

"I saw that man. He was killed. I saw the donkey get killed too. I know you helped one donkey pull the cart here. But what is Pompeii?"

"It is a town like our home in Rome, only smaller. We are safe here. There is no fire here," Ruth said.

David dissolved into soft sobs. Ruth had no idea of God's

plan, but two things were apparent: one, their lives were forever changed, and two, she had to remain strong for David. She reached to embrace him, holding him tightly. "We will be well. God is always looking over us. He will show us the way." Looking up, she sighed, then kissed the top of her son's head, and they fell asleep once again.

Under their window, commotion from commerce on the streets stirred Ruth and David awake. A slight breeze wafted in the stench from the waste below warmed by the late morning sun. Reminded it had been a while since David had used a latrine pot, Ruth hustled him out of bed and pointed to the pot in the corner.

When he was finished, Ruth said, "Let's go downstairs to see the nice lady who let us sleep here." With her hand on his shoulder, Ruth guided David down the stairs.

They passed down a long hall following the delicious smell of freshly baked bread. They had never been around the actual baking of bread; it was always sliced neatly on a plate for them at meals. Mother and son trailed the enticing aroma until the hall opened to an entrance under a flight of stairs. They made their way from under the stairs noticing that there were separate stairs leading up to a storage space full of grain sacks. The room was full of slaves working at separate stations in various phases of bread making. The heat was intense as fresh wheels of bread were pulled from the oven on long wooden handled pulls. There were four stone grinders with men pouring grain into two of them, while the other two were pushed in circles by oxen tethered to tall wooden dowels. Stone mills crushed, then ground the grain into fine flour which was collected below in lead boxes at the base. A man dressed in the brown loin cloth of a laborer slave finished pouring a sack of grain into the grinder and looked sideways at her but did not meet her eye.

"Have you seen Justine?" Ruth asked.

"Domina, she will be at the front of the bakery." The slave did not look up.

"I am grateful." His bare chest was powerful, no doubt gained from lifting grain sacks, then forcing the mill in circles for many hours. She realized, though unkempt, she still presented as a domina. David sidled up next to her as they moved past the grinders to the front, where Justine was selling bread to a patron. Stacks of warm bread carried right from the oven neatly lined shelves by the counter ready for sale.

"Justine?" Ruth approached her and touched her shoulder.

"Ah, Ruth," Justine looked down at David, fidgeting with his mother's toga. "Please help yourself to anything you desire in the culina. I will be in shortly to talk with you." Justine brushed her hair out of her eyes and turned back to the counter.

Ruth nodded.

"Mama, does that mean we can eat?" David asked rubbing his stomach with a frown. "I'm hungry." Having spent his five years on this earth in the comfort of a large domus, he was unaccustomed to hunger and enjoyed the care of doting slaves who met his every need.

Ruth guided him back through the bakery under the stairs to the hall, recalling that the culina was to the right. No one was in the room; the house slave must be at market. She had never been expected nor knew how to prepare a meal; Ushriya and the other slaves were always there to serve her. Though now, if she and David were to eat, Ruth must prepare something. She decided the easiest solution was to pick fruit and bread from baskets on the floor or up on the shelves. She handed David grapes from one basket and tore bread from another. Newly cracked nuts were next with olives and apples. They ate in silence until David patted his stomach once more.

"I'm full!" He smiled as his mother wiped his face with a nearby cloth.

Justine bustled into the culina, wiping her hands on her apron. She ladled a cool cup of water from a clay pot.

"Did you find plenty? I can prepare..." Justine began.

"No. We are grateful, although we can't pay you. I have no money," Ruth said.

"Don't worry. I know you have lost everything. What are your plans?" Justine leaned against a table; her arms crossed.

"We have nowhere to go, no way to make our way." An idea occurred to her. "Would you consider allowing me to work in your bakery?"

"A matron such as you? With a young child? Do you have any family? You have never labored before!" Justine said.

"We have no family and I have no choice. I know I can learn," Ruth said.

"We have slaves. We can't pay you," Justine said.

"We will work for a warm bed and food," Ruth bartered.

"Hmm. Come with me," Justine grabbed an apron from the hook beside the table and threw a glance at David. "I can always use more help. He will grow to be a strong man, just like my sons. From domina to laboring in a bakery with a child will be quite a change, but I can see your situation. You say you can learn? Well, let's try. I'll give you a chance. You and David may stay in the room you have just left. Three meals a day. We start before dawn."

Justine led them back into the bakery. She stopped in front of the station where the dough was made, then kneaded.

"Ruth, help with mixing ingredients. David, bring your mother flour from the sacks over by the stairs when she needs it." She said nothing further, instead taking her place at the counter, leaving Ruth confused at her change in manner. Four patrons were waiting to buy bread.

"Patience, my patrons. I have lots of bread to sell!" Justine laughed.

At the end of the long day, David was playing under the stairs making roads and paths through the dusty spilled flour waiting for his mother to finish the last batch of dough. Thump. Thump. Crash. A wailing scream rang through the bakery as one of the slaves bringing flour down from the storage space upstairs tripped, toppling head-first down the flight of steps. Heavy sacks of grain pitched into the air, bursting as they hit the rock floor. David peeked through the rungs. The man had landed on the floor face down, eyes wide open. Ruth ran to David and turned his head into her toga.

"Mama! That man…" David cried.

Justine hurried to the still slave, kneeling beside him. "Is he alive?" A slave who knew medicine rushed to his side. Other slaves slowly gathered around their friend.

The kneeling slave looked up at Justine and shook his head. "He's gone."

"Servius, take him to the slave yard. Put him in for the next burial. Now, the rest of you, salvage all the grain you can, clean up what he ruined, and get back to work! We have bread to finish for tomorrow's deliveries. The day is almost done," Justine demanded.

Ruth was shocked at Justine's insensitivity. In Rome, at her domus, when a slave left the earth, she made sure they were mourned and prepared according to the Torah. Ruth's head turned as the slave woman who'd smiled at her and played with David just this morning, tried to stifle her grief. She stood at the door, handing baskets of bread to wagons stopping to pick up their deliveries, tears streaming down her cheeks.

Another slave woman crying closest to Ruth leaned in and whispered. "She weeps because she is with child. His child."

"Why do you whisper?" Ruth asked.

"Domina does not like us to stop progress for any reason in the breadmaking. She will be angry and violent. We fear her son who whips us with leather," the woman said. "I am Lucretia."

Ruth nodded and glanced over at Justine standing at the counter selling bread. Justine was smiling, now. Ruth dropped her head exhaling deeply.

What just happened? A woman had violently lost her husband, the father of the baby she was carrying, and Justine had no compassion. Ruth had seen Justine mourn her own husband, so she knew her heart was not made of stone, but here she is able to dismiss a slave's life as nothing. Marcus and Ruth had treated their slaves as family. She remembered one celebration for a visitation that took tremendous amounts of planning, time, and labor. All the slaves, including Ushriya, worked long hours preparing food, gathering the needed tables and chairs, hanging garland and arranging flowers.

"Leave the decorations up. Ruth, David, and I will take a cart ride in the country. I trust you will clean up after your celebration!" Marcus announced. A cheer went up from the slaves. The three returned the next day to an immaculate domus. Consequently, their slaves would do anything for them. Ruth smiled at the memory. She missed Marcus. She missed her life in Rome, but now there was a new reality; a new life and she knew if she were to survive, she would need all her strength.

CHAPTER 18

JULY AD 65

Ushriya sat alone in the culina. One elbow resting on the table, she moved the food around on her plate and thought about the past year. With a wince, she reflected on her escape from the fire. She sent thanks to God, not just for her safety, but for Priscilla. God had placed Priscilla in her life for a reason and even though a meretrix was not the station she wanted, she understood that this was her path to becoming a freedwoman. Absorbing Priscilla's expertise as the owner of the Lupanare, she was beginning to understand how to anticipate the needs of a business. She slid off the chair, hid some figs and nuts under her toga, and scooped up a handful of olives as she left the culina.

With no one around, Ushriya visited the girls confined on the bottom floor. There was one girl she was particularly fond of, whose sparkle shone through her misery. They were all resting now from a long night of unwanted sex. Ushriya longed to open the metal doors and set them all free. Pangs of remorse surged when she caught sight of her friend, Melita. Priscilla frowned upon friendships with the "girls".

"Leave them. They are not to be pitied," she had ordered. Ushriya had her private room upstairs, along with her pay as the most desirable meretrix in Pompeii, while these women languished in rooms with bars, waiting to service the next drunk who fell into their stone beds for no pay. Priscilla had paid little or nothing for them at auction. They were the ones who couldn't work because of deformities or illness. Occasionally, there was a young boy in their midst, but only because he was also deemed worthless as a work slave, usually because he was slight or effeminate.

"Tell me how you are feeling, Melita." Ushriya leaned against the bars, pushing figs and nuts through to Melita's eager hands.

Melita shoved the food into her mouth as quickly as Ushriya gave it to her. Her coarse black hair was tied back with small piece of cloth torn from her stained tunic. "Four men since the sun rose. One of them struck me in the face because I appeared tired." She touched her bruised cheek. "I am tired, domina. I am so very tired…and with no rest, I am growing weaker. My tunic smells of old blood. The men ridicule me and do not want me. They call me unclean, but lena Priscilla does not allow us out to the baths very often. I am becoming worthless to her." Ushriya pressed her palm to Melita's palm.

"Why do you call me domina? I'm not. I only wish you good health." Ushriya looked over her shoulder as she slipped extra figs and nuts between the bars. "Where is Silvia?" Ushriya glanced around to the other rooms in search of Melita's friend.

"Silvia left this earth before the sun set last. She was taken to the slave burial yard." Melita wept. "With no rest, I am next."

A sense of urgency surged through Ushriya.

"How long have you been here?" She asked.

"I have no idea. Time has no meaning; just one sun and one moon over and over. I have been here since the domus unloaded us from the big boat. There were brown, black, and yellow-skinned women taken on board at every port. No one understood each other. We cried the entire passage." She lifted her soiled tunic. "I was born with a leg that makes me limp, so the dominus sold me to lena Priscilla as a prostitute slave. I am worth nothing, so I am here." Melita explained.

"But you are quite beautiful, Melita." Ushriya said.

"Ah, thank you, domina. When I first arrived, that might have been true. Now, I am withering into something not even I recognize."

Ushriya dropped her head and turned away to leave, eyes brimming with tears. *What can I do? They are powerless to the lust and cruel desires of the dregs of Pompeii.*

Ushriya allowed her mind to wander as she brushed her long golden red hair. She swathed a green strip of cloth around the top of her head tying it behind her neck in attempt to hide the white hair above her forehead. The streak had been a source of ridicule since childhood. She had tried rubbing clay and flowers to disguise it, but nothing worked. It seemed to have brought value, though, as a slave and now as a meretrix. As soon as the temperature rose or her hair was wet, it was a like a candle in the night. Setting the brush down, she dragged a bag bulging with aeses from under her lectus. The coins were the reason she endured this life. Saving five of the nine aeses from every patron, Ushriya grew closer to freedom. A thin smile stretched across her lips. Tonight, she would lay with five men adding twenty-five aeses to her stash. After counting each coin, she gazed upon the shiny luster, gathered them together, and carefully put them back into the bag. They hardly fit; she would need another bag before she set the entire cache before Priscilla, the day she announced her freedom. Convincing Priscilla she was a beautiful moron was her pathway to freedom and she had done that quite well. The more money she made for Priscilla, the more valuable she became.

Lifting her newly cleaned rose-colored toga over the top of her head, she was pleased it fit more tightly than those the matrons of Pompeii wear. The snug garment accentuated her curves rounding to her breasts. Wearing a colorful toga awakened a long-silenced desire within her. In Rome, Ushriya had worn the tunic of a famulus, but coveted domina Ruth's vibrant togas as she carried them to and from the fullonica to be cleaned. Although the stench of urine in the cleaning process was repulsive, hanging the togas outside in the dry summer air lessened the odor. Wearing the toga of a domina, Ushriya felt confident and beautiful.

She hoped Alexis would be in the house tonight.

"Priscilla!" Augusta shrieked. Ushriya jolted alert from the culina and bounded for the stairs, lifting her toga to her knees.

As she rounded the corner, she found Augusta cradling Priscilla's head in her arms. Priscilla's toga was soaked with blood from her waist down.

"Ushriya, get Alexis. Tell him to find Lucius!" Augusta shouted.

Ushriya turned on her heels and dashed to the back of the house, where Alexis was in his room, servicing a matron. She burst through the unlocked door. Both Alexis and the matron sat up.

"Ushriya, leave at once!" Alexis shouted.

"Alexis, something has happened to Priscilla! Augusta is with her. You must find Lucius!" Alexis grabbed his tunic, covered his nakedness, and brushed past Ushriya through the door. Her heart skipped. She took half an instant to throw a smirk at the matron who pulled a woolen blanket over herself. Alexis raced down the hall and disappeared, making his way out the door for Lucius who was working to repair a wall cracked by the earthquake.

"Lucius, come at once. Something has happened to Priscilla!" Alexis motioned him to follow. Lucius dropped his tools and was behind Alexis in an instant.

Ushriya returned to Priscilla and Augusta, fell to her knees and circled Augusta's shoulders with one arm. Alexis and Lucius arrived at Priscilla's side. Augusta and Ushriya backed away to let Lucius work.

"Is she with child?" Lucius tore the toga away from Priscilla.

"I have no idea. She didn't say anything to me." August turned to Alexis. "Go get the cloths by the door in the culina. Bring the hot pot of water from the fire."

Alexis left to get the wraps as Ushriya stood motionless.

"She is losing a great deal of blood," Lucius said. Alexis returned with the cloth and water. He bound Priscilla's abdomen while Augusta cradled her head and Ushriya held her hand.

"Alexis, help me compress her tightly to stop the bleeding." But as he knelt to the floor, Priscilla gasped for air.

"My daughter!!" Augusta wailed. Lucius and Alexis finished binding the wraps.

"Alexis, help me lift her." Lucius gently guided his hands under Priscilla's shoulders as Alexis lifted her feet. Ushriya followed them into the nearest cubiculum with her arms around Augusta. They gently placed Priscilla on the soft lectus. Lucius motioned to Alexis to bring more water.

"Ushriya." Priscilla's eyes fluttered open. Ushriya knelt at Priscilla's side and took her hand in both of hers.

"Yes, my lena." Ushriya said.

"You must listen carefully," she whispered. Ushriya nodded.

"My child and I will leave you now. I have watched you study me. You have not fooled me; you are far more intelligent than you would have me know. I have watched you grow in your faith in yourself and your knowledge of the world, and I know you have not always agreed with my ways. That is why I am leaving the Lupanare to you." Priscilla's voice grew faint. Her eyes fluttered closed. "You are young and have many years. Take the Lupanare. Make it right. Make it yours." Priscilla exhaled her last breath.

CHAPTER 19

JULY 21, AD 65

"You swine! How dare you waste my flour!" A thick rod struck the back of Camas' head as he crouched down to sweep up a bag of flour that split open. His hand shot up to protect himself. "Put your imbecile hand down and take your punishment!" Justine screeched. She raised her arm a second time.

Without a thought, Ruth jumped in front of Camas. "Stop domina! Camas is one of your strongest and best bakers! You need him. Calm yourself."

Justine hit Ruth with the rod and backhanded her across the face, opening a wound in her lip. Ruth staggered backwards, falling on stacked flour sacks.

Justine caught herself, dropped the stick and covered her face, breaking down in sobs. "Do not tell me how to treat my slaves!" she cried. "Oh, how can this be? It just never ends. Work never ends. Where are you, Hanoch? Why did you leave me?" Ruth heaved an angry sigh. She stepped away from Justine, wiping the blood from her lip with the back of her hand.

"They work so hard…." Ruth said.

Wheezing and gagging sounded from under the mix table beside the flour sacks.

"David!" Ruth turned away from Justine and reached under the table. Lack of air sucked the blush from her son's cheeks. A boy with a gray pallor covered in flour dust crawled into the light. Ruth brushed off the flour and carried him away.

"Mama...can't carry the sack... resting under the ..." David fell limp in her arms. A man scooped his limp form from her and rushed inside to the culina. Servius laid the still body on the table in the middle of the room, turned David on his side, and slapped his back. David didn't move.

"Cough, David." Servius waved to Ruth. "He needs to inhale the scent of the mint leaf...boil some water, check behind the figs. You'll find some there." Ruth dipped water into a pot, sat it on the hot fire, and went searching for the mint leaf. When she found it, she grabbed two handfuls and dumped the fragrant herb into the water. Immediately, the mint aroma filled the room.

"Fill a ladle and bring it to David's nose" Servius told her. "The mist will loosen the flour in his lungs. How long has he been like this?"

"He has had a cough since the fire, but it has worsened lately," Ruth whimpered.

David finally coughed like a braying donkey, a dry hack from deep below his throat. The coughs quieted, then ceased. He labored to breathe.

Servius turned to one of the slaves. "Go upstairs. Find any perfume bottle you can with the smallest neck. I need something to use as a tube." The slave dashed off and quickly returned with a tiny bottle.

"Will this work?" he asked.

Without answering, Servius smashed the little bottle against the table and broke the bottom from the stem, handing it to the other slave.

"Rinse it in the hot water." Servius whisked a knife from the shelf and stepped toward David.

"I have to open his airways." David's chest rose and fell in shallow breaths as he struggled for air. Servius turned him over on his back, tipped his head back, making an incision with the knife right beside his throat. He opened the incision with his finger and inserted the perfume bottle stem. Air bubbles came through the thick red blood flowing down his neck in long slow tendrils.

Ruth screamed. "Stop!! You're killing my son!" Ruth lunged at Servius as two slaves gently pulled Ruth away from David. Justine rushed to her side.

"I have seen Servius do this before. He needs to clear the dust. I had no idea David was sick," Justine consoled her.

Ruth pulled away from her and went to David's side. Justine withdrew.

Servius continued working on David until his chest began to rise and fall. "At least he can breathe again, but we have a ways to go. I can hear the blockage of grain and flour. Bring me some wraps." The two slaves who were assisting reappeared with long strips of cotton cloth that had been dipped in the mint water, along with more boiling water so that the steam could loosen the blockages in his chest. Servius held the cylindrical top of the cask in place, then wrapped his throat with the cloth to stop the bleeding. David fought hard; his chest rose, paused, then fell. Servius watched closely. Ruth stayed silent now that Servius was in charge. "Put your hands around his feet and talk to him. He needs to know you are here." Ruth instantly grabbed David's small feet with her warm hands.

"David. Remember our song? Our mountain song. I will sing it to you. There is a mountain…." Her voice cracked. Servius shot her a glance that said-no tears, show him you're strong and not worried.

"I need you to be brave like the strong boy you are. I am here. I will not leave." She continued singing, "…high above our head. We can see it from our bed." Ruth rubbed David's feet. "We have much to do my little man, many things to see." Squeezing his feet, Ruth felt David's toes wiggle. "I'm here."

"He hears you. Come around to his head. Lean in close." Servius finished the last wrap around the perfume bottle tube and positioned Ruth close to David. Quiet settled over the culina. Justine stood back, her brow furrowed, and hands clasped in prayer.

"Will he…" Servius' hand went up to signal for silence. Justine obeyed.

"Ruth and David need rest. Everyone out." Servius went to the corner beside the fire and sat down. "I will stay close." He ladled himself a cup of water.

"Maker of Wonders, where are you now?" Justine looked to the heavens. She touched Ruth's shoulder with a reassuring smile and left. Ruth had no response.

David fought through the rest of the day and labored all evening. His breathing eased, and then he struggled. Servius stayed with Ruth, soothing her when she needed it, at the same time working alongside David to keep him as comfortable as possible. Servius knew this sickness. Once the flour was in the lungs, the body fought back with another sickness; a kind of messy, thick mucus that blocked air. Rarely did he see a recovery.

Evening shadows made it necessary to light the gas lamps in the culina. Justine told the kitchen slaves to distribute foods needing no heating or cooking. They all dined on nuts, bread, fruit, and raw vegetables leaving the culina to David, Ruth and Servius. David fell into a deep sleep as the evening wore on.

"When will he awake?" Ruth asked. Just as Servius started to answer, David's eyes opened wide. Though he couldn't talk, Ruth rushed to his side.

"My love? Are you here?" She asked, leaning over to touch his cheeks.

The corners of David's mouth turned up and he gazed at his mother for a moment. Then the light went out of his eyes, the corners of his mouth relaxed, and he was gone.

Ruth screamed with all her soul. "Noooo! My baby! Noooo!" She dropped to the floor.

CHAPTER 20

Leaning into her knees on the steps of the Lupanare, steadfast torrents of warm summer rain formed tiny streams between cobblestones. Ushriya's toga grew heavier. Dark, angry skies reflected the past months. Priscilla was dead. Ruth and David were gone. And the biggest change: she was free. Free to think, feel and do whatever she wanted. And now she owned the Lupanare. She owned the Lupanare!

All at once, warm arms circled her wet shoulders. A woolen wrap draped around her. Alexis was beside her. They silently rocked back and forth together.

"Priscilla is gone. I have known her wishes for some time, that she wanted you to have the Lupanare. She saw brilliance in you," Alexis whispered.

He tipped her chin with a single finger, his soft lips almost meeting hers.

Her shoulders drew back. "Have you heard of the Wonder Maker?" Ushriya asked.

A bit surprised at the abrupt change in her demeanor, he answered. "Who?"

"The Wonder Maker. He taught the equality of men and women. His closest follower Mary, who may still be of this earth, heard the Wonder Maker's lessons and then taught them to followers. She was the one who relayed that a person's self is spirit and has nothing to do whether you are a man or a woman. She also proclaimed that leaders could be either," Ushriya said.

"Your spirit is not man or woman? Whoever heard of such a thing?" Alexis said. "Of course, my spirit is a man."

"But think of it. Such a powerful idea: being equal to a man; being treated the same as a man. I am completely captivated hearing the teachings of this man through a *woman*. Before I left Rome, word traveled through the gatherings that Mary had been a prostitute, that she repented when she became a follower. In one of the last gatherings, I attended before escaping the fire, mostly women slaves whispered of the other close followers of the Wonder Maker, who were all men. They said Mary would not have received most intimate teachings because she was a woman," Ushriya said. "They were envious that a great teacher could convey his teachings to her."

"How can women lead? They have no power...and who would listen to them?" Alexis asked.

Ushriya pushed away. "Well, obviously I am now to own a business. And now, at last, I have some power. Sharing wisdom with a woman makes sense to me. Why wouldn't the Wonder Maker pass on such knowledge if, in fact, he viewed men and women as equals? And over and over in the gatherings, I heard, 'Whoever has two ears to hear should listen.' Doesn't that include both men and women?"

"Well, both men and women have two ears," Alexis mused.

"You have no idea what I'm talking about. And I am aware men are not inherently more superior just because of their physical strength," she said. "Occasionally, many men, both dominus and slaves, appear quite the contrary to me; some are undeniably dim. You know, I have saved many coins because I know that one of the biggest weaknesses of men are seductive women. And it was you who taught me that great lesson." She softened and leaned into his shoulder, smiling. As the angry rain softened to mist, Ushriya looked up to the heavens.

"You're quite clever, as was Priscilla. She understood how women could lead because she did." Alexis stood, extending his hand.

"I'm a thinker, and now I intend to be a leader," Ushriya stated, taking his hand.

Warm clothing and a dry room did nothing to ease Ushriya. Flopping down on her bed, mixed emotions disoriented her. Alexis' mistimed, almost kiss, along with becoming the lena of a bordello, eclipsed any logic she could muster. And she was free. All three sent her mind reeling. Her spirit soared because the rest of her life, decisions were hers…and she would not waste it. Second, she was a lena. The business of the Lupanare needed immediate attention and she had no idea where to start, but one thing for sure, there would be changes. Third: Alexis. Ah, Alexis. She would tuck that one away for later and savor his lusciousness.

She called up memories of Priscilla abusing the lowliest slaves yet petting her dog. Ushriya understood slavery; after all, she was a slave. She saw how many slave owners caged and mistreated theirs, but Priscilla had been kind to her from the very day she arrived in Pompeii from the fire. The only other example Ushriya had were the slaves of the House of Acacia who'd been treated with compassion. Domina Ruth encouraged them to marry, to take time for the birth of a child. She even mourned at the loss of family members of her slaves. Ushriya remembered the wedding of Ruth's best friend, Calista, last year. And although dominus Marcus frowned upon it, domina Ruth danced and laughed with their slaves until dawn.

Ushriya recalled a memory of a heated discussion with Priscilla. She had locked Silvia in a dark back room after she lost the strength to service one more man. Priscilla had harshly reminded Ushriya that it was she who was the lena in this house, and she would run it her way. But now Ushriya smiled.

If Ushriya were honest with herself, were she to run the Lupanare the way Priscilla had, she would indeed lead a privileged life, and what a lovely fantasy. Allowing perverted men to mistreat defenseless people in order to live a comfortable life disgusted her, so she decided she would be a little less privileged. Even though she had benefited working as a meretrix, now there was a different way. Trying to make sense of it all, Ushriya remembered a woman called Thecla who was but a few years older than her. A virgin martyr and a student of Paul of Tarsus, who renounced prostitution and laying with men, Ushriya recalled her preaching in the Forum in Rome while delivering papyrus to dominus Marcus. She had stopped to listen. Thecla would have considered Ushriya a sinner, especially as the lena of the Lupanare. What would Thecla suggest in this situation? Ushriya fell on her knees and surrendered to prayer. When she arose, streaks of sun peeked through the window. She slipped on her sandals and went in search of a bath and fresh air to clear her mind.

Clouds from the afternoon storm gave way to bright sun.

Streets steamed with warmth, rekindling the stench. As the skies cleared, the majesty of Vesuvius loomed great over Pompeii. Somehow that monstrous mountain comforted Ushriya. Statuesque in its view, the people of Pompeii feared its fury, yet worshipped its power. Ushriya saw similarities between Priscilla and Vesuvius. Maybe anger was her power. Maybe that was the only way she could reign over such a large enterprise. Her rage created fear in the slave prostitutes. That was the only way she knew to oversee them.

Nodding to a bureaucrat strolling with another woman, she recognized him as one of her patrons. His gaze did not meet hers. She wondered if he was aware of Priscilla's death. Word spread fast in Pompeii so it would certainly be a topic of conversation at the baths. She decided to forego a bath and avoid the clamor of inquiries.

"Ushriya!" Cornelia ran up behind her, breathless. "You are needed at the Lupanare. There is chaos. Alexis is telling all that you will be our new lena. Come quickly." She grabbed Ushriya's hand and then dropped it, respectfully bowing away.

Ushriya grabbed Cornelia's hand and led them through the crowded streets.

"Ushriya!" She heard her name frequently passing groups of people. "What has happened to Priscilla?"

Not stopping to answer, she gained momentum with every step.

"Slow down!" Cornelia was breathless.

"Take your time. I will see you when you get back." Ushriya let go of Cornelia's hand, raised her toga above her knees, and ran the last block to the Lupanare.

As she burst through the door, she was instantly surrounded. Forlorn stares followed her as she gently touched each slave passing through the small crowd until she caught sight of Alexis.

"What will you do with us?" The group surged towards her. She felt their panic.

"How will we survive?" the slaves demanded.

Her head turned towards the clanking cages. Alexis stepped up on the edge of the small pool of water in the middle of the impluvium. "Silence! Give Ushriya some air. This is new to her as well. She will..."

Ushriya gently tugged Alexis' hand. "Come down. I am capable of speaking." Impressed at her confidence, Alexis stepped down.

"Cornelia, now that you are back, please get the keys from the culina and unlock the cages." "Bring the girls here. If they cannot walk, ask others to help. We will wait," Ushriya declared.

Minutes later, girls with bruises and scabs covering their bodies emerged slowly into the foyer. One young man trailed behind, naked and bent over. Limping and weak, they sat on the floor around Ushriya.

"What are you doing? They are filthy and unable to present themselves in pleasant company," Alexis said.

"I am not Priscilla." Ushriya retorted.

Augusta stifled a cough, then stepped from behind the door of the culina wiping her eyes.

"Priscilla's body has been prepared for burial...Ushriya, what are you doing?" Augusta asked.

Ushriya stood tall and addressed the group. "Priscilla has left this world. She has left the Lupanare to me and as the lena of the Lupanare, I will not allow you to be kept in cages."

The entire room erupted in applause. Now, she spoke deliberately.

"From this day forward, you will be cared for by the Lupanare. You will be paid a stipend, and it is your choice to stay or leave." Facing the slaves, her voice became assertive. "If you stay, you will not be caged." Now there was silence. Turning to the others, she charged, "Those who are able, go to the culina and begin heating water for baths. Find some tunics that are not rags."

Extending a hand, Ushriya helped Melita stand, wiping tears with her toga. Melita couldn't speak; her lips widened in a weak smile. Ushriya whispered, "My dear friend, your spirit has been one of my true treasures. I ask that you help me as I learn to oversee the Lupanare." Ushriya's lips rested on Melita's head.

CHAPTER 21

Ruth dropped a sack of flour from her shoulder.

"How can I help you, domina?" A slightly built young woman with light brown hair tapped Ruth's shoulder. Ruth looked up and recognized Flavia.

"Please don't call me domina," Ruth snapped. "Oh Flavia, I'm sorry, but it reminds me of my past life. I am here now, but I feel as if I am in another world, another time."

"And you are. You have lost your son. I understand because I, too, lost a child and am here against my will." Gently leading Ruth under the stairs, Flavia motioned to the flour sacks. "Would you like to sit and talk?" Ruth nodded, but warily looked around in case Justine was lurking close by. "Justine is visiting an ill friend. She will be gone for a while. And I would like you to know that Justine hasn't always been this angry. She is lost without Hanoch." Flavia folded her hands in her lap.

"Flavia, I don't know you or where you came from," Ruth began.

"I was brought here from Judea, from a small town called Caesarea."

"Then you are a Jewess?" Ruth was pleased. "How did you come to Pompeii?" Motioning around, she added sourly, "And to this place."

"Yes, I am a Jewess, but how I came to Pompeii is not pleasant."

"Tell me." Ruth said.

"When the village leaders along with our Rabbi began opposing high taxes from the Roman Empire, our Rabbi quit prayers and sacrifices at the Temple, causing the emperor to become angry. Roman soldiers were suddenly everywhere, and they began destroying our village. I have heard since that that was only the beginning; the Roman Army has now completely taken over Caesarea."

"The Roman army, you say? Are you sure it was the Roman army?" Ruth asked.

"I could see their red tunics under the armor on their shoulders, chests and legs. They had javelins, and their helmets looked just like the soldiers who sometimes march through Pompeii. It was the Roman Emperor who was angry. It was he who sent his filthy soldiers."

Slightly offended, Ruth said, "My husband was a consul in the Roman army, but I know he was not in Judea...at least, I don't think...What happened to your family? Where are they?"

"When the soldiers charged the village from horseback, one killed my husband with a javelin, and another scooped my little girl from the ground beside him. She was just learning to walk..." Flavia hesitated. "Then they threw her off the horse. She died when her head hit the ground." Flavia cried. "Just as I ran to her side, they dragged me away and threw me in the back of a wagon with other women. Many of them were my friends and relatives; they raped us over and over on the trip to Rome, where we were sold into slavery." She calmed. "Hanoch bought me, and not long after my arrival in Pompeii, I found I was with child. Part of me celebrated with the daydream of having a new baby, but since the child would be the result of rape, it could not be blessed by God, so I prayed he would take it. Servius and Justine cared for me after I awoke one morning and lost the child. I was sad, yet relieved because I know the child would not have had a good life. That was almost two years past." Flavia's eyes filled with tears again. Ruth's head swiveled at the sound of Justine bursting through the door.

"Too much idle time while I'm away will bring the rod to your back!" Justine stormed into the bakery. Loud cracks from the rod at first hit the table; then her wrath came down on Ruth's back like thunder, harder and harder.

"It was my fault!" Flavia cried.

"I hate you! You wicked woman!" Ruth lunged back at Justine.

Servius stopped the grinding mill, unyoked himself, sprang in between Justine and Ruth and stopped the rod in mid-swing.

Justine turned on Servius, but he caught the rod in his hand. Justine tried with all her might to pull it away from him. His strength overcame her.

"Domina, she has lost her son. Can't you give her a little pity?" Servius pleaded. Justine raised her rod to him one last time; he caught it, and finally, she surrendered and released her arm.

Ruth crawled into a corner to compose herself. "No one has ever treated me like this!" Ruth yelled at Justine.

"A spoiled woman who has never worked. You are a slave! I gave you pity when you came to me after my Hanoch was killed. Poor girl of riches. You've been pitied enough!" With her back to them, Justine yelled at no one in particular.

"Take a deep breath. She lost her temper. It wasn't you. She is still mourning, herself." Servius said quietly. He turned to the other slaves. "Everybody get back to work."

"But I have just lost my one and only son! How could she....?" Ruth collapsed sobbing.

Not yet daylight, a loud bell clanged to wake the slaves. Rolling onto her side, Ruth winced. With one leg draping over the side of her bed, she reached back to touch her wound. She could feel that her shoulder had bruised during the night, and she dreaded the heavy weight of the flour sacks she would lift that day. Just as she was getting ready for bed last night, Servius had brought his medicine bag and wrapped her shoulder after treating the wound with aloe to speed the healing. Noticing he lingered while rubbing the aloe in sent a thrill through her.

After lighting her candle, Ruth walked slowly to the culina to help prepare ientaculum for the slaves and Justine. Since she'd arrived at the bakery, her cooking skills hadn't improved, so running errands, boiling water, gathering eggs, and keeping bread supplied were her chief duties. Wondering if she should go into the bakery for more bread, or if there was some left over from the day before, the peace and quiet of the morning soothed her. Wiggling sore feet into worn sandals, she stood up straight to get some semblance of her former self. The toga she wore was the same one she'd worn since the fire. The same two places where she'd torn strips for David and Ushriya were still there. Lovingly, she ran her fingers over the frayed edges. It felt like an eternity since she'd watched Marcus and David giggling in the garden while Ushriya stirred garum on the fire. Tattered and stained, her toga smelled like sweat with an occasional whiff of smoke, even though Justine had let her wash it when she went to the baths. *Oh David, I'm so glad you are with God, your father and Ushriya.* She grabbed the door handle and stumbled into the bakery.

CHAPTER 22

"A pleasure, Ushriya." Shielding her eyes from the glaring sun, Ushriya squinted as one of her patrons came into focus. "How was the bath?"

"Fine, thank you," Ushriya answered. "Yours?" Ushriya's jade toga accented her golden red hair as she walked past.

"Very fine. May I have a moment of your time?" Ushriya turned and paused. "I wonder if you might join my wife and me tomorrow? We will be hosting a rather large banquet. I would hope we could have the pleasure of your company."

Ushriya was not acquainted with the wife of Jovian Varius, but it didn't matter. Social invitations still caused a bit of insecurity, yet she was becoming accustomed to her newly acquired notoriety as lena. Reasons for these kinds of invitations were unspoken but understood. It would be a lucrative day; providing girls for the elites' banquets had substantially increased the income of the Lupanare in recent months. Besides the benefit of added revenue, she was learning the inner workings of the governing body and the power wielded by those in charge, especially the influence of bureaucratic intimidation. She'd also learned she could manipulate these men. Pondering the invitation for only a moment, she answered coyly, "M'lord, have you extended your invitations to any others?" Ushriya wanted to know her competition.

"Why no. We are inviting the best," Jovian Varius winked.

"I will consider it. Melita will arrive before sunset with a reply," Ushriya tipped her head.

"Your answer is eagerly awaited. We have invited Numerius Popidius Ampliatus, to join us for a banquet in his honor. It is his son, Numerius Popidius Celcinus, although only six years, who is sponsoring the rebuilding of the Temple of Isis, so badly damaged by the earthquake. We will have elites from Rome as well," Jovian boasted.

"I didn't know of him. Only six years? How does a child know he would like to rebuild The Temple of Isis?" Ushriya asked in a patronizing tone.

"He will be the sponsor, using his father's wealth. Although quite young, the father has assured his son a political future, having just been elected a decurion," the patron answered with a nod. "I look forward to your acceptance."

His large frame bowed before her. With an arm across his body tucked inside his white toga, the other reached behind his back. Jovian Varius' slave lifted the back of the heavy toga as they made their way from the Stabian Baths.

Unimpressed, Ushriya planned the following day; how many and which girls would suit the occasion. But the idea of a small boy having his entire future planned for him stayed with her.

Ushriya awoke to a knock at her door.

"Lena Ushriya, it is Melita. So sorry to disturb your rest, but there is a woman waiting for you downstairs, by the impluvium. She says she will speak with you and no other."

"She can wait. Come in." Ushriya embraced Melita. "How are you, my friend?"

"I am well, Iena. Sitting in the sun and eating good food has helped so much. And regular baths. I feel wonderful," Melita beamed.

Melita's new vigor brought a smile to Ushriya. "Please go to the house of Jovian Varius before the sun sets and accept his banquet invitation for tomorrow." Melita nodded. "And we will need six girls dressed in their most alluring tunics for the day. Pick girls who enjoy such banquets. I will attend for a short while, but I will not participate."

"Yes, Iena."

"Now who is this lady who waits downstairs and why is she here?" Ushriya asked.

"She is called Phoebe. She has traveled from Rome to see you," Melita answered.

At the bottom of the stairs, a lady dressed in an indigo toga sat on a bench next to a large amaranth plant. Phoebe looked up to see Melita and Ushriya descending and smiled broadly.

"It is you, Ushriya, the woman whose reputation spreads to Rome!" Phoebe rose from the bench and extended her hand. "May we talk?" Phoebe tentatively stepped towards Ushriya.

Ushriya was doubtful of the woman's sincerity and expected confrontation. Most patron women who came to the Lupanare were furious and sometimes violent about a philandering husband.

"It is not my responsibility if your husband has not stayed in the confines of your marriage. It is..." Ushriya began.

"I have no husband. I am not here to discuss infidelity." Phoebe smiled again. "May we speak in private?" She glanced at Melita.

"Melita is welcome to hear what you have come to say. We will hear you upstairs," Ushriya replied stiffly. Phoebe nodded. Solemnly, the three women climbed the stairs to Ushriya's room. Waving Phoebe to a chair in the corner, Ushriya and Melita sat on the lectus.

"How may I help you, domina?" Ushriya intently gazed at the woman.

"It is you who have become the domina." Cordially, the woman continued. "My name is Phoebe. Word of your faith in the gatherings in Rome before the fire has spread to others."

"My faith?" Ushriya asked.

"Yes, some of the slaves recalled that it was you that attended the gatherings to learn the teachings of Jesus of Nazareth. It's said that you were among the most faithful," Phoebe added. "Is that true?"

Ushriya thought for a moment. "This man, of all the miracle workers I've heard of, touches my heart the most deeply. His lessons are for everyone. Men, women, and children, young and old, rich and poor. He teaches through his followers that everyone is equal. He made me feel that I'm capable of anything. However, how did word spread?" Ushriya interrupted herself.

"Your patrons' gossip. It's told that many who have visited from Rome have seen great changes in the women and men here. Even though they are free, they choose to stay because you feed and clothe them. Why did you free them?" Phoebe asked.

"Because I was one of them. I still am. They are me, and I am them," Ushriya answered. "Why are you here?"

"Well, now I know for certain that I have been led here. I've come to ask a favor."

"And what might that be?" Still wary of Phoebe's intentions, Ushriya continued to listen.

"I've come to ask if you would welcome a gathering...here at your Lupanare."

"A gathering? Here?" Ushriya was surprised." "This is a brothel. Men and women pay to commit adultery or have illicit sex here," Ushriya declared.

"Since it is a brothel, it would be such an unusual place to gather; it might not be noticed. I'm sent by no one, but I delivered Paul's letters of the teachings of Jesus to the Romans. I've been a teacher, so it was my notion to travel further on to Pompeii to reach new followers by finding a place to assemble."

"How do you know you have found the right person?" Ushriya asked.

"Because I was told you would have the white hair above your eyes, and you are the lena of the Lupanare. I can see that the slaves have left their cages, yet willingly stay for the woman who freed them." Phoebe leaned towards Ushriya. "The only thing I ask of you is to allow a gathering of people who want to hear a message; who want to hear of a new way. Will you consent?"

"I am flattered. In Rome, I pursued the gatherings of the slaves to learn. So much has happened since the fire, and every day confusion clouds my mind. This is a house of prostitution. It is NOT the way." Ushriya said. "I have known the name Thecla from Rome, who teaches that women who marry should stay as chaste as possible. How can that be? Then the teacher Mary, who herself may have been a repentant prostitute, teaches that the Wonder Maker sees both men and women as equals; that achievement and success is spiritual and does not mean you have to be a man. I am indeed confused. What is your teaching?"

"Since I brought the letters to Rome from the disciple Paul, I know his writings of the teachings of Jesus. He teaches that adultery is a form of slavery to passion," Phoebe explained.

"Then why would you want a gathering in a brothel?" Ushriya repeated. "It would be directly against everything he is saying!"

"But don't you see? There are people who go against the teachings everywhere. They need to hear, even those who patronize a brothel. Have you heard the saying, 'Whoever has two ears should listen?' Those who are deemed immoral or corrupt should especially listen. And as for a brothel? A brothel is a place Nero will not suspect a gathering," Phoebe reasoned.

"This is the first place the soldiers come when they visit Pompeii. Word will leak. He will hear," Ushriya said nervously.

"Is there a time when the house is quiet; when everyone is asleep?"

"Yes, just before dawn until late morning. That is also when we bathe and eat."

"Then the gathering will be in the morning-just after the sun rises. What do you think?"

Pursing her lips, Ushriya heaved a big sigh, nodding, "We will do it. But it must be kept secret until after Nero's celebration. I have heard his visit is soon."

Phoebe kissed Ushriya's hand, then replied, "I will leave tomorrow, then travel back to Pompeii after Nero's celebration. I'm sure I will hear of it in Rome, then return to help plan the gathering."

CHAPTER 23

Servius plopped his bowl of blackberries, cherries, and grapes down on the great table in the slave's culina and scooted a chair next to Ruth.

"You interrupted my daydream." She glanced sideways at his bare chest.

"What were you dreaming about?" Servius asked, scooting a bit closer. "Or *who* were you day-dreaming about?" He chuckled.

"It will be my secret," Ruth smiled.

"Very well. Word in the slave quarters tells that you were once the domina of a great house. I think it just may be true." He bit a cherry from its stem and popped it into his mouth.

"How did you come to hear of such things?" Ruth tossed her dark hair. "And why are you curious about my past?"

Servius leaned towards her. "Watching you…."

"You've been watching me?" Ruth asked.

"I have, and don't pretend you haven't noticed…but watching you makes me aware that you are from a higher ilk than a slave baker. It is like gazing at a white swan on a smooth lake in the middle of a flock of geese, honking and flapping." Ruth giggled, hiding a mischievous smile behind her dark curls. Servius' handsome face broke into a seductive grin. "Won't you tell me?" He tossed a walnut into his mouth. "Your toga, for instance, is red, the color of a domina. Not one slave I have ever known has owned a tunic, much less a toga, of that color," he motioned up and down.

"It was indeed a beautiful toga the day of the fire," Ruth sighed. Now it is filthy, faded and torn. As for my life, there is nothing to hide. Yes, before the fire, things were quite different. My husband was a consul in the Roman army, we lived in a domus in Rome; but Marcus was killed by Nero's soldiers-I suspect because he attended some such gatherings of a man they called the Wonder Maker. I left with nothing, except the pride of my life, David. Now, without him, I am lost."

"But you..." Servius' hand found hers and lingered. She looked at his hand, then gazed up. He was focused on her, just her. Heart fluttering, she felt light-headed.

A deafening bell penetrated the culina. Slaves scattered, bustling to the call of their duties. Another glance at his delicious face, and Ruth's heart raced as she hurried out to the bakery.

The sun was high in the sky when Ruth kneaded her third batch of bread with wooden paddles. She carefully distributed the dough into round, bronze pans to give them their shape. Then she passed the pans to two other slaves, who used dividing string to indent the dough so there were eight individual pieces. They scooped the dough out of the pans after it was shaped and divided, and laid it in the hot ovens, where it baked until golden brown. Slaves carrying wood from the pile outside kept the fires burning from dawn until dusk. Ruth wiped sweat from her brow between trips to the dividing table. Yesterday, two slaves fell ill from lack of water, so she stopped to drink a ladle from the cove between the ovens and the slave culina.

"We are assigned the delivery today. Meet you by the cart," Servius whispered from behind her. Before she could reply, he spun around and disappeared. She turned quickly to the wash basin to freshen up, pinching her cheeks.

By the time Ruth met Servius at the cart, the bread was loaded into baskets separated for each delivery. She stepped up to the cart and Servius' strong hands circled her waist hoisting her into the seat beside him.

"Ready to go?" he asked gently, clasping his hand over hers. Ruth nodded. "Six stops. Last one is the Lupanare." Servius grabbed the reins and shook the donkeys into a slow trot.

"The Lupanare? Isn't it a brothel?" Ruth asked.

"Yes. Augusta always requests the spelt bread. Lena Ushriya loves it straight from the ovens."

"Ushriya? The domina's name is Ushriya?" Ruth stared ahead. "My famulus in Rome had the same name. It is not a common name, but it couldn't be her." On second thought, Ruth wondered if somehow Ushriya had survived the fire and made it to Pompeii. "The last time I saw her, she was lying in the street as David, and I were escaping the fire. I wrapped a wet cloth around her mouth so she wouldn't inhale smoke if she were alive, but I honestly thought if she were, she would not live; that she would be trampled or die of the smoke. Do you think she could have lived?"

"Possibly. But someone would have had to have helped her. Then she would have had to have made it out of Rome, as you and David did. Miracles do happen, but chances are, she didn't make it." Servius snapped the reins. "Was she sturdy?"

"Strong of will, that's for sure. She had an authority about her. She could take any problem, solve it, and move on to the next. She embraced new things, new adventures, new places like no one I have ever known." Ruth said wistfully. "You have reminded me how very much I miss her." Servius reached over and squeezed her hand.

"She is still with you. Right here." He pounded his chest.

The donkeys knew the route and sidled up to the curb in front of the Macellum. Servius jumped off his seat and helped Ruth down. He lifted two baskets from the cart, handed one to Ruth, and took two more for himself.

"If you deliver the one on the right side, I will do the three on the left." Ruth nodded, raising the basket of twelve loaves to her head. She hurried to her first delivery at the thermopolium, because Justine was angry the last time when she wasn't back in time to help prepare the noon meal.

"Put the bread on the second shelf and make haste with it." Ruth nodded with a smile to the impatient proprietor. She hummed while walking to her next delivery. Swinging the empty basket back and forth like a child going out to play, she rushed to the cart. Servius was at the end of the street to pick her up.

"Last stop, the Lupanare!" Servius teased Ruth, but now she didn't care. She realized she would go anywhere with this man; he nurtured her soul. Stepping up to sit alongside him on the cart, she felt safer than at any time in her entire life. Safer than being married to a consul of the Roman army because she felt Servius would protect her...from anyone.

"How did you come to learn medicine?" Ruth asked.

"My father was a medicine slave who came from Greece, and

so was my uncle. They were both slaves of Hanoch's and admired him very much. He took care of my family," Servius answered. "Medicine and healing have been in my family for generations."

"Were you ever married?" Ruth asked shyly.

"Yes, but my wife died of the same sickness as David." He looked away with a sad expression.

"That is why you knew what to do with David; why you knew exactly what was needed." Ruth put it together. "Was your wife a slave of Justine and Hanoch?"

"Yes, and she loved them as her own parents. That is why I have stayed, and why I told you Justine hasn't always been this way."

A small rift in the cobblestone, probably from the earthquake, jerked the cart sideways. Servius grabbed Ruth's knee and saved her from falling. She clutched his bicep. Both smiled at her touch, and the donkeys plodded on.

Arriving at the Lupanare, Servius jumped down with the basket of bread.

"Wait here..." he said.

"No, I'm coming with you." Ruth determinedly swung her legs to the side of the cart. Servius reached up to her and gripped her arm to soften the landing. "I would like to meet the lena. What if she is my Ushriya? I've never been inside a brothel...and word through the slave quarter is that the caged slaves that lena had freed have stayed on. Why?"

"She was a prostitute herself, and the lena Priscilla bequeathed it to her," Servius said.

"How do you know so much about a brothel?" Ruth asked.

Servius laughed. "Pompeii is small, and the slaves talk to each other just as much as the elites," he winked.

Ruth blushed. "Well, my Ushriya would never have become a prostitute."

Servius used his solid shoulder to push open the posticum, the entry for slaves and deliveries. A slightly built girl with black hair and bronzed skin greeted them pleasantly.

"Augusta is expecting this bread," she said.

"Is Iena Ushriya present?" Servius asked politely. "We have brought her spelt bread fresh from the ovens. Please let her know."

"Yes, I will. She has taken Melita for the afternoon and did not say when they would return." The delicate slave girl took the basket of bread and disappeared behind a door into the culina, brought the empty basket back and handed it to Servius. "Thank you. I will tell Iena you asked for her."

Servius draped his brawny arm around Ruth's shoulder protectively and guided her back to the cart.

"Deliveries with you are a pleasure." Servius said as he grabbed the reins. "I have you all to myself."

CHAPTER 24

Ruth looked forward to daily deliveries with Servius. Expecting him to be a while longer because Justine sent him to the domus of a friend who was suffering back pain, she relaxed in the sun. Before they left the bakery, he scooped up his medicine bag.

"Dominus Atticus hurts his back every year just before the grape harvest," Servius explained. "After a day of moving casks, he sends Felix, his wine slave, to ask domina Justine if I may visit to help with the pain. When I arrive at his domus, he is wrought with pain and can't move."

"What will you do for him?" Ruth wondered.

"A good rub-down and guiding him through some stretching helps. It is usually his lower back, so I ask to him to bend from his waist, touch his toes then lie down on his back, bringing one knee up to his chest, then the other. There are many stretches to help with back pain. One would think he'd remember them, but I think he enjoys the rub-down with liniments the most, so here we are making my yearly trip," Servius grinned.

As Ruth settled on the seat waiting for Servius, a glimmer of tousled dark hair caught her eye in the midday sun. Her heart quickened. For a flicker of a moment, it was David, his pudgy face framing two missing front teeth. Laughing with another boy, the child yanked himself up off the curb with a crutch, picked up a rock and hurled it at a carved phallus on the side of the tonstinae, where most of the elites had their hair cut. The rock missed its target and the boys scuffled off, giggling, down the street. Grief swelled in Ruth like the water gushing upwards in the Forum fountain. She closed her eyes to assuage overpowering sorrow. Ruth's head fell into her hands. The lead donkey startled, lurching the wagon forward. A firm hand grabbed the reins.

"Whoa!" The donkeys calmed, settling the wagon.

"Centaurus, it is you. I am waiting for Servius to finish deliveries." Ruth looked away. Some of the slaves found him handsome, his short shaggy light brown hair capping his square jaw, but the way he treated women was disgusting.

"He told me to tell you he would meet you at the bakery and asked that I escort you back." Centaurus moved around the cart towards her.

"I will wait a while longer for Servius," Ruth replied firmly, sitting up staring straight ahead. Just a few days past, she witnessed Centaurus grab Acantha's breast and laughingly squeeze Eliana's buttocks as they strained to bring sacks of grain up the stairs at the bakery. Ruth had heard Nero had closed the school of gladiators over a trivial skirmish in 59 that caused riots between the people of Pompeii and neighboring Nuceria. The owners and trainers would salivate at Centaurus' sizeable hulk.

"I am going back to the bakery anyway, and I'd love the company of a beautiful woman," Centaurus leered.

Ruth had no choice but to move as Centaurus climbed up into the seat beside her. His odor was repulsive as he settled close to her. He brushed her thigh with his shoulder when he reached down to pick up the reins. Turning his head, he gave Ruth a sideways grin, and snapped the reins motioning the donkeys forward. Comfortable with their destination, the donkeys needed little direction, but Centaurus steered them off their path. Feeling wary, Ruth leaned away.

Without warning, Centaurus jerked the reins, pulling into a seldom used alley between the wine and produce shops. The donkeys obeyed, drawing the wagon snugly against the curb between the stone walls of the narrow walkway.

"What are you….?" Ruth panicked. Too late, since the cart was close to the wall, there was no room to throw herself over the side. She struggled to jump backwards over the backboard of the seat. Centaurus pushed her over the backboard, into the bottom of the wagon. His immense body followed, dropping down on top of her, taking her breath away. Nostrils flaring, pouncing, he was like a lion seizing its prey. The donkeys, sensing trouble, reacted to the shift in weight and jerked the wagon forward. Tightly pinning Ruth down by the waist, her tormentor reached back and clutched the reins. The donkeys halted as Ruth cried out, twisting, and kicking. Her head bounced off the wooden floor of the wagon and her shoulders cracked audibly. His eyes blackened and the power of his lust rendered her helpless. His breathing came in foul, stinking, heavy waves of hot, putrid air as he mashed his meaty lips into hers. Ruth threw her head from one side to another, trying to avoid his rotten breath, squirming with all her might. She gasped for air, but the weight of his massive body on top of her depleted her strength. With both hands and a swift jerk, he bunched her red toga at her neck and ripped the whole garment down the middle, exposing her naked body. Wrenching her legs apart, he thrust himself inside her. Overcome, Ruth retched the contents of her stomach into his face. Centaurus fell backwards, his lust immediately tempered.

"The gods damn you! I should kill you!" Centaurus flung the vomit from his face, drew his arm back and slammed his fist into her face. Ruth's blood splattered in all directions.

All at once, a huge club landed on the back of Centaurus's head. He dropped towards Ruth and shook his head, then turned around and reared up on his knees. He wrapped both arms tightly around Servius' legs, throwing him over the side of the cart into the street. Servius caught the top of the wheel with his hand, landing on his feet. Centaurus lunged over the side of the cart right behind him, but Servius found a loose cobblestone, and shoved it into Centaurus' face. Centaurus staggered and fell to his knees, disoriented. Servius scrambled back into the cart, found the club, vaulted over the side, and pounded Centaurus' head. Centaurus fell forward face-first into his own blood. Servius dropped the club and choked Centaurus with his bare hands making certain he would never move again.

Servius climbed back into the cart and slid an arm underneath Ruth's shoulders, cradling her head.

As she slowly regained consciousness, Ruth strained to focus her rapidly swelling eyes. "Servius? Is that you?" she whispered.

"I'm here." Blood dripping from his hands, breathing hard and still quaking with anger, he lifted a clay water jug from beneath the seat. He poured cold water on Ruth's shredded toga and gently daubed at her face.

"Centaurus...I was sitting in the cart, and he...he said you asked..." Ruth's eyes fluttered.

"Shhhh. Don't worry, he's dead. I killed him. I saw what he

was doing. We will leave his corpse here in the alley, where it will rot. The animals can devour it. I wanted to tear his arms from his body, that rotten, worthless…" Jaw set, teeth clenched, Servius' shoulders heaved as he offered sips of water to her bleeding lips. Ruth closed her eyes and felt Servius wrap her torn toga around her body while cushioning her head with straw from the cart. The last thing she remembered was Servius climbing into the seat and shaking the reins.

CHAPTER 25

"Why you would want to see an evil man is quite beyond me." Augusta was disgusted and it surprised Ushriya. "Torching people as lamp lights! Engaging in debauchery...I have never seen such horrific deviancy." Augusta bustled around the culina.

"Such venom, coming from a lupa!" Ushriya flashed a smile, then sobered. "Was Emperor Nero actually guilty? When I escaped the fire in Rome, I saw the horror, but I thought it was the work of the drunken soldiers." Ushriya stared intently at Augusta while nibbling on a grape.

"I'm sure it was the dim soldiers who carried out his wishes, but Nero believed the followers of the Wonder Maker started the great fire and thus spread the word over the whole of Rome and Pompeii. Two women, with whom I am well acquainted, have said Nero was playing his lyre and singing in another town while Rome burned. I should think that you, of all people, would not want to waste your time gawking at such filth," Augusta said.

"Augusta, do you follow the teachings?" Ushriya asked.

"I've not quite decided. But there was a time-in a visit to Rome-I heard a woman speak. The words she spoke moved me, and I haven't forgotten her," Augusta said.

"Who was she? What did she say?"

"Her name was Mary..."

"Mary! It was Mary herself? The woman who teaches that men and women are equal? That all with two ears should listen to the Wonder Maker?" Ushriya's voice rose.

"Why, yes. She said she knew him. She walked with him. She taught that a connection to God was created through dialogue with him, the Wonder Maker, the one she called Jesus of Nazareth; that a bond between him as the teacher and we as the students would lead to the understanding of virtue and righteousness and thus a path to God. I was forever changed after that day. But until now, there was no other teaching of the message. Now I hear of the followers gathering from Jerusalem to Rome," Augusta said.

"And here at the Lupanare," Ushriya added with wink.

"What? What are you are saying?" Augusta exclaimed.

"A messenger from Rome visited with me some days ago. She had heard of me, and that I'd decided to change how we oversee the Lupanare. Her name was Phoebe. She delivered Paul of Tarsus'…"

"Paul of Tarsus! He was also a great teacher of the Wonder Maker." Augusta declared.

"I'm impressed that you know of him. Yes, she delivered his letters to the Romans, and since her mission is to spread the message, she made the trip to Pompeii to speak with me. I have given her my permission," Ushriya said.

Augusta's excitement lessened. "We will all be killed, once Nero hears of this."

"The gathering will be in the morning just after sunrise, when the Lupanare is quiet, and Emperor Nero has finished his visit; maybe days after he has left. If any of his soldiers are still in town, they will still be drunk anyway, so they won't care what we are doing. They will be gone from the Lupanare by then," Ushriya explained.

"What about the ones who pass out lying in the street?" Augusta said sarcastically. "What if they come out of their drunken stupor and hear?"

Ushriya laughed. "Have faith! I will have Alexis haul them away!"

Augusta waved her hand. "You amaze me. Priscilla would be proud of you."

Ushriya giggled and hugged Augusta. "Besides, I find it hard to believe a man great enough to rule Rome would do such evil things; he wouldn't be right in the head. I do want to see the celebration, though. So exciting! Alexis…"

"Are you my son's lover?" Augusta looked up from her task and asked. "You don't have to answer, because I would be delighted if the answer were yes, but you know how rumors spread, besides it seems you two have become close lately."

"Augusta! You ask such personal questions. Alexis and I have become, well, close as you describe. He has agreed to accompany me. He wants to see the royal entourage, too. Besides, what could be more thrilling? I hear that Emperor Nero is visiting his wife, Poppaea Sabina's family." Ushriya turned to leave.

A knife forcefully thudded onto the table and echoed throughout the culina. Ushriya froze and turned to Augusta. "You were not in Pompeii before his reign." Augusta walked towards Ushriya, waving the knife. "It is true there are twice as many brothels now, and we have benefited from his perversion. But I refuse to think it is right to hang people from poles just because of their faith. As a follower and now a business owner, I would think it should be concerning to you. But then you have been a slave, and not privy to his rule," Augusta said sarcastically.

"You are wrong! Just because I have been a slave doesn't mean I didn't hear when Emperor Claudius died. That I didn't hear the rumor that his wife, Agrippina, poisoned him so her son, Nero, could be Emperor. And that Nero killed her, because she was such an overbearing mother and didn't like the way he was ruling. I pay attention to the people that rule us. Even with all that, I don't believe that a man of such high stature would slay his own citizens," Ushriya said firmly. "Besides, who would he rule if he killed everyone? And as for tomorrow, I have heard that along with the royal chariots, there will be music and dancing in the streets, a great celebration." Ushriya twirled her toga as she danced between the table and oven to the door.

"The fire is built, the oven is getting hot, lena Ushriya. I must get the vegetables ready," Augusta's ire was palpable.

"Don't be so cross. Come with us, Augusta! Have you ever seen the grandeur we will see?"

"I have seen grandeur. This is not the only time there has been a celebration in Pompeii. You with your youthful exuberance! Can't you listen? You need to learn about what this supposed emperor has done. This man has slain the very people you have befriended because of a new messenger you are growing closer to. He has massacred the followers for his belief they have committed crimes against mankind, that they would set fire to Rome. No, I cannot be part of such a revolting, foul display of honor for a man who should be put to death himself!" Augusta yanked her apron off, threw it on the floor, and stomped out of the culina.

Ushriya wandered into the garden. She understood why Augusta was angry. All of Augusta's life, she'd longed for the right way, the way she could lead her life. Instead, she'd become a prostitute and had a child with a man she didn't know. It had never been what she wanted for her life. It was what life, what God, gave her. *Now I know she has heard Mary, the very woman whose ideas intrigue me,* she thought. Equality between men and women was such a powerful notion. One that could change the world; the very idea that all souls were the same as spirits and that the physical body was simply earthly, energized her.

A timid girl with long dusky tan hair giggled at the whispers of another. Ushriya recognized the girls, all thirteen years, sitting on the benches strewn amongst the foliage. Celia hushed their chatter. Celia had been at the Lupanare since she was twelve when she first started her monthly bleeding. Ushriya had been thinking of mentoring girls, of teaching them how to save the stipend they were earning, of educating and encouraging them to leave and find a husband; maybe have some children. But working as a prostitute wasn't respectable and being treated as an object by men spoiled intimate love for most girls. Their journeys would be long, but there was hope in youth.

"Hello, girls." Customers were sparse in the early afternoon. "Have you looked at the papyrus I gave you yet? If you haven't, I would like you to learn the symbols of the alphabet, so we may begin putting words together. Wouldn't it be wonderful if you could read, then write?"

Celia glanced at the other girls. "Yes, domina. But do you think we are clever enough?" Celia asked. A strand of hair fell into her small almond shaped eyes.

"Without a doubt. We will begin meeting in the morning before the afternoon patrons arrive. Please be ready by the impluvium, the day after the emperor's visit."

A feeling of concern came over her as she sauntered by them. Deep in thought, she picked a rose, careful to avoid the thorns. Something Augusta had said, "This man has slain the very people you have befriended." *If the followers were killed by Nero in Rome, would the emperor be watchful of the followers in Pompeii? If indeed they were sought and then killed, it will be on my heart. I must learn for myself about Emperor Nero. Is he evil? Was he responsible for the torture in Rome?* Ushriya thought.

"Ahh, Ushriya, there you are. Augusta is dismayed at our plans to observe the royal entourage tomorrow. Quite dismayed, I think. No! Furious!" Alexis laughed. "However, she did tell me you had admitted we are lovers."

"I didn't tell her in those words," Ushriya smiled.

"She also told me your thoughts of a gathering here. What are these followers? Who are they following? What do they do at a gathering?" Alexis reached for her hand.

"Oh Alexis. Such a long and detailed story, and one you might not be ready to hear-but after the gathering, a feeling like you've never felt before comes over you and you feel like you can do anything!"

"Anything?" He raised an eyebrow.

"Oh you! Can't you be serious?" Ushriya asked.

"I'm looking at something I can be serious about," he answered wistfully. Ushriya's heart felt like it would leap from her chest.

He changed the subject. "I calmed Augusta. She has relented, and is no longer angry, although she is concerned. But you can explain why, later. Besides I'm anxious to spend the day with you and see the revelry." Alexis clasped both her hands and brought them to his lips. Her face flushed hot.

CHAPTER 26

The lamps on the street outside Ushriya's window faded. She bounded from her blankets and fumbled with her sandals. Melita tapped at the door and peeked inside.

"Come, lena. The sun is rising. The celebration has surely started without us," Melita sighed. Ushriya knew Melita had already put in a full workday. By now, she had been to the Macellum, bought bread and food for the day, and hauled water.

"You don't have to attend the celebration. I know you've been working since long before the sun," Ushriya said.

"I wouldn't miss it. I've never seen you so eager to be in anyone's presence, not even dominus Alexis," Melita chuckled.

Ushriya pulled her toga over her head and tied a thick purple sash around her slim waist. "I can't help myself. I feel as if I need to see him. And I want to dance." Ushriya spun Melita around.

"Lena!" Melita giggled then tripped, and both friends fell onto Ushriya's soft lectus.

"We must bring some light into our lives. We work all the time!" Ushriya stood and pulled her friend up. She threw her brush to Melita. "Please help me with this tangled mess."

After Melita finished brushing Ushriya's thick golden red hair, she admired her toga.

"You are so daring to wear purple, the color of the elite, to an imperial procession!" Melita exclaimed.

"I have been saving it just for this day. Wearing purple may be for royalty, but it's my favorite color. Today I feel royal!" Ushriya twirled around, toga and sash circling her.

Outside the second-floor window, the feverish hum of a gathering crowd lent a fresh energy to the day. Ushriya took Melita's arm, and they ventured down the steps and out into the street.

"Do you think he will be handsome?" Ushriya asked in anticipation of setting eyes on the ruler of Rome. "They will probably enter through the Porta Marina. That is where I arrived from Rome after the fire. The shortest street is past the Forum. Let's go!" They squirmed through throngs of people. Small children with baskets of flowers to throw at the feet of the emperor ducked through the crowds and made their way to the street. Dancers swayed to cymbals, and the whole city vibrated with excitement. Most citizens had never seen an emperor. This was Nero's first procession through Pompeii, although Ushriya heard the rumor he had visited in secret.

"Wait! Ushriya! Melita!" Alexis raised his arm, annoyed by a young boy tugging on a goat in his path. He was at once beside them, hustling them through the multitudes.

"Go if you like, but you will have to work through the night to get the baking done! And…" Ruth and Servius looked at each other. "You may take the donkeys. Do not let them wander."

Justine scowled and turned back to her work. With a shrug,

Ruth smiled up at Servius. Since the loss of Hanoch, Justine had aged. Appearing much older than her years, her wispy thin hair flew around her skeletal face. Haggard and scrawny, she never left the bakery. However, since the attack of Centaurus, Justine had become kind, more tolerant, even maternal. Servius put his arm around Ruth as they took advantage of their freedom and scampered out the door. Ruth wore a soft orange toga Justine had given her. She had never been prouder of a toga-even the custom-made togas she'd worn in Rome. For the first time in many suns, she felt attractive. Dusting the flour from the bottom of the toga, and running her fingers through her hair, she said, "I am such a sight." She looked at Servius. "Can you still see my bruises?" No one questioned the absence of Centaurus. Ruth presumed his evil was well known. Good riddance to such filth.

Servius leaned into her, kissed her warmly on the lips and said softly, "You are as beautiful as ever." She hugged him.

Taller than Melita, Ushriya was frustrated with her inability to look over the sea of heads, so she stood on her tiptoes, breathless. Alexis stooped down to let her climb onto his shoulders. Gladly accepting his offer, she hiked up her toga and threw a leg over each of his shoulders.

"Sorry Melita. I only have two shoulders," Alexis grinned. Melita smiled.

Once propped up, Ushriya was mesmerized and reported observations from all around them. The sounds of the horns and trumpets announced the emperor's progression. "Here comes the emperor! I can't quite tell, but he doesn't look tall. Oh! Now! I can see. His legs look short, like the stumps of a tree...he has a big belly under his toga... he's so ordinary!" As the procession grew closer, she could see more details. "Not at all appealing. His eyes might be blue... not pretty... he has a fat neck. And there are little spots on his face and hands and his hair is the color of wheat, and... he has a white streak of hair... in the front!!" She lost her balance, almost toppling both she and Alexis. Alexis' strong muscles steadied them.

"Why do you care so much what he looks like..." Alexis asked with a bit of resentment. "What did you say? A streak..."

"Yes, under his crown in the front... above his forehead. It's silvery, like mine!" Ushriya declared.

Mclita found a nearby bench by a fountain to climb on for a better view.

At that moment, Emperor Nero turned slowly and caught Ushriya's gaze. He straightened. Ushriya became unsteady. He uttered something to a soldier walking beside him. The soldier looked over his shoulder as the procession slowed, and Emperor Nero gestured toward Ushriya.

"Lena Ushriya!" Melita shrieked, jumping down from the bench.

"Alexis! Lower me!" Alexis bent over, trying to gently lower Ushriya to the ground. Her toga caught on his head; she toppled and fell. She got up and brushed herself off.

"I'm going to see for myself...." Alexis left Ushriya and Melita, pushing through the crowd, but they couldn't resist; they followed close behind him. Just in time to see the procession pass directly in front of them once again, Ushriya felt Emperor Nero's stare as Alexis wrapped his arm around her and pivoted her in the opposite direction away from the emperor. Feeling confused and disoriented, Ushriya surrendered to Alexis.

He whispered loudly to Ushriya and Melita. "I saw it. I saw the patch in his hair. It's the same as yours."

Still stunned, Ushriya was whirled around by a woman shrieking her name. "Ushriya!" Squinting into the sun, she focused on Ruth's face.

"Domina! Domina!" Ushriya screamed over the loud crowd.

"Ushriya. I knew it was you...your shimmering hair!" Ruth hugged her tightly.

"You know lena Ushriya?" Servius was astounded.

"Yes, it *is* my Ushriya. Remember, when I told you my famulus had the name Ushriya?" she said to Servius, then turned to Ushriya. "But never would I have imagined you were...here in Pompeii and ...the lena...of the Lupanare?"

Dazed, and without an answer, Ushriya responded again. "Ruth! My domina! What happened to your face? Why are you bruised?"

Both ignored each other's questions and continued with their joy. "How can it be you? I thought you had left this earth in the fire!" Tears streamed down Ruth's cheeks, then she sobbed. "Where have you been? I have missed you. I have needed you."

Ushriya forgot the emperor's stare, disregarded the procession, and soaked in the discovery of Ruth.

"Oh domina. I am so happy." Ushriya noticed that Ruth's toga was not its normal quality, her hair was not plaited in the grand style she'd worn in Rome, and she had a slight scent of a body odor, something domina would have never tolerated before. She knew there would be much to learn, but, for now, soaked in the glorious feeling of knowing Ruth was alive. "Dominus Marcus and my precious David?" She asked as her eyes took stock of Servius.

Ruth sadly shook her head as she noticed Ushriya's scrutiny of Servius. "What about you? Look at this fine toga, with a purple sash? Such daring!"

Alexis quickly interrupted, "I suggest we continue this reunion at the Lupanare, where you may talk safely." Ushriya appreciated Alexis' understanding of the need to turn the group in the direction of the brothel to lead them out of the crowd.

"I can see we have much to catch up on." Looking bewildered, Ruth swiveled her head as they followed Alexis, his arm protectively around Ushriya.

After arriving at the Lupanare, Alexis momentarily left Ushriya, Ruth, and Servius in the atrium alone to catch up on the last two years. A slow trickle of water in the fountain soothed their mood as Ruth told the story of her escape from Rome, the death of Marcus, her passage over the Via Appia, the death of Hanoch, and the arrival of the donkey at the bakery of Hanoch and Justine. She fell into tears at the recounting of David's death, and the two friends collapsed into each other's arms. "And you? My sweet Ushriya? What happened to you? How did you arrive in Pompeii?" Ruth asked. "I can't wait to hear!"

Ushriya told Ruth of her passage on the Via Appia, her acquaintance with Priscilla, and the necessity to become a prostitute at the Lupanare to support herself. She told of the subsequent death of Priscilla, and how she saved her coins to buy her freedom but became the lena at Priscilla's last request.

"Ushriya, this is Servius. He has become a close, well, er... he is the one who tried to save my David. He has knowledge of medicine and has helped me through my grief and melancholy. He was a slave at the bakery of Hanoch before David and I arrived. He taught us the way of the slaves," Ruth described.

"Oh, Domina! You? a slave? This cannot be!" Ushriya was stunned.

"...and you, Ushriya, a domina lena? We have traded lives, it seems," Ruth laughed. "At first, I didn't know how I would survive, but with God's help, I did. Although, I didn't think I could live after the loss of David." She glanced lovingly at Servius. "But with this man's help, I am here."

Then her expression turned serious. She took Ushriya's hands in hers. "My dear Ushriya, how is it that you and Emperor Nero have the same white streak in your hair? I noticed it on his forehead in the procession and saw him search the crowd. Then I saw you on someone's shoulders above the crowd. I wouldn't have seen you if it weren't for that. You are the only person I have ever known to have such an unusual mark in your hair. Emperor Nero noticed you. Are you afraid? You told me you were stolen by slave traders and have always been a slave. Can it be true? Who was your father?" Ruth's questions spilled out.

"My earliest memories are of a bakery. I am as confused as you, my domina." Ushriya said.

Ruth shook her head. "Please do not call me domina. Not now. Not here."

Alexis overheard the discussion. "I have never seen another white streak in anyone's hair either. Now we see there is one in our Emperor's hair. And he noticed you on my shoulders. Did you see? He stared straight at you, then leaned over to his soldier-the one walking beside his carriage. Ah, Ushriya, either this will bode very well for you, or not. If there is blood between you and Nero, he might believe there could be a compromise in his lineage."

"Wait!" Ruth's voice was shrill. "Now I remember Hanoch talking of the daughter they picked up when it became obvious the father wanted to expose the baby. Could it be...?"

"Justine can tell us," Servius calmly interjected. "I know there is much to talk about, but Ruth, we must go. We have left the bakery cart with the donkeys, and Justine will surely wield the rod on our backs if we are late." Ushriya's wide eyes looked at Ruth with worry.

Ruth gazed deeply into Ushriya's eyes and took her face into her hands. "My Ushriya." She kissed her forehead. "I have found you. It is the will of God that we are together again. I must go now, but please know that we will see each other soon, and often. Nothing in this world has made me happier than to find you." After a quick hug, Servius' arm went around Ruth's shoulder, and they walked swiftly to the bakery cart.

As Ruth settled into the cart, her hand found his as he grabbed the reins, "There is one more thing that has made me happy."

CHAPTER 27

Ruth and Servius fell through the dense rickety door of the bakery, out of breath as Justine forced it open.

"You're late! Have you had too much wine?" she demanded. "The others have started preparing the pans for the morning's baking without you. You should have been back long ago."

"Domina, you have to listen. Punish us later if you must, but you have to listen," Ruth pleaded. She touched Justine's shoulder.

"Do not touch me!"

"Please forgive us, but we have news. News of the baby you and Hanoch lost to the slave traders..." Ruth blurted out.

"Whaaa—aat?" Justine dropped down in the closest chair. "What are you talking about?"

"What was your baby's name?" Ruth asked.

"Ushriya." Justine answered.

"What? Your daughter Ushriya and my famulus Ushriya might be the same? While David and I were in the cart from Rome, Hanoch told me of a baby stolen by slave traders, a daughter. He might have told me her name, but if he did, I did not hear. So much has happened and I have tried to forget my past life, but my Ushriya, my famulus is here! Here in Pompeii!" Justine inhaled. "I had forgotten about her white spot," Justine gasped. "But how many people have the name Ushriya and a white spot of hair? She must be the same. I did not connect the two until now. Nero bears the same mark. As his carriage passed, he noticed a woman in the crowd who was sitting on the shoulders of a man. That is when I saw her; I knew it was Ushriya. Her golden red hair glistened in the sun, and I heard her laugh. It was her. I thought she had left this earth in the fire in Rome, but there she was! Before my eyes! I ran to her. I couldn't believe it," Ruth explained.

"You spoke with her?" Justine wanted to know.

"Yes, it was Ushriya." Ruth answered. "She was so happy to see me. We went to where she lives, to talk. Servius hurried us along because he knew you would be looking for us. We agreed to see each other again."

Justine sighed. Looking down at her feet, she started to rock back and forth.

"It is her." Ruth turned Justine's face to look into her eyes. "I know she has to be Ushriya, the baby you and Hanoch lost as a small child to slave traders. And the little girl my husband's father bought for us at a slave auction for our wedding, but you are the only one who knows for certain. Where did she come from? Did she have the same golden red hair of my Ushriya? Did she have the white streak?" Ruth asked.

Justine's head sank into her hands. "Her little head was covered in golden red hair, and she did have a white streak. Hanoch and I picked up a child, a daughter that was left to exposure. But we thought the baby was the illegitimate child of a vestal virgin."

Ruth fell to her knees at Justine's side, "Tell us the rest of the story."

Justine lifted her head as locks of gray hair fell around her ears, then stared off into the bakery and divulged her long-hidden story.

"Hanoch and I were in Rome at the palace," Justine sniffed, tears trickling down her brown wrinkles. "We had just delivered bread to the emperor and were leaving the palace grounds. After passing the Temple of the Vestal Virgins, we heard a wailing scream from around a far corner," Justine smiled. "I remember Hanoch was angry because the cart was stuck in a rut." She continued, "We hurried to the corner and peeked into the vestal courtyard. There was a woman rocking a baby. When I rushed into the Temple, she heard me, quickly put the baby down and disappeared. I looked for her, but she was gone. I went back to the child laying on the cold floor and picked her up." Justine relaxed but resumed her rocking. "I knew if the woman was a vestal and had a baby, she would be killed, so of course she would leave the baby to exposure." Justine inhaled deeply. "I took the baby out to Hanoch, who was waiting by the cart; men are not allowed in the Temple." Justine wept. "It is like yesterday; the poor woman was in such haste to leave the courtyard. I was so sad for her." Justine's words became more deliberate. "When we opened the blanket and saw a baby girl only hours old, we assumed she could only have been born of a vestal. Then we saw the lock of white hair. We told no one where we found her; just that when we returned to Pompeii, we found a daughter that was left to exposure. We named her Ushriya, which means a blessing from God, and cared for her until she was taken by slave traders; at least we thought she was taken by them and now it seems that it was true."

"Did you know Nero had the white..." Ruth wondered.

Justine sighed deeply and looked down. Hands clasped, she continued.

"Not until now. We didn't know Emperor Nero had the same streak of white...and why would we know such a thing? But do you know what this means? It most certainly means Ushriya has his blood. As a child, I do not think Nero ever left the palace. When we delivered bread, we caught glimpses of him, but not closely. About the time of our trips to bring Emperor Claudius our bread, rumors spread in Pompeii of slave traders stealing small children to be sold in Rome to the great houses of the wealthy. We watched our children closely, but Ushriya was an able child, very curious about the world around her. She loved Hanoch, never left his side, but that day she did." Justine broke down and a melancholy overcame her. "I miss them both. I miss him. I miss the curls of Ushriya's golden red hair. And her curiosity, oh, her curiosity." She wiped her eyes with her apron. "Everything was 'why.' Why, moma?' She called me Mo-ma instead of Ma-ma."

Ruth stroked Justine's face. "Now, we know what happened to her. She is alive. She is Ushriya, the lena of the Lupanare."

A sour look came over Justine. "If she is royal, she is the sister of Emperor Nero, the daughter of Empress Agrippina." Then wistfully added. "I hope she remembers me in some small way."

Ruth felt Justine's pain. "I fear it is true, and I don't think anyone knew until now, not even Ushriya or Emperor Nero. If she was stolen by slave traders, they obviously brought her to Rome, where she was sold to my father-in-law for our wedding. She was awfully young when she came to us and, of course, I certainly did not know anything of her background. She became the famulus, the head slave, of the house. And yes, Ushriya, was beyond her years in the ways of the world. She had something about her that told us her ancestors were not slaves. When the great fire tore through Rome, that was the last time I saw her. She was lying in the street, barely breathing. I thought she wouldn't make it. I didn't think there was anything I could do for her." Ruth closed her eyes and sighed deeply. "I didn't know she was still alive, but somehow, by the grace of God, she made it to Pompeii. I don't know the entire story of her survival, but I do know she has not only survived, but become a wealthy matron."

"If she is the daughter of Emperor Claudius and Empress Agrippina, we can count back the years. Justine, when did you and Hanoch go to the palace? Can you remember when?" Servius asked.

"Yes, it was the year of our lord forty-eight. I remember because it was the year of Ushriya's birth." Justine confirmed.

"Emperor Claudius and Empress Agrippina were not married then, but rumor had it she was with child and carrying his illegitimate baby. Word spread that the child died shortly after birth, but now we know the baby did not die! They must have left it to exposure in the Temple of the Vestal Virgins. And Hanoch and Justine just happened by at the right time. Thus, Ushriya has the same white streak as Emperor Nero. Both Claudius and Agrippina have left the earth, but their baby has not. It is Ushriya." Servius sighed, satisfied that he had put the pieces of the mystery together. "We must tell Ushriya."

"Justine! We have found our Ushriya. Your daughter and my famulus, my friend," Ruth beamed.

"If she has been in Pompeii all this time, why hasn't she looked for me?" Justine insisted.

"If she was just a small child, she might not remember. I think we will hear her story," Ruth answered.

Justine's gray eyes teared. "Will you bring her to me?"

CHAPTER 28

An olive tree does not know from whence it came. And neither do I.

A tiny olive branch swished across her face as Ushriya strolled through the orchard haphazardly reaching for ripening olives. Her mind raced. Reflecting on the events of the previous day, she felt bothered. *Can it be true? Am I related to an Emperor? What if Augusta is right and he is evil?* Ushriya shivered as she recalled Emperor Nero's gaze. As the procession moved down the street, the emperor had taken a second glance at her. *I have never seen another person with the same white streak I have in my hair. It is in the same place as mine, and he has the same red hair...though he is quite disgusting. He looks more like a pumpkin!*

Ushriya giggled nervously to herself.

And domina Ruth! She is here in Pompeii. She is alive. I will go to the bakery as soon...

A loud crack startled her. She turned toward the noise. A blurry image of a man wearing a red tunic vanished behind a tree and disappeared through the orchard. Frightened, Ushriya instinctively ran in the opposite direction, the leaves crunching beneath her sandals. She altered her route at the end of the orchard and briskly walked down the side of the cobblestone street toward the Lupanare, slowing her pace so as not to alarm anyone.

Not minding her path, Ushriya plunged forward into a hunched elderly man, knocking him off balance and almost toppling him. His walking stick was flung several steps away.

"Oh, I am indeed sorry! Let me help you…." Ushriya circled around and retrieved his walking stick. As she raised the frail man from the dusty cobblestone street, she caught another fleeting sight of the man in the red tunic and a wave of panic shot through her. The old man mumbled to himself and did not respond. Steadying himself, he dusted himself off, grabbed his walking stick, and proceeded on his way. "I wish you well," Ushriya whispered, turning away.

Rushing through the door at the Lupanare, she slammed into Alexis' back.

"I was looking for you," he said softly.

"Why? I was in the orchard thinking…where is everyone?" Ushriya asked. Alexis slowly took her hand and began walking toward the stairs.

"Where are we…" His eyes answered her question. She followed him up the stairs to her room.

The man wearing the red tunic was soon forgotten. After her fast walk to the Lupanare, Alexis' touch didn't slow her breath or her heart. Inside her room, Alexis closed the door behind them and gazing into her eyes, he passionately lowered his lips to hers. Little by little, he slid the soft blue toga off her shoulders, dropping it to the floor. Just as her knees buckled, he reached down, sweeping her up into his arms. Nuzzling her face as he carried her to the lectus, she abruptly sat up.

"I am a meretrix. You do not need to teach me any further!" Ushriya playfully proclaimed as she fell backwards into the softness of the lectus.

On his hands and knees, Alexis took short strides over her until she was completely underneath him. He gently lowered himself on top of her.

The sun was hot on their faces as they sluggishly awoke from a sensual sleep.

"That was not how I expected to spend my afternoon," Ushriya smiled.

"It was exactly the way I expected to spend my afternoon. I knew Augusta would be at market, and most of the girls are sleeping," Alexis said kissing the top of her head. He curled her hair around his finger. "I've wanted to make love to you for a long time but didn't think you would take me seriously. I thought you might look upon me as Priscilla's little brother and therefore your brother as well."

"I've never regarded you as a brother. I didn't think you found me beautiful enough for your liking since you have lain with every woman in Pompeii. I thought you saw me as a sister!" Ushriya reasoned.

"No, I didn't. And none of those women are like you. You are more beautiful and more intelligent than any woman I have ever met. I thought Priscilla was bright and very clever, but she was nothing compared to you. Now we know there is a story in your blood!" Alexis sat up.

"Yes, but what is it? Truly? Because the Emperor and I have the same color of hair with the same white streak, does that mean we are of the same blood? I have never known exactly who my mother was, because I lived with domina Ruth since I was a small child. If I am related to Nero, that would mean Empress Agrippina is my mother. Well, if she had the streak, then we would know for certain. I've never met or seen anyone else that had one. How do we find out? Domina Ruth says it was Justine who raised me, and she is at the bakery. Maybe she will know. But it is an odd feeling to know the woman who raised me has been here all along and I didn't know. I grew up thinking my parents were dead and that's why I was put into slavery." Ushriya got up off the lectus as she dressed herself. "It is almost time for the evening hordes to arrive with their coins in hand!"

"You are much more fun." Alexis got up and draped his loincloth around his waist.

Ushriya ran her fingers over Alexis's chest, standing on her tiptoes. He tipped his head down to meet her kiss.

At the bottom of the stairs, Ushriya grabbed Alexis' hand and sighed deeply. "When I returned this morning, I was out of breath and upset."

"We remedied that, my dear," Alexis quipped.

Ushriya smiled. "You definitely distracted me. But I must tell you why I was so upset. While walking in the olive orchard, a man was following me. After I saw him in the orchard, I saw him again on the street. He was wearing a red tunic. We've seen that tunic enough times on drunk soldiers. It's the clothing Roman soldiers wear under their military regalia," Ushriya said. "What if Emperor Nero has ordered a soldier to follow me? Do you think I'm in danger?"

"I'm going to see if he is still lurking around the Lupanare." Alexis started for the door.

"Wait." Ushriya grasped his arm. "If Emperor Nero thinks there's a reason that both of us have the white streak, I can see why he would send a soldier. Maybe he would not want to hurt me but is interested to see if what he thinks he saw is true. And to be quite honest, I'm also interested. If my blood flows to the house of Augustus, shouldn't I be aware? And if it is true, I don't think Nero would want to hurt me."

"Yes, you should know about your blood, but I am not so sure about Nero not wanting to hurt you. Augusta says he is mad, and you know what a mother bear she can be." Alexis stepped back. "You are indeed much more attractive than Nero, although the hair color and streak are quite confusing."

"I intend to sort it all out," Ushriya said.

CHAPTER 29

Since she and Servius returned from the procession, two suns past, Ruth noticed Justine had taken on a serene, pensive demeanor. She, indeed, lacked the rage she had held inside her since losing Hanoch, and Ruth came to believe what Servius had said about her not always being so angry.

"Domina, thank you for your blessing of my time with Ushriya. Will you change your mind and accompany me to the Macellum to meet with her?" Ruth said.

"No, I would like to see her alone. Now that I know I have seen her before, I am certain she is my Ushriya. When she came to the bakery, I did not notice her white hair because she frequently wore braids with flowers, and now, I wonder if that was to deliberately cover it up? She has bought bread at our bakery for several years. Since becoming a lena, a great deal of Pompeii knows her. She freed her slaves and now they are paid. I know her reputation. She is well regarded among the followers, and I wonder..." Justine brought her fingers to her lips to silence herself.

"The followers? What do you know of them?" Ruth remembered overhearing whispers of the followers in Rome. She recalled hearing of the persecution they faced when Nero's soldiers found them together in numbers, though she did not witness it.

It was a death sentence to be a follower. "Are you suggesting Ushriya is a follower?"

"She might be. There were times we discussed her grand ideas. And Hanoch must have thought you a follower, or…" Justine said.

"I AM A JEW!" Ruth stood up in defiance. "When I arrived in Pompeii, we began this discussion, but I was much too thankful to you for rescuing us to offend you. But domina, my father was a priest, one of the highest order in Rome. Are you telling me you are a follower? You told me you and Hanoch were Jews," Ruth caught herself overstepping her boundaries.

"Yes, we are Jews, but so was the Wonder Maker," Justine's hands settled on her hips defiantly, looking sternly into Ruth's eyes. "And if the gossip in Pompeii of a gathering at the Lupanare is true, Ushriya is a follower."

Ruth remembered the word from Calista. "Gatherings? I have heard of them before. What exactly *are* gatherings?"

"The followers gather at homes or at a merchant shop to learn the Way, the teachings of the Wonder Maker. Why are you so surprised?" Justine asked.

"Because that is where my husband, Marcus, told me he went on many nights. He called them 'gatherings'. I thought it was to learn the ways of government with the elites," Ruth remembered.

"Your Marcus must have been a follower. That is probably why Hanoch granted transport to you and your son. Did you tell him?" Justine asked.

"I told him I was a Jew, but he did seem to know of Marcus."

"Then that is why Hanoch allowed you and David aboard our cart. He knew Marcus was a follower and thought that you would eventually be a follower," Justine surmised. "Lots of Jews are listening."

Ruth dropped her head in disbelief. "Marcus was a follower. Now it is evident that is why he is dead. Nero impaled him in the streets of Rome! I hate Nero! He killed my Marcus…and Marcus knew I would never abandon my faith. He knew it. My father…Oh Marcus!" Lamenting the death of her husband, Ruth released her long-stored deep sorrow of loss. Slowing her tears, she reasoned, "Ushriya is most certainly a follower and may be Nero's sister. If she is, she's in danger."

Ushriya admired the purple wool in the textile shop as she casually strolled down the street to the Macellum. She daydreamed of the day before and fantasized of making love with Alexis. At last, she knew his desire for her, and the feeling was mutual.

"Hello, domina!" Ushriya recognized Ruth walking toward her in the distance and quickened her pace, greeting her with a quick hug. Then Ruth shouted to someone behind her.

"Hello!" Ruth shouted to a man behind Ushriya. "Avunculus Solomon! I am surprised you are here in Pompeii. I need to ask you something! Now." Ruth was angry. The man spun around and hastily ran away. Ushriya turned, just in time to see his red tunic disappear around the corner of the wine shop.

"Do you know that man? I think he has been following me!" Ushriya asked.

"I believe him to be my Avunculus Solomon, my father's brother. I believe he is here on behalf of Emperor Nero, which means no good to either of us," Ruth said. She reflected on her talk with Justine and sighed deeply. Gripping Ushriya's arm tightly, turning to look over her shoulder, she led Ushriya to a nearby doorway, out of sight, just in case Solomon was nearby.

"What is it? Who is your Avunculus?"

"Quickly, I need to ask you a question, and I need you to be truthful," Ruth said.

"Of course, I will be truthful. If you, in turn, will answer a question I have for you. What is it domina?" Ushriya responded.

"When you were the famulus in Rome of Marcus and me, were you a follower? Was he?" Ruth was indignant. "Tell me! I think Avunculus Solomon murdered Marcus because of it!"

"Murder! How? Why? Yes, to both questions, but why is he following me?" Ushriya asked.

Ruth sighed. "Justine told me the people in Pompeii know about your gatherings. I didn't know what a gathering was, until Justine explained. They know you are a follower. I think my Avunculus Solomon was sent by Nero to kill Marcus in Rome because he was a follower. Since the procession, and since Nero has visited Pompeii and knows of the white mark in your hair which most certainly confirms your tie to the house of Augustus, he is here again."

"How do you know all of this?" Ushriya probed.

"No time to explain now. Come with me, quickly," Ruth tugged at Ushriya's arm.

"Wait. Now you must answer my question." Ushriya planted herself firmly.

"What is it? You must ask quickly." Ruth said.

"Why was your face bruised? Have you been beaten? Who beat you, and why? Was it the man who was with you at the procession?" Ushriya asked.

Ruth relented. "Let's sit in the shade." She motioned to a stone bench along the street. "I will tell you. I have not spoken of it to anyone since it happened." Both women sat.

"What is it, domina? What happened?" Ushriya asked again.

"First of all, would you mind calling me Ruth? It is you who are the domina now," Ruth smiled at Ushriya. "Please never call me domina again. We shall be Ruth and Ushriya from now forward." Ushriya hugged Ruth.

Ruth let out another big sigh. "I was delivering bread with Servius. He is such a reputable man. You will like him once you know him. He is a medicine slave and is the man who tried to save David. You remember David's weak breathing had always been a problem, but after we'd been in the bakery for so long, all the dust he'd inhaled killed him. I will never forgive myself for not noticing sooner." Ruth sighed again. "Servius is a thoughtful man, and we have become close." Ushriya smiled.

"So, he did not do this to you?" Ushriya said.

"No, as I said we were delivering bread and I was waiting for Servius' last delivery, when a man named Centaurus...." Ruth sobbed. "Ushriya, he, he violently raped me," Ruth looked up from her hands, and Ushriya's arms circled her shoulders. "He was a bakery slave who I'd thought quite awful, but he said Servius had asked him to drive me back to the bakery. I was frightened, but Centaurus was quite forceful, so I had no choice but to let him climb up in the seat of the cart. He drove the cart into an alley, stopped the donkeys and threw me over the seat into the back. Everything went black; when I awoke, Servius was beside me, out of breath. He said he had killed Centaurus."

"Good." Ushriya said. "Did he..."

"I don't think I can be with his child because I remember vomiting in his face, and he fell backwards. That is when he hit me in the face, and I do not remember anything after that until I awoke with Servius beside me," Ruth sniffed. "I am healing well on the outside, but on the inside, I am struggling. Servius has been so patient. I cry when I'm alone, because I feel soiled and unworthy, but Servius continually reassures me. I know almost every woman is violated by a man at some time or another, but I have not, until now." Ruth explained.

"I'm glad you have Servius. My heart aches for you. I haven't been through such violence either, although there were many times, I thought it might happen. As a lena, I keep watch that violent men are not allowed in the Lupanare. I know the man you speak of. He'd not been allowed in the Lupanare for a while, because of his rage. He does not treat men this way, but women make him truly angry. I'm glad he's dead, and I'm glad it was your Servius who killed him. Is there anything I can do to help you through this?" Ushriya soothed.

"Knowing you are alive, well, and here with me has already helped more than you know," Ruth said. "We will have many more days together."

CHAPTER 30

"Where are we going? Why are you rushing me?" Annoyed, Ushriya followed Ruth to the back door of the bakery.

"Domina! Where are you?" Ruth called to Justine, pushing the door open with her shoulder and pulling Ushriya inside.

"Domina? Who is domina?" Ushriya asked resisting Ruth's insistent tugs.

Kneading dough for the next batch of bread, Justine clutched her apron, wiping her hands and pausing as the two women entered the mixing room. In an instant, her eyes met Ushriya's.

The two women gazed at each other for what seemed like an eternity. "It is you." Justine's gray eyes wandered to Ushriya's white streak of hair shining in the sunlight. A slow glow brightened her face. And your green eyes, they are like emeralds as I remember."

"Hello Justine. Why yes, it is me, but you know me. I buy bread from you frequently. What do you mean it is me and you remember my green eyes?" Ushriya glanced at Ruth, eyebrows questioning.

Justine walked slowly to Ushriya and ran her hand lovingly through her hair. Ushriya pulled away, astounded at Justine's forward gesture.

"What is happening? What are you doing? I am no longer a

slave. I'm not for sale." Ushriya was firm but confused. "Ruth, why am I here? I don't need bread."

Ruth stepped in between the two, meeting Ushriya's glare then gestured to Justine in a calm voice, "She is so glad to see you."

"Why?" Ushriya's head swiveled from Ruth to Justine to Ruth and back again. "She knows me. She does not approve of me. I am the lena of the Lupanare and she hasn't always treated me well when I buy bread." Ushriya spoke to Ruth as if Justine could not hear her and stepped away. "Why is she smiling?"

"You're her daughter." Ruth gently rested her hand on Ushriya's arm.

"What are you saying? I'm her daughter? How can that be? Yesterday, I'm the sister of Nero and today I'm the daughter of the baker. Is the Emperor of her blood, too?" Ushriya's face flushed crimson as she breathed in deeply, eyes widening. "What more could there possibly be that I don't know?"

"You're the daughter Justine lost many years ago to the slave traders of Rome when you were just four years." Ruth took Ushriya's hand and gently placed it in Justine's. Justine embraced Ushriya and wept deeply into her shoulder, the tears of a mother's joy. She took Ushriya's face into her hands and smiled up through her tears.

"Ushriya. Since you became the lena of the Lupanare I have never known your name. It was not important to me, and I did not need to study you closely. My head was down in the bakery working. Had I known your name was Ushriya, I would have observed you closer. I would have asked more questions. It is the name Hanoch and I bestowed upon you as an infant. Our little Ushriya. Our child with the kiss of God in her golden red curls.

He would be so happy I have found you." Justine's tear-filled eyes did not leave Ushriya. Standing and staring at each other, Justine tenderly ushered Ushriya toward two nearby chairs, "Come, sit, my daughter and listen to the story of how you came to Hanoch and me." Ushriya surrendered and listened intently. When Justine finished, Ushriya lightly embraced the woman who claimed to be her mother.

"Where is apa?" The words slipped out before Ushriya realized what she said. Justine nodded to Ruth.

Ruth explained. "He was killed by bandits on the Via Appia from Rome."

"How do you know how he was killed?" Ushriya asked. "This is all…"

"… both a miracle and a coincidence. When David and I escaped the fire, Hanoch's cart was outside the exit. We climbed under the wheat; he had no idea we were aboard his cart. A little down the road, when he found us, he was at first a bit irritated, then saw how desperate we were, and he allowed our passage; what a kind man he was. After he was killed, it was a miracle David and I made our way to Pompeii, not having any idea where we were going or how we were going to survive. The bandits also killed one of the donkeys, but the remaining donkey somehow knew its way. We let it lead. God watched over us that day. He sent Hanoch to save us, and then He took him," Ruth explained.

"When did you know Justine and Hanoch had a daughter with my name?"

"While Hanoch, David and I were traveling from Rome, Hanoch was telling me about his family. I was half asleep, but I now know I heard the name Ushriya. I thought I was dreaming, yet it was such an unusual name, it remained with me. Then Justine told of a daughter with a white streak in her hair that she and Hanoch had lost to slave traders, and I realized Hanoch had said the name Ushriya. God's hand is in this."

"That is one thing I can understand at this point. It is God's hand…and here we are, all together." Ushriya shook her head in disbelief.

"If that hungry donkey hadn't led us to the barn; to *its* barn, Justine wouldn't ever have known what happened to her husband, and none of this would have unfolded," Ruth said.

"I knew I came from a far-away place when I came to Rome, but I had no idea from where, because I was so young." Ushriya's eyes watered, glancing over at Justine. "I didn't look for you because I was such a young child. I really can't remember much. I have foggy recollections of a family. Are there others?"

"Your oldest brother, Cyrus, is a father with children. He toils in his father-in-law's vineyard. Julius passed when he was ten years," Justine answered.

"I'm sorry to hear of his passing," Ushriya said.

"You were quite a clever little girl," Justine smiled. "But the day you disappeared has haunted me since. I knew there were slave traders in Pompeii, but that day I thought you were with Hanoch, and he thought you were with me." Justine cried. "But now you are here. I wish Hanoch could see you. He would be bursting with love. He had red hair, and no one ever questioned you as our daughter."

"I hope you will give me some time to grasp this, to understand I have a moma and a brother?" Ushriya said mother the same way she had as a child. Justine smiled. "Of course. I may need some time myself."

"Now the biggest mystery left is why Emperor Nero and I both have white streaks in our hair. Since I have never seen another, am I of the blood of the house of Augustus? Can someone please tell me?" Ushriya asked again, "Justine?"

"I can't tell you for certain because we thought you were the illegitimate child of a vestal virgin, but we didn't see your birth, nor could we have confirmed you were her child. And we did not know Nero had the same white spot. But where else would it have come from?" Justine said.

"He obviously thinks there is a relation, or he wouldn't have sent Solomon," Ruth interjected.

Servius rushed into the bakery, sandals grinding across the gritty floor.

"There is a man outside the door. I fear he has followed both of you to the bakery. Go up to the flour storage where I know you will be safe." He hurried the women to the stairs and turned on his heel toward the outside. Camas started to follow him, but the door banged closed before he could get there. Screams of pain at once pierced the busyness of the outside road. Ruth flew down the stairs chasing Servius' cries. Just outside the door, she found Servius slumped against the wall. Warm blood trickled down his chest, soaking his tunic a bright red. Ruth collapsed to her knees. Hearing Ushriya and Justine close behind her, she called for their help.

"Someone has tried to kill Servius!"

Servius' eyes fluttered open. "Get inside. There is danger here," Servius mumbled, struggling to keep himself conscious.

Slaves poured from the bakery and gathered around their friend, forming a protective wall.

"Bring him inside!" Justine ordered. Camas and two other slaves tenderly lifted Servius, carrying him through the door to the cooling table. Flavia and another woman cleared the table of bread, putting the loaves into baskets to make room for Servius. The three slaves slowly placed him on the table, and Servius took charge of his own treatment.

He gasped, "...there is knife wound in my chest, not too deep...get bleeding stopped...vinegar... bandages." The medicinal knowledge Servius possessed, cut through the grogginess, and he worked to save himself. Justine hurried to the water basin with a clay ladle, scooped clear water into a large pot, and carried it to an already hot oven. Two female slaves tore bandages. Ushriya daubed the wound with vinegar, then Ruth wrapped a bandage tightly around his chest while Camas lifted his shoulders. The bleeding slowed. Servius succumbed to unconsciousness.

Ruth reached for his hand. Servius' lips quivered. Ruth felt his finger move against her palm. Her head fell to his chest listening for a heart beat. "He is alive." Everyone heaved a sigh of relief.

CHAPTER 31

Ushriya dumped a bag of coins on the lectus. Faces of Nero stared sideways on each coin, his thick neck and pudgy chin elucidating his excesses. She turned them over and over between her fingers while pondering her new identities as the lena of the Lupanare, the daughter of the baker, and the sister of the man whose picture these coins bore. She had landed directly in the opposite status of a slave, the only class she had ever known. Shaking her head, she sighed while carefully sorting the coins into piles. There were five more bags under her bed, and much more hidden in carefully chosen spots throughout the Lupanare. Working as a meretrix had been lucrative. Suspecting an opportunity would eventually present itself, she was grateful for the money she'd saved.

She had spent most of the night praying about how she might find gathering places for the followers, and how she might help Ruth. By the time the sun rose, God answered both prayers with one plan. *The money I have saved is enough to buy the bakery for Ruth, and I would keep an interest in the business. While she would have to agree, Justine would probably want to rid herself of such a burden. The ownership of the bakery will answer two prayers. Ruth will own her own business, and although Ruth is a Jew, I know that if I asked to use the bakery as a gathering place, she would consent. And as a bonus, we would agree to free the bakery slaves to work as freedmen and women, just as we did here at the Lupanare*. Ushriya heaved a big sigh.

"Lena!" Melita knocked, then opened the door, not waiting for an answer.

"Melita! You frightened me!" Ushriya exclaimed.

"My apologies, lena, what are you....? Melita was shocked at the mounds of coins on Ushriya's lectus.

"Shut the door!" Ushriya began scooping up the coins and stuffing them back into the bag as Melita slammed the door.

"Help me put these away and please do not talk to the others about this. I have a plan of what I'm going to do with all these coins. I don't want anyone to know, not just yet, but that's not why you came rushing in," Ushriya said, head down, gathering coins.

"Lena, I won't say anything about your coins to anyone. I came to tell you Alexis wants you to know there is a man outside the Lupanare. He has been there since the sun and wears the red tunic of Emperor Nero's soldiers. Alexis said to tell you he has been watching the man from the windows. He goes outside, circles around the back streets and follows until the man suspects he is being followed. Alexis said the man stays close to the Lupanare. He knows the man is not a patron, because he never comes inside. What do you think he is doing?" Melita asked.

"I know what he is doing. He has been following me. Ruth's Servius was stabbed by a man of the same description, and Ruth thinks it is her Avunculus from Rome. She thinks he murdered her husband at Nero's command to kill the followers, and Servius thinks he is also here at the request of Emperor Nero to see if I really do have a white streak in my hair, as he does." Ushriya jumped off the lectus and charged down the stairs to the culina. Melita followed close behind.

"What do you know of the man wearing the red tunic?" Ushriya brusquely asked Alexis as he looked up from a plate of fruit and bread.

"I know you don't intend to have such a demanding tone, but I'll answer your question because I am trying to protect you."

Ushriya's expression softened. "Yes, I'm sorry."

Alexis explained. "There is the insignia of the Roman army on his tunic, so he is one of Emperor Nero's soldiers, but he is gone now. The only probable reason for him to be here is if he is sent to find you for the emperor. I'm afraid he intends harm. It's rumored Nero has become deranged and is taking over the land inside Rome, building his new palace. People are whispering of great gold and ivory delivered from faraway places. He orders the people of Rome to listen to him sing from sun until the moon rises in the amphitheater. They cannot leave for food, water, or to use a latrine. Some have died in the heat of the sun, but he doesn't care. What a cruel idiot."

"If all that's true, he is, indeed, a cruel idiot. Where did the man go? When did he go?" Ushriya demanded. It is obvious this is all happening because of Nero's sighting of my hair at the celebration. But I've heard also that his behavior is becoming more absurd. He kicked Empress Poppaea to death in a fit of rage because she asked about his late-night revelry while she was carrying his unborn child. He is touched." Ushriya paced the culina. "I know of his hatred of the followers, and if he thinks I'm of his blood, has he sent a soldier to kill me or is he simply curious? I would think his curiosity would overpower him and he would…"

Ushriya abruptly turned and vomited into a basket of fruit by the table.

Rushing to her, Alexis grabbed a cloth and scooped a cup water from the basin. Ushriya sipped the water sliding down to the floor beside the basket. He dipped the cloth in the water gently wiping her chin.

"Have you eaten something rotten?"

Ushriya gagged again into the basket. Alexis rubbed her back while Ushriya regained her composure.

Interrupted by a knock, Alexis went to the door. Servius, breathing hard, collapsed against the culina wall. Still recovering from his recent wound, he struggled for breath. Alexis helped Servius to a chair, then helped Ushriya to her feet. Both wrinkled their noses and Ushriya threw a cloth over the soiled basket.

"What is it, Servius? What has happened?" Alexis asked.

"I may ask the same thing of you two. It smells quite awful in here." Servius wrinkled his nose.

"Ushriya became ill suddenly. We haven't had time to clean up," Alexis said.

His breath returning, Servius relayed the reason for his visit. "Ruth sent me to let domina Ushriya know that she is certain the man wearing the red tunic is her Avunculus, from Rome. The people are gossiping of your mark, and now they have seen the same on Emperor Nero. Everyone has heard he killed his own mother, Empress Agrippina, and Empress Poppaea and their unborn child. The most bizarre of all the rumors is that he has brought one of his eunuchs dressed as Poppaea to Pompeii and is telling everyone that that is his wife." He turned to Ushriya, catching his breath. "Ushriya, Nero is mad. Ruth fears what he will do to you--he might think that when you realize you are of the House of Augustus, you will want to become Empress."

"Me? Empress? I have only just changed from a slave to a lena. I have not had time to think about becoming Empress." She was amused, then sighed, "I have to admit, the story about the eunuch is repulsive, but then, I'm beginning to believe, so is Nero. He's obviously lost his mind, but I hear he is coherent on some days. It's quite difficult to believe that I'm his bloodline when I find him so, so, oh there is no other word for it; ugly. He is ugly. I hope I have no resemblance, except the color of my hair and white streak." Ushriya caught herself. "I don't mean to sound vain."

Alexis hugged her. "Of course, you don't look like him! After all, you are the highest-paid meretrix in Pompeii."

"This is all moving too fast. I know Ruth supposes he wants to kill me. I don't think he wants to kill me, at least not yet. I think he is curious. Let's confront the soldier and ask him Emperor Nero's intentions. Servius, please tell Ruth thank you for her message." Ushriya took a step back, hand to chin, studying Servius.

"Excuse me, domina. What are you contemplating?" Servius asked, his face reddening.

"You are a sturdy, imposing man who could appear threatening. Would you mind seeking the man wearing the red tunic and questioning him? Are you feeling well enough? Would you do this for me?" she asked.

"Of course, I will, domina. Although running still tires me, I'm feeling sturdier each passing sun. I think I know where the man is staying, just outside the front entrance to Pompeii, in the orchard."

Where I met Priscilla when I arrived in Pompeii, Ushriya reflected. *So long ago.*

CHAPTER 32

With determination, Servius made his way onto the street of Vicco del Lupanare. The sun was high in the blue sky. He followed the Via Degli Augustau passing the Macellum, stopping in his tracks. There, directly in front of him was the man wearing the red tunic. Servius lowered his head as he wove toward him through the Fish Market. The man was nonchalantly shopping, appearing to waste time, though several people did take a second look at his tunic, probably at the insignia of the Roman army. Servius watched and waited. Not knowing what the man would do if he was any closer, Servius decided to stay his distance and follow patiently. If this was Ruth's Avunculus, *he has the blood of the woman I love running through his veins*, Servius thought. He glanced away for a moment and didn't notice when the man spied him. The man swiveled on his sandals and slithered quickly through the crowd.

Tearing past the shoppers, Servius knocked over a jar of garum at the edge of the Fish Market, spurring the merchant to follow the chase. Interrupted, Servius lost sight of the man he was chasing between the columns of the Forum Baths. As a slave, he knew he could not enter the Baths without a dominus, so he waited at the opposite corner for the man. He apologized to the merchant, who remembered Servius as the slave who had administered medicine to his youngest daughter when she became ill. Servius knew the man he was chasing would have to stay on the Via Dell Termeon to get to the Porto Ercolano, one of the entries to Pompeii, under the biggest of olive trees. That was where Servius suspected he was spending his nights.

Servius waited, hidden behind a column at the top of the steps. Several minutes later, the man stepped out of the Baths and looked over his shoulder. He crept slowly down the steps, glancing side to side, following the route Servius knew he would take. Servius stalked him to the street of the Via Consulare at the steps of the Porta Ercolano.

Spotting Servius again, the man ran to a smaller grove of olive trees. Servius knew he could overpower him; he was stronger and faster than this man, who was at least ten years his senior. Even though Servius was not back at full strength, he caught him handily, bringing his prey down like a big cat, pinning his shoulders in the dirt with his knees.

"It is you! The man who stabbed and left me for dead." Servius drew his fist back. The man twisted his head, trying to avoid Servius' fury, grinding against the sharp stones in the dusty dirt. Servius' fist landed on the side of his face causing blood to spray from his mouth. One of the man's hands wriggled free and reached for Servius' jaw. Servius' powerful arm chopped the hand away, and he smote the man square in the face. Another blow crushed his eye; the sound of bone against bone caused Servius to hesitate. He knew he could kill him right here, right now, but he wouldn't. Ushriya's wish rang in his mind. Blood gurgling in his throat, the man tried to talk.

"Don't kill me! I...I am Solomon from the Emperor's army. I want nothing to do with you."

"So, you ARE Ruth's avunculus. If you want nothing to do with me, why did you try to kill me?" Servius drew his fist back again.

"Please! Please let me live!" Solomon mumbled. Servius eased his hold and stood up.

"Speak!" Servius demanded.

Lying in a pool of blood, trying to spit broken teeth, the man could neither sit up nor get to his feet. The bright sun in his blood-filled eyes blinded him. Breathing heavily, he grabbed the bottom of his tunic to wipe the blood from his eyes, exposing his scratched loins. He warbled, "Yes, she is the daughter of my brother."

"Did you kill her husband, Marcus?" Servius crossed his arms, staring down at the helpless man. Though badly hurt, Solomon rolled to his side and rose to his elbow, trying to focus on the large man towering over him.

"I had no choice because he was a follower. I'm at the leisure of the Emperor of Rome who had an edict that all followers be impaled...that they be set afire to light Rome's way." Solomon strained to talk.

"Light Rome's way? Let the gods curse you! You are an impaler. You slime!" Servius lunged at Solomon again wanting to pound his face and body. Instead, he gained self-control. "Ushriya asked me not to kill you. I will honor her wishes."

The wounded man attempted again to sit up, then fell back into the dirt. He stayed on the ground, struggling to talk. "I have not come for Ruth, but for the one with the streak in her hair. I understand my niece hates me. For that I understand. Is my nephew..."

"If you mean her harm, I will kill you. Although you do not deserve to know, David has passed from this earth," Servius said.

Solomon spoke slowly, eyes closed. "I am sorry. I do not mean any harm to Ruth. It is Emperor Nero that has sent me to find the one with the white streak. He means her no harm. He is at the domus Oplontis at Empress Poppaea's family residence. It will be at her leisure that I extend his invitation to visit the domus."

"Why does he want to see her?" Servius demanded.

"It is… obvious to everyone in Pompeii by now…that she shares the white streak in her hair with Emperor Nero. He saw it. He knows there's only one reason that she can have the touch of the Gods; that she has the bloodline of the House of Augustus. The reason I'm sent is because I've seen the slave with the streak at my niece's domus in Rome. I didn't realize Emperor Nero had the same mark until I was a guard at the palace, and I gasped when I saw his. He asked me why I responded with such surprise. I told him I had seen someone with the same mark. He did not seem to care at first, but then remembered that I'd told him when he visited Pompeii and saw her in the crowd. He sent me to confirm his suspicions." Solomon's shoulder gave way; he lost consciousness and fell face first in the rocky soil. Servius left him where he lay.

Ushriya sat with Alexis and Augusta, chopping nuts and dates as Servius entered the culina.

"I will be at market, then to the bath." Augusta gathered up the dates and nuts, put them in baskets, threw her cloth on the cutting table and left the culina. "I will return before the sun sets."

Ushriya waved at her. "What have you to tell us, Servius?

"Heh!" He grinned. "I almost killed him, but remembered your wishes, lena, and left him lay after he'd told me of his intentions."

"What are his intentions?" Ushriya asked.

"He did kill Ruth's husband, and for the reason she suspected. He killed him under an edict of Nero to impale the followers… to light the way in Rome!" Servius raised his arms in a grand gesture. "What a rotten man. He was indeed the one who stabbed me. I didn't beat him as hard as my strength would allow. But it is true, Iena, he has come for you."

Ushriya inhaled and held her breath. Alexis leaned forward; eyebrows knitted.

"Not for the reasons we thought. He does not want to harm you. Solomon saw your white hair when he was at the house of Marcus and Ruth! He told Nero about it, but Nero had forgotten until this visit to Pompeii. Emperor Nero sent Solomon to invite you to the residence of Poppaea Sabina's family in Oplontis for audience. Nero knows it can only be a mark from the house of Augustus. "He wants to see for himself," Servius explained.

"Of course, it is. If I was picked up by Hanoch and Justine at the palace of Emperor Claudius before they wed, before Agrippina was Empress, then they are my true parents. The streak comes from the line of Agrippina. Nero is my brother." Ushriya sighed heavily. "I'll go. I'll see Emperor Nero."

"You can't go alone to have audience with a murderer. You have no idea of what he is capable. I'll go with you," Alexis told her.

"No, you won't. I must do this myself. I'm not frightened of him. For some reason, I know I'll be safe. But I won't go right away. I need to take care of some things here.

CHAPTER 33

As she turned the corner onto the Vi Degli Augustau, a hefty basket full of coins cradled under her elbow, Ushriya lovingly laid her other hand on her budding belly. Though excited to start a partnership in the bakery with Ruth, a small flutter under her palm thrilled her. Ushriya's joy boosted her pace, walking as fast as both burdens would allow while her blue toga wafted in the hot wind. A soon-to-be mother is no longer desirable to the customers of the Lupanare. Relief enveloped her, spawning a tiny sneer of satisfaction when she realized she would never lay with another man for coins. Ah, Thecla: threat to the Roman Empire because of her disavowal of marriage and therefore never having children. Although she hadn't ever met Thecla, she had heard of Thecla's devotion to the teacher, Paul of Tarsus. Thecla was a woman in Rome who had almost married but rejected the man who wanted to marry her. She became an ardent follower of Paul, and consequently, an enemy of the Roman Empire because the survival of the empire depended on a woman's obligation to marry and bear sons. *Thecla, if I could talk to you, I would tell you I have laid with men. I'm going to have a child, and even though I love Alexis, it will be my decision if I am to marry. Thecla! Finally, I hear you. I have choices!* Ushriya thought.

Close to the bakery, Ushriya found herself out of breath and heart racing. She saw a woman she didn't recognize sitting on a bench just ahead. Skin the color of walnuts, she wore an elegant red toga.

"May I sit with you while I catch my breath?" Ushriya asked.

"Yes, dear one. I see you are with child. You must take care of that baby," the woman answered. "Rest yourself." She patted the bench next to her. The shade of the lemon tree cooled them while the scent of warm lemons drifted through the soft breeze. A group of children were playing under the tree behind them.

"What a lovely hat. I see every color of the rainbow in the beads," Ushriya said.

"It was a gift from my husband, who loved to make things from beads. We are from Afri-terra and came to Pompeii because my husband loved to travel to sell our hand-made wares." Her spirit sparkled through her smile like light bouncing off the water of a lake. She reached down and touched Ushriya's knee, "Tell me something, dear one. Is this your first child?"

"Yes. I am hoping to have a girl," Ushriya said

The woman's smile was broad and warm. "A girl would be wonderful, but you are carrying a boy. He will have the dark hair of his father and will know you as the strong one."

Astonished, Ushriya asked the woman, "How do you know this?"

"I know this because I can see you are just beginning your life; that people will follow you and children will love you."

Ushriya suddenly remembered that she was on her way to the bakery. "I have to go. I am so glad to meet you."

"You have my blessing, dear one." The lady smiled.

Ushriya hoisted her basket up to her elbow and bade the woman good-bye. When she reached the end of the block, it occurred to her she would like to get to know this fascinating woman who had told her she was going to have a son. She turned around and walked back, but the woman was gone from the bench.

"Do any of you know which direction the woman I was sitting with went? She was wearing the red toga and the beaded hat," Ushriya called to the children still playing behind the bench.

"What woman?" one child asked. "You were sitting alone." They all giggled and scampered away.

"But.." Ushriya raised her finger, scanning the area for any sign of red. Shaking her head, she walked to the bakery.

"Hello, Justine. May I have a word with you?" Ushriya shouted over a bakery customer. She was not yet comfortable with Justine's maternal role in her life.

"Can't you see I'm busy?" Justine, head down, curtly replied, but upon seeing it was Ushriya, she smiled. Knowing Justine had worked hard all her life, Ushriya understood her annoyance, and began to appreciate her adopted mother.

"It will be short. Please?" Ushriya asked.

Justine wiped her hands on her toga, nodded, and motioned Flavia over to the counter. Justine waved Ushriya around the counter and with a hand on her shoulder, guided her towards the bakery culina. Ushriya dropped her heavy basket on the floor.

"We carry different burdens. Mine has made me tired," Justine sighed.

"I know you're exhausted from this work. I bring good news,

or at least I hope you will see it as good news. May we ask Ruth to join us?" Ushriya asked.

"Why do we need her?" Justine asked. "She is busy pulling bread from the ovens; the bread will burn if it is not pulled soon." She noticed Ushriya's expanding girth and impulsively said, "And how will you know the father of this baby?" She calmed. "I'm sorry. That was rude."

Justine called from the culina. "Ruth! Come to hear what my daughter has to say!" Ruth soon appeared at the door to the culina.

"What is it, domina?" Ruth looked at Justine, then saw Ushriya. "Oh, Ushriya! So good to see you! What brings you to the bakery? We have fresh bread almost ready to pull from the ovens."

"Tell the other oven slaves to pull the bread, so you may sit with us for a short while," Justine said. Ruth turned back towards the ovens to relay the message, then returned.

Ushriya heaved her heavy basket from the floor to the table, smiling as she put one arm around Justine and the other around Ruth. "Justine, this is on behalf of Ruth and me." Ruth looked confused. "I have come to buy the bakery. I have come to make life easier for you and Ruth."

Justine looked at the basket, then to Ushriya, then to Ruth, then back to the basket. She walked to the basket, uncovered the yellow cloth revealing the glimmer of golden coins inside a bag. "Why, there must be…" Justine was bewildered. "You should not have been carrying this heavy a load; you are with child!"

Ushriya laughed, "Yes, I have been saving for a long time. And don't worry, I didn't bring it all at once," Ushriya smiled. "The time has come at last to do something good with all of these old coins gathering dust under my table."

Ruth could hardly speak. "I don't know what to say."

"You don't have to say anything. If Justine agrees, she will be free of the bakery. If you agree, you will be the new owner. There are three conditions. The first is that I will retain a part ownership silently and you will make payments to me. As far as the patrons know, you are the owner. Second, you must free the bakery slaves as I have done with the Lupanare. They will have the option to work for you. And dear Ruth, third: you must provide a place for the gatherings of the followers. What do you say?"

"I am Jewish, domina," Ruth said. "I will remain a Jewess."

"I know your faith. I know you are not a follower, but I also know your heart. And I know you know God. I will ask you to think and pray about it," Ushriya replied.

Ruth's demeanor changed, becoming firm. "I don't have to think about it. Meet with your followers; I will stand guard." She grabbed Ushriya, hugged her tightly, then turned to Justine.

"Can you believe this? Justine...er, domina. What do you think?" Ruth asked. "This is your opportunity to live with Cyrus and to be with your grandchildren; to be part of their lives and live out your life with those who love you the most."

A warm glow swept over Justine like the rising sun. Tears followed, cascading down her face. Ushriya and Ruth were at once beside her. All the sadness, misery, worry and fatigue pent up inside her since the loss of Hanoch, burst forth like a breaking dam.

"There is nothing to think about. Hanoch and I built this bakery for our children; it was to be our legacy, but all that has changed. Hanoch is gone and working this hard has made me a bitter old woman. That is not who I am, nor who I want to be." Justine turned to Ushriya. "I'll accept your offer, and I know it will be fair. Ruth is capable, kind and patient. She has Servius to help her. The bakery will be well taken care of." She took Ushriya's hands in hers as the tears returned.

Ushriya nodded. "I will take both your words as agreement to what I have offered. It will be your responsibility to make plans according to your own timelines. Justine, I will leave these coins here as the first payment. I will bring the balance when you have both agreed on what you will do next. I know you will want this to go forward as soon as possible. Now, I am needed at the Lupanare. I'll expect to hear from you soon."

CHAPTER 34

Ushriya stopped in her tracks. "Before we walk, I have to tell you I met the most interesting woman while walking to the bakery. At least I think I met her."

"How can you think you met her? Either you did or you didn't," Ruth said.

"Do you believe in spirit guides or angels?" Ushriya asked.

"Of course, I do," Ruth said. "They are messengers of God."

"I met her at the bench on the way to the bakery. I needed to rest, so asked her if I could sit down beside her. She agreed, patted the bench, and I sat down. She was lovely. Dark skin, wearing a beautiful red toga with a colorful hat made of beads. After she told me about herself, she asked if this was my first child. I said yes that I was hoping for a girl. She said I was going to have a boy with dark hair like his father and he would know me as the strong one."

"Strong one?" Ruth asked. "You are strong..."

"Yes, the strong one! Since I was in a hurry to get to the bakery, I left abruptly. But, at the end of the street, I thought about the woman I had just met; I wanted to make more of an acquaintance. By the time I walked back, she was nowhere in sight. I thought I would at least be able to call for her. I looked around to see if I could find her, but she was gone. There were children playing by the lemon tree. They said they had seen me sitting on the bench-alone. Ruth, did I meet an angel?"

"I hope you did. You may need one." Ruth stretched her arms above her head.

They walked in silence for a short while, enjoying the brief coolness of the summer morning.

Ushriya looked sideways at Ruth. Escaping the bustle outside Pompeii always made her feel calm. A hint of a soft summer breeze whispered through the bent grass heating up the day. With her hands clasped on top of her belly, she gazed up at the restless Vesuvius. "You know I'm planning to have an audience with Emperor Nero."

"I do. And I also know Nero might kill you," Ruth answered brusquely. "Ye God! If he killed his own wife and unborn child, what makes you think he won't kill you? And I now know why he pierced my Marcus on a stake and lit him like a torch. And what about the idea that if your child is related to him, he will take it? And you are a follower of that 'Wonder' person? How do you know he doesn't know that? Word travels fast."

Ushriya rolled her eyes, "I want to see the man who may be my brother. Can't you understand that? I've never had family." Ushriya changed the subject and softened her tone. "Is Justine temporarily moving to the dwelling in the back of the bakery?" Ushriya reached for Ruth's hand. "She will be quite comfortable there." Ruth jerked her hand away.

"Curses to you Ushriya! Can't you hear what I'm saying? He will kill you. You are...and why are you a follower anyway? This 'Wonder' man may be the death of you. Why does God need another messenger? And what will the messenger do for us? What will he save us from? He cannot take on the sins of others, no man can do that. If you believe such things, you are senseless." Ruth stared angrily ahead, her long legs doubling her stride. With her increased girth, Ushriya struggled to keep pace.

"Slow down, my domina. Calm yourself." Ushriya caught up to Ruth. Ruth stopped and crossed her arms. Ushriya continued, "Your husband is dead because he believed in something so strongly and passionately. Have you wondered why?"

"Do not call me domina! I know that whatever... or whomever, it was, was not worth losing my husband. My Avunculus killed him at the behest of Nero. I hate..."

"Please do not hate. I know you. You do not have room in your heart. You have lost so much yet gained so much. We both know God has blessed us and allowed us to survive. And now the Wonder Maker has come to show us a new way," Ushriya said.

"What way? He is not the Messiah. Pontius Pilate has killed hundreds of so-called messiahs. How do you know this man is the One? And just what have I gained? I have lost my home, my husband, and my son. I have been a slave until you freed me with money you have earned as a common whore!" Ruth gasped and burst into tears. "Now that I've found you again, I can't lose you, too." Ushriya's wrapped her arms around Ruth's shoulders.

"You will not lose me. Neither will this child I'm carrying," Ushriya patted her stomach. "Now we have new lives, new futures. You with Servius at the bakery, and I with this baby. I have the same plan with Melita for the Lupanare as we did with the bakery. It will serve a higher purpose."

"I will accept and respect the gatherings, but only because you ask me to. It is for you that I am considerate of this man. Ushriya, there is only one God. You know that. I will be true to my faith. Man cannot be God. He cannot be delivered of a virgin birth. He cannot rise from the dead to walk the earth again. How can you believe such nonsense?" Ruth demanded.

Ushriya sighed, "Ruth, there are several things I have learned for certain. The first is that nothing stays the same; nothing is forever. Not long ago, I was your famulus in Rome. Then a prostitute in Pompeii, now the lena of the brothel, and for all I know, the sister of the Emperor of Rome and-if I am, I need you to understand that I need to discover the truth. The second thing is that I've learned to trust my own intuition. Every time I don't listen to it, I fail. The last is that I've never felt as strong, as capable, and as confident as when I listen to the teachings. If he is not the messiah, so be it, but I know in my heart his message is the one I will follow."

There was a long silence between the two friends, each reflecting on what the other had said. Their walk slowed to a stroll, a thoughtful contemplation of the past years. So many changes had occurred since they left Rome.

Ruth broke the silence. "I'm in awe of your determination and your ability to reshape things. Your vision is greater than most people around you and better than their best. I knew when you were a small child that your curiosity and ambition would lift you to heights most only dream of. I hear your devotion when you speak of this man." She paused. "And honestly, sometimes I'm envious. I'm envious of your momentum. You don't question if you are able to do something, you just do it. These are God-given gifts that are only now blooming."

"Thank you, but curiosity has led me to trouble, too!" Ushriya lightened the moment. "The world is so fascinating. People are interesting. I want to meet everyone, turn over rocks and look over fences! And I want this baby to see all there is to see."

"If the child is anything like the mother, there is a good possibility." Ruth softened.

"Will you have more children?" Ushriya asked. "Will you marry Servius?"

"Since you have bestowed the gift of the bakery and Servius is now free, he has asked me to be his wife."

"And when were you going to tell me this grand news?" Ushriya exclaimed.

"I was waiting for you to tell me you were intended for Alexis!"

"I've not decided if I will marry," Ushriya said matter-of-factly.

"But you are with child-probably his child."

"Yes, there is no doubt this is his child. And I love Alexis. Yes, we will probably marry, but I want it to be our decision, not just his."

"What? The baby will be illegitimate," Ruth stated.

"No baby of mine will be illegitimate. With or without Alexis, I can provide for this baby."

"Where are you getting these ideas?" Ruth was curious.

"Nothing new. I have always provided for myself and now it warms me to be in service of others. But there is a woman with the idea that male and female are equal of spirit, that they are neither man nor woman, but simply human. All spirits are the same and made in the image of God. Her name is Mary of Magdala and there are rumors she was a repentant prostitute."

"That is why you relate to her," Ruth understood.

"But she was so much more than that. She was the closest

woman to the Wonder Maker. She was with him when he died. Since then, she has become an important conveyor of his teachings." Ushriya explained.

"Why is he called the Wonder Maker? Did he have a name?" Ruth asked.

"His name was Jesus," Ushriya answered.

CHAPTER 35

Ruth helped Justine lift a dense wooden box filled with her possessions into the cart. Justine leaned against the back panel and wiped her brow. The slaves were bustling with early morning tasks and wondered why Justine was loading a heavy box into a cart without demanding they help her.

"That is all. Now, shall we tell them?" Justine heaved a big sigh. "I'm ready."

Ruth put her arm around Justine's delicate shoulders and nodded to Servius. They walked into the center of the bakery, all three standing by the millstones. Servius halted the donkeys from grinding grain.

"Come, gather with me. I have a message for you." Justine motioned two men slaves and a woman slave down from the loft. Five men, glistening with sweat, stopped pushing on the other millstone and hesitated to step forward. Servius stood behind Ruth. All the slaves moved in closer. Two women finished kneading bread, wiped their hands, and approached Justine-eyes averted. Two others cautiously watched the ovens, fretful the bread would burn, but knowing they should obey. Justine gestured to take the bread out of the ovens.

After the bread was pulled, Justine began to speak. "I never thought this day would come, but it has. There were many times

I've been so cruel, beat you and treated you all so beastly. I hope you remember a time when I wasn't so angry. Today I have great regret and sorrow in my heart. I apologize. Had I known what God had in store for me, I might not have been consumed with resentment. I don't know that I deserve what God has provided." She turned to Ruth, sighed, and continued. "The bakery has been bought by a gracious domina. She has bought it for Ruth. So...I will leave you in her hands." Ruth stepped forward, a wide smile on her face. Gasps flooded the room as the realization of Justine's message seeped in. The slaves erupted with applause. Justine held her hand up. "Ruth will no longer be a slave. And you..."

The slaves exploded again in loud applause. Ruth interrupted the cheer, "Thank you, my friends, and yes, you will always be my friends, but now I have more good news." A hush. "You will all have the ability to buy your freedom. You may stay here and work until you have enough coins to exchange them for a place to live. You will now receive coins for your work." A loud jubilant cry went up. "For today, I ask that you return to work, so that we may fill the orders of our customers. But tomorrow you will be paid with coins." Ruth noticed not one slave asked what amount they would be paid, and she knew why; they had no idea of what being paid meant. All they heard was "free." Ruth tilted her head toward Justine as Servius' muscular arms encircled both.

"Servius will drive your things out to your new home." Ruth felt Justine smiling at Servius. "There is one more bit of good news though." She took Servius' hands and looked lovingly into his eyes."

"Just when were you going to share this happy news with me?" Justine folded her arms. Ruth smiled recalling Ushriya had asked the same thing.

"We have been keeping this secret for some time, but with all the good news, why not add more?" Servius beamed.

Justine laughed. "I've known this was coming. Your amorous stares when you think no one was watching were more apparent than you thought, and besides, I have also known Ruth doesn't sleep alone. I have a habit of checking on things when I cannot sleep at night. Giggles and sighs do echo in the halls!" Justine shook her head. "Nonetheless. I congratulate your betrothal and will expect to celebrate your wedding." Servius helped Justine into the seat of the cart, circled to the other side and climbed in beside her.

"I'll return by sun set," he called to Ruth as he shook the reins.

The cart bumped over the cobblestones, jostling both. Servius threw a protective arm in front of Justine when she lurched forward.

"Servius. Are you a Jew?" Justine asked.

"I was born a Jew," he answered. "Why do you ask?

"Are you now a practicing Jew?" Justine asked further.

"No. If you're asking about my faith, and I'm supposing you are, I had been to the gatherings with Hanoch when I had traveled with him to Rome. I began questioning my Jewish faith when we saw Paul of Tarsus spread the teachings of the 'Wonder Maker' whom the followers have suggested is the messiah. At first, I didn't listen closely, but then I realized that it didn't matter if he was the messiah. I knew how I felt after hearing his message. So, I'm not a practicing Jew nor am I a follower. You have never asked, and I suppose it didn't matter that your slaves would have thoughts of faith," Servius answered.

Justine ignored Servius' last comment. "You know Ruth's father was a Jewish priest in Rome-quite elite, I hear. It would be my recommendation that if you are to wed and don't intend to continue in your faith as a Jew, she should know," Justine said. "Just an old woman's thoughts."

Servius returned at sun set as promised and found Ruth by the mixing table finishing the last batch of bread to be ready for the ovens first thing in the morning.

"How are you, my love?" Servius wheeled Ruth around passionately kissing her.

"Servius! This bread must be ready for morning."

"Who cares?" Servius exclaimed, then became serious, "Justine asked me something interesting on our ride to the vineyard."

Ruth busily put the kneaded dough in a pan. "What was that?"

"She asked if I was a Jew."

Ruth hastily pushed the pan aside, dropped her hands and asked, "Well, what did you say?"

"It occurred to me that neither have you asked of my beliefs."

"What is the answer? I assumed you were a Jew."

"I was born a Jew..."

"Oh good! I was..."

"Let me finish," Servius interjected, watching Ruth's face and shoulders fall.

"I have been to Rome to hear the teachings..." Servius said

Ruth became indignant. "What is with this 'Wonder'? All around me, there are people with ridiculous thinking, full of foolish, impossible ideas. Ushriya told me he is dead, yet he lives? Impossible."

"He has died but now he is alive," Servius answered nonchalantly, then changed the subject. "Will you still marry me now that you know I am not a practicing Jew who may or may not be a follower?"

"First Justine, then Ushriya, now you. Servius!" Ruth suddenly pulled Servius's face to hers, "Too late. I am in love and can't imagine my life without you. Can *you* marry a Jew is the real question?" Servius lifted her, whirling her around, tunic sliding up her legs. "Put me down!"

"Yes, I will marry you, my Jewish princess!" Servius put Ruth down and kissed her firmly.

"From sunrise to sunset, our lives have changed. An owner of the bakery soon to be married, with three of the most important people in my life following a man they call the 'Wonder Maker'," Ruth said.

"Two for sure."

"Two people I love and respect who are alive. Marcus, who had become a more kind man in the days before the fire, was impaled because he chose to follow, and now the man I am about to marry is considering. What am I missing?" Ruth asked. My father would have told me if the Jews had acknowledged this Wonder Maker as the messiah. He said nothing. He did, however, tell me about a man from Nazareth that was a Jew who was teaching a message of morals and a path to a good life. I thought nothing of it. Could that be him?" Ruth asked.

"Yes, because I have heard him called Jesus of Nazareth," Servius said. "I wonder if your father, as a Jewish priest, would have acknowledged him as the messiah had he lived longer and heard the teachings."

Ruth reasoned, "I think he would have heard him as a Jew; a good man, who understood the will of God. He wouldn't have leapt to the notion that this man was the messiah because it was known that Pontius Pilate killed 'messiahs' every day. Justine says Hanoch was also a follower. So now there are five people in my life, three living, two dead. How did you hear?"

"I didn't know about this man until I heard Paul of Tarsus in Rome with Hanoch. As Hanoch's slave, I had no choice but to accompany him. Along with the Emperor Claudius' appetite for his spelt bread, hearing Paul speak was one of the main reasons Hanoch traveled to Rome so frequently using the excuse to buy wheat. He could have bought wheat here but chose to trudge to Rome. One of those trips resulted in his death." Servius explained.

"I know."

CHAPTER 36

JUNE 1, AD 68

Augusta slid a bowl of fruits and nuts in front of Ushriya. "You need to eat before you go. That baby needs food."

Ushriya glared at Augusta. "Just so you know: This is Alexis' baby." Ushriya's stomach gurgled, the child growing inside her was not cooperating with neither the idea of a bumpy ride over cobblestones to Villa Poppaea Sabina nor meeting its new avunculus.

"I'm not hungry," Ushriya snapped.

The rumors of Empress Poppaea being murdered in the last days of her pregnancy tinged Ushriya's decision to meet Nero. *Did he indeed kick his wife and unborn baby to death?* Too late, the sound of clacking metal against stone reverberated from around the corner and since it was coming from the wrong direction for carts and wagons during the daytime, Ushriya knew it had to be Emperor Nero's royal carriage. She shielded her eyes from the morning sun. Augusta and Alexis craned their necks to catch the first glimpse of the arrival of the carpentum. A message two suns ago informed Ushriya that a royal carriage would arrive to carry her to Nero's audience. She was determined to make this trip alone. Her stomach gurgled.

As the carpentum approached, she wavered. *Am I doing the right thing?* She needed to know where she came from; why she had the same mark as Emperor Nero. *Because if I don't live through this birth, I need to know the truth now. I don't want Nero to raise my child. When I return from the trip and the baby is born, I will know how to move forward knowing if my child carries the blood of the house of Augustus or not.*

All three inhaled deeply as a magnificent carriage drawn by two white horses materialized from around the corner in the brilliant morning sun. Wooden wheels painted white with iron shod rims encased carved spokes. An arched roof enclosed the sitting area. The resplendent carpentum halted at the door of the Lupanare. A soldier dressed in the scarlet finery of the drivers Ushriya had witnessed at the procession wielded the horses in the highest noble fashion. He did not get down from his pretend throne to assist Ushriya. Girls from the Lupanare hung from the windows to witness the spectacle, keeping silent in respect. Patrons lingering on the street stood still, but the gossip, nonetheless, of the lena getting into a royal carriage began spreading through Pompeii. Alexis took Ushriya's hand, balancing her up the steps into the grand carriage and placed her bag under the seat. The soldier stared forward.

"I will expect you in two suns, my Ushriya. If you do not arrive, know that I will come to Oplontis to fetch you." Ushriya nodded and gave him a quick kiss good-bye. The driver snapped the horses to a trot.

Blowing another kiss from the window, then ducking inside the spacious sitting area, she snuggled into the pillows of purple silk with gold tassels. Frescoes of lemon trees with birds woven in silks decorated the red shimmering fabric inside the carriage. Another window on the opposite side allowed Ushriya to view the countryside. Even the ceiling was painted with red and yellow flowers. She settled in for the ride.

Vineyards and groves of lush green olive trees lined the road from Pompeii to Oplontis. Ushriya reached under her seat for a sip of water. Soon, she laid down, and fell into a deep slumber, the constant rhythmic metallic clicking of the wheels lulling her.

A lurch of the carriage roused her. She sat up as the driver stepped down to open the door to the majesty of the Villa Poppaea Sabina, the domus of the family of Nero's dead wife. Nero resided here as a stop-over when he visited Pompeii and the neighboring towns. A cluster of women slaves, dressed in small tan tunics, with their heads down, bustled around the carriage nodding in deference. The famulus stepped forward. Ushriya recognized their order.

"My name is Pauline, and I will serve you."

"I am Ushriya. I am pleased to know you."

Pauline bowed again, noticing Ushriya's soft lavender toga. She offered a pillow with oils and lotions. "Please follow me to your bath. Will you be changing your toga?"

"Yes, I have brought an extra." Ushriya followed Pauline.

"Please pardon if I am forward, but his royal emperor will not be pleased if you are wearing any shades of purple for his audience, so if you are in need..."

"I will wear the toga I brought with me," Ushriya stated. Pauline nodded.

"Very well. You will have an audience with the emperor tomorrow. Today, we will prepare you with a bath, grooming, and the foods of your choice. We will plait your hair and…does the emperor know you are with child?" Pauline asked cautiously.

"I don't know, but why should he care?" A foolish remark, Ushriya realized. Pauline was silent. Ushriya touched the white streak in her hair. A feeling of nausea came over her with a twinge of cramping. "And yes, I will have my hair plaited, but I should like it tied back so that it falls to my back." Ushriya fondly remembered domina Ruth's plaited hair piled around her head.

Leading Ushriya into the grand entrance where the blue sky bounced off the cerulean water of the impluvium, red frescoes illustrating columns, doors, and teal drapery covered the triclinium on their right where the dominus of the house received guests. The frescoes made the domus look even larger than it was. They walked through the colonnade lined by gigantic white granite columns; she followed Pauline on sparkling marble floors, around the corner of carefully manicured bushes. There were blossoming plants, cherry, and plum trees, along with lemon trees laden with bright yellow fruit. The ceilings were excessively high and glimmered in the sun. *Gold everywhere*! Even the impluvium, almost empty of rainwater, was immaculately decorated with statues of golden nymphs and cherubs. Azure blue peacocks peeked from more frescoes. Pauline guided Ushriya around a pool meant for swimming and a spa under construction. Patched walls and columns betrayed the earthquake of several years ago.

When they arrived at the bath, hearty young slaves eased her out of her toga and into warm water. Fragrance swirling over her swollen belly soothed her. Ahhh, such relief. Every few minutes, a spray of fragrance filled the air. Pauline appeared with a soft cloth and scented oils to assist Ushriya from the bath. As she emerged,

Pauline carefully wrapped her in a scented toga and guided her to a chair. Ushriya lowered herself into the chair. Pauline hovered close by. Ushriya took a deep breath. "I am completely exhausted...not sure this trip was a good idea."

"Domina Ushriya. The baby might be closer than you think. I've seen many into this world. When the water comes, we will know," Pauline advised.

"I can't have this baby here. I will have my audience, and soon make my way back to Pompeii. Can you tell the driver to be ready?" Ushriya asked.

"Yes, I can let him know to be prepared to leave. Now, after the body oils, I will plait your hair, then I will add some highlights to your face." Pauline fluffed Ushriya's hair. "Your hair is the color of Emperor Nero's, and you have the silvery white streak of hair in the front..."

"That is precisely why I am here, Pauline. I both fear and wonder if we are of the same blood. I suspect we are. My past is uncertain, and more and more I fear..."

"I would say you are his blood...but certainly more attractive than he." Pauline giggled, putting her hands over her mouth.

Ushriya laughed. "I have seen him. I think he looks like a pumpkin. However, my hair color and the spot in my hair are clues."

"Then, domina, you won't mind me saying you seem a bit more..." Pauline grasped for the right word.

"Sound? Stable?" Ushriya finished. "I have been a slave. Now, I am a lena. I have had to survive on my own."

Pauline relaxed. "It might be a blessing. I know you will find the answers you seek."

"I don't think this Emperor, or any other elite is better or more worthy than those who toil as slaves. Since arriving here and having seen him in Pompeii, I am putting the pieces together; I'm certain I am of his blood. Now I'm concerned; how will he react when he sees I am big with a child who may be of royal blood also?" Ushriya at once felt vulnerable.

"May I be honest, domina?" Pauline asked.

"Please," Ushriya answered.

"You have heard the rumors of Empress Poppaea. They are true. He is capable of murdering a pregnant woman. I will stay as close as I can to you during his audience. Be on guard. Do not turn your back to him."

CHAPTER 37

JUNE 2, AD 68

"Agrippina, the daughter of Germanicus, wife of Claudius?" Nero stood gazing out a full-length window, framed in the same gold silk-tasseled curtains as the carriage that had carried her here. Ushriya was blinded by the late morning sun bouncing off the gilded ceiling. His back to Ushriya, a long silk Tyrian purple toga draping to the floor, Nero's voice was shrill and small. He did not turn around.

"I am Ushriya. I am not Agrippina."

"Your mother! Was Agrippina your mother?" he demanded.

"I don't know that for certain, my Emperor...."

"You don't know? How could you not know? You have the white streak of my mother Agrippina!" Nero's high-pitched voice rose. He abruptly turned to face Ushriya, raising his hand to his hair. "The same as mine!"

"I didn't know Agrippina had the white streak until just this moment," Ushriya said.

Suddenly, Nero's demeanor changed. Dropping a silk handkerchief he was holding, his head tilted as if seeing a kitten for the first time. Both sides of his petite mouth rose to meet his fleshy cheeks in a demented smile. He slowly offered his hand to her. "It is you, my Poppaea. You have come back to me…and you have brought our child."

Ushriya backed away. Nero tilted his head the other way scuffling towards her.

"Why are you afraid, my Poppaea? It is me, your beloved."

"No, you are mistaken. I am Ushriya, the lena of the Lupanare."

"Poppaea, I knew you would not leave me." The emperor stared at Ushriya's belly. She backed into a fresco on a red wall as he reached for her abdomen. His eyes were glazed, distant and crazed. Frightened, Ushriya frantically searched for Pauline. Aware of Ushriya's distress, Pauline slowly walked towards Nero, gently edging between them so as not to arouse him. She leaned to Ushriya and whispered, "He thinks you are his dead wife." She turned to Nero. "My Emperor, I will take Poppaea for…"

"No!" Nero thrusts both arms. "She has just come back. Leave her to me."

"I am not Poppaea, and I wish to leave," Ushriya said, staring at him.

Nero reached forward slowly as if moving in mud. He put his pudgy hand on Ushriya's head to touch the white streak in her hair, then pulled his hand back and touched the streak in his own reddish hair. Ushriya jerked away, glaring at Pauline to let her know she would take her leave. Nero stepped in her path to the door.

"Poppaea, I see you have matched my white streak just like my mother. To please me? Oh, don't you see? There is no reason for you to be angry. I have not been out late driving my chariot. I am here now with you." He cocked his head. "Have you brought Claudia Augusta with you? Where is she? Does she play in the forum?" Pauline inched closer to Ushriya and whispered once again.

Pauline became alarmed. "He is having such imagination. Claudia Augusta is his dead daughter by Empress Poppaea."

Clearly, the Emperor was delusional. Even so, Ushriya attempted to reason with him.

"I am not Empress Poppaea, my Emperor, but I may, indeed, be your sister. You see, we both have the white streak in our red hair. If your mother did also, there is chance I am her daughter. I am told I was rescued from exposure at the palace of Claudius by two people who raised me until I was stolen by slave traders. I have been a famulus at the house of Marcus in Rome since I was a small child." The words tumbled out.

"Sister?" With the recognition of "sister", a bit of reality seemed to creep back into Nero's consciousness. He paced the room with the strides his squat legs would allow.

Ushriya didn't want to upset his momentary fragile sanity. "My Emperor. Is there a chance your mother, Agrippina, lay with Claudius before he took her to be his wife? It is the only explanation I may offer," Ushriya rationalized.

"Oh, there is every possibility Agrippina lay with Claudius before they betrothed. She was a whore, you see, and a good one at that! Look who she took to be my stepfather! She is the reason I am Emperor." Nero stared at Ushriya's belly and switched realities. "But Poppaea. I am so pleased our son will be here soon. He will be the heir to my throne, so that I may leave this awful office to once again sing and dance in the theater."

Ushriya whispered to Pauline. "How long has he been this way? Sing and dance in the theater? He seems tormented," she whispered.

"He believes he is the best singer and dancer in Rome. He

forces the people to sit for hours in the Amphitheater to watch him. They sit in the hot sun without food, drink, or latrine. Some die," Pauline explained. Ushriya heaved a big sigh.

"So, I have heard."

Nero gazed out the window, unaware of the conversation going on around him. "Domina, he has been completely out of touch since the death of Empress Poppaea. He was not quite this vile before now, but he goes in and out of reality. You see, he became angry with her when she questioned his late nights out, disguised, carousing, whoring, and driving his chariot. So angry that he kicked Queen Poppaea and their unborn child to death. He has since turned his sickening affections to a boy. He had him castrated, makes him up, dressing him in her clothing. He treats the boy in the cardinal way and forces him to accompany him to state affairs. I know you have heard the unspeakable deeds he has done to the cult of the followers."

"Yes, the husband of my domina in Rome was among them," Ushriya answered, speaking as if Nero was not in the room.

"You had mentioned you were a slave. He must have been a follower," Pauline said.

A scream erupted from Nero. "The child you bear is of the house of Augustus! You will stay here. Live in the Villa until the child is born. Then the child will travel to Rome and live as a member of the Royal family." Nero stared hard at Ushriya. Her worst fears had come true.

"I will do no such thing!" Ushriya replied. "This child is mine, and will live with me..."

"Who is the father? Who have you laid with? How much longer..." Nero became agitated and shook his fist at her. Ushriya stepped towards him and gazed into his wicked, muddy green eyes.

"Certainly, no business of yours!" Ushriya exclaimed.

He clenched his fist, then dropped it. "Guards!" Nero's red hair now matched his red face. The door opened and two soldiers rushed in. "Take this woman who claims to be my sister! Lock her in with this slave until the baby she carries is born." He motioned to Pauline. Both women were grabbed by their arms and taken out of the room, pulling from the soldiers. By chance, Ushriya broke free and fell crashing to the floor. Paulina rushed to her. Ushriya cried out, grabbing her abdomen.

"If you've hurt my baby, I will kill you!" she screamed.

Nero stood back; arms crossed. "You and the rest of my empire!" His eyes narrowed and his thick lips pulled back in a wicked grin.

Pauline struggled against Ushriya's weight. The soldiers intervened, roughly yanking her by the arm to her feet, then shoving the two women ahead of them. Pauline looked back at the soldiers, both of whom she knew. "Put us in the healing room," she instructed. The men obeyed, guiding them along the corridor, past the front atrium where Ushriya had arrived at the front of the villa. Ushriya stumbled into the hedge before they turned to a corridor leading around the lush estate garden to the room used for healing purposes. When they arrived, Ushriya was panting. Pauline pointed to a chair padded with pillows and drew a footstool close to prop up her feet.

"I need air," Ushriya gasped. "I'm so hot. Can you remove my toga?"

"Can you stand?" Ushriya wobbled while Pauline inched the

toga up from the floor to her waist. "Now lift your arms and I will slip it over the top of your head." With some effort, the toga was up and off, exposing Ushriya's naked girth. "I'll bring some thin cloth to wrap around you. You will get cooler as you rest. If I knock at the door, the two guards will allow me to leave. I'll also bring back some cool water and food." Ushriya felt fortunate to have Pauline attending her.

"Please rest. I will be back soon." The guards opened the door as soon as Pauline knocked twice.

Ushriya dozed in the comfortable chair. By the time Pauline returned, she had regained her breath. Pauline used a large cloth to wrap around Ushriya, then poured some water.

"I must be on my way back to Pompeii. There are people expecting me," Ushriya said. A cramp doubled her over. Pauline rubbed her shoulders. "They will come for me if I don't return by sunset."

"I know the guards won't allow you to leave, given the emperor's orders. And I think this baby is coming soon," Pauline said.

CHAPTER 38

JUNE 3, AD 68

As Ruth approached the Lupanare, Alexis stepped into the morning light, a stuffed cloth bag in hand and a determined look on his face.

"I've come to tell Ushriya that Phoebe is arriving tonight from Rome for the first of her gatherings, and while I'm not in favor...." Ruth's tone changed to serious when she saw the worry in Alexis' eyes. "What's wrong? Hasn't she returned from Oplontis?"

"No, she hasn't. I was on my way to the bakery to get your permission to use the cart and donkeys. I'm going to Oplontis," Alexis said.

"Of course! Go! When you are at the bakery, ask Servius to accompany you, that it's at my request. I will greet Phoebe to tell her...never mind, just go."

Alexis hurried down the street, running toward the bakery, arm in the air, shouting, "Thank you. We'll return tomorrow!" He disappeared around the corner.

Ruth worried about Ushriya and her unborn baby. David was her only child, but she remembered how she felt before he was born. During the last days, she ached, wobbled, and continually visited the latrine. At the end, she kept a latrine pot beside her lectus. Her mother was with her when David made his entrance into the world. Marcus had been there to examine his new son. Going through childbirth alone was beyond anything she could imagine.

Ruth opened the door to the Lupanare and made her way to the culina. Augusta was bustling about, tossing newly sliced onions, parsnips, and asparagus in a pot of steaming garum. The scent of onions and fish wafted through the culina. Grabbing a spoon to mix herbs and cheese, she nodded towards the bread on the table.

"Just finishing some moratum. Are you hungry? Help yourself to some bread." Augusta loved feeding people. She placed the bowl of cheese mixture in front of her. Ruth settled in a chair closest to Augusta and tore off a serving of bread.

"Alexis is off to fetch Ushriya...." Augusta paused to stir the boiling vegetables.

"I met him as he left. He is using the cart and donkeys and Servius is accompanying him. Augusta, I'm worried. There can only be one reason Ushriya has not returned. Nero is holding her there until she has the child, so he may keep the baby. Why did we allow her to make this trip?"

"There is no "allow" in Ushriya's world. Since she learned to use her own gifts, nothing has been able to stop her. She is stubborn, that one. But being so big with child, she should never have made such a trip, especially meeting with a mad Emperor." Augusta shook her head, wiped her hands on her toga, and began chopping cabbage. "Servius and Alexis will find her. I have faith."

Ruth agreed. "How was she feeling before she left? Do you have an idea of the time the baby is to arrive?"

"Her stomach was bothering her during sunset, and she didn't sleep well."

"Do you know if Alexis is the father? Surely, as a meretrix, she would…"

"She made that clear to me before she left." A bit perturbed, Augusta held up her hand. "As soon as she became the lena, she stopped laying with others. The only one I know to have lain with Ushriya is Alexis. I thought she had surely fallen in love with him. You do know that means Ushriya is carrying my grandchild."

Ruth snickered. "How wonderful that your blood will mix with the house of Augustus, Augusta!"

Augusta sat the knife down and looked into Ruth's eyes. "Before I celebrate, I need to know they are both safe. She and my grandchild are certainly in a great deal of danger. I can feel it. Why, that mad Nero kills people for no reason, and if he suspects…"

"…she is his sister, then he will know she is carrying an heir!" Ruth finished Augusta's thought.

Augusta glanced away. "And I know he has killed the followers. It's times like this when I ask myself why I'm following."

Ruth replied with anger. "Why are you following? I'm putting myself in danger to meet a woman I don't know so that she may relay the teachings of this man to a lot of people I also don't know! Why am I doing this?" Ruth didn't wait for an answer. "So that I can keep a promise to Ushriya? Because she is a follower? …and who, as we speak, is in mortal danger because she is the sister of the emperor and is carrying a royal baby, through no fault of her own." Ruth wrung her hands and paced back and forth. "Your declaration of a crucified messiah who has been raised from the dead by God hasn't been predicted by God himself. It is written that all kings will worship God and all nations will follow him and it is not by any

Jewish authority that this man is the messiah. My father would've been such an authority. Why do you think this man is the savior? I haven't heard of kings or nations falling before him!" Ruth was indignant. "So far, he hasn't saved anyone from anything."

"Paul of Tarsus saw the Wonder Maker for himself. This man revealed himself to Paul," Augusta said calmly. "He is also known as Jesus of Nazareth."

"Who is this Paul of Tarsus? What authority is he? And how can you believe the word of one man? Against the teachings of the ancient traditions, which came from God?" Ruth cried out.

"I have heard that Paul was a Jew, that his name was Saul. He acknowledged that the Wonder Maker's message would be resisted by Jews. He has said that the rebellion of the Jews is part of God's plan, so the Jews will oppose this man, so the teachings could be taken to others," Augusta said.

"What does all that mean now? We will lose our Ushriya, no matter what this Paul says, if Nero sees she is his sister. Alexis and Servius have just left; they won't be back until tomorrow; we can only hope we see any of them again." Ruth's thoughts skipped around. "I will be overcome with worry tonight when I'm opening the bakery for the gathering. The word has spread that Phoebe will be in Pompeii. I have been stopped on the street many times by people asking me about the gathering."

"If people are asking, don't you think it's a sign there is interest in a messenger of God?"

"If he's a messenger of God, is he, himself, now a God?" Ruth asked.

"I didn't say that, but if he was resurrected and seen by Paul, wouldn't that suggest he is a God?"

"No. There is only one God. This Jesus was a Jew, a mortal man teaching the ancient traditions, nothing more," Ruth answered. "And if Paul saw a resurrected man, there is always the possibility he could be lying."

"If he's not the messiah, then he was sent to bring righteousness back into our world. There's a great hunger for a message of love and goodness. I became a follower because even if he isn't the messiah, his message is uplifting and sends warmth and love. That is all I know," Augusta said. "Ushriya became a follower in Rome when she was your famulus. She didn't know Marcus was a follower. There were gatherings of the slaves separate from the elites. She knew Marcus was attending the gatherings; she told me she saw him leaving a gathering late one night when Paul of Tarsus was teaching. Ushriya told me Marcus knew he needed to be cautious; he was a soldier who took his orders from Pontius Pilate, who had killed multitudes of false messiahs, so he was careful," Augusta stated.

"I did know he was a follower. I knew he thought his life as a soldier wasn't fulfilling anymore. He told me he had seen Paul teach in Rome. We argued; he said the Wonder Maker pleased him. I said this man was teaching the same traditions we have always known; to love God with all our hearts, souls, and minds. Why are people thinking he is different than any of the other Jewish teachers?" Ruth asked.

"You are Jewish, and from what I'm hearing, you are steadfast in your belief that there is no new messiah," August assumed.

Ruth sighed. "You're right. I am resolved in my faith, and Marcus wouldn't have tried to convert me, given who my father was. He had no choice, and now he is gone."

"Will you have the gathering at the bakery tonight?"

"It is Ushriya's wish that I will allow Phoebe to teach, and it is a promise I will keep. I will return to the bakery to greet her."

"Do you pray?" Augusta asked.

"Of course, I pray," Ruth answered.

"Then pray."

CHAPTER 39

JUNE 3, AD 68

Ushriya retched. From the daze of nausea, she heard the massive door of Nero's palace thunderously close behind Pauline. A pot of steaming water in one hand, folded cloths under her arm, Pauline hurried to Ushriya's side. She moved a birthing chair close to Ushriya and helped her sit up in position over the hole in the seat for the baby to drop through. She placed her hands between Ushriya's legs, gently spreading them apart as her convulsing body prepared for impending life.

Pauline laid a wet cloth on Ushriya's forehead, but she ripped it from her face. Pauline patiently positioned another cloth underneath Ushriya, sopping small gushes of blood. Ushriya rocked from side-to-side moaning and vomiting into a nearby latrine pot.

Pauline stood beside her. "Domina! Please! You must stay still in the chair of birth!"

Leaning on her elbows, sweat poured from Ushriya's brow as she struggled to focus on the blurry image of two men coming through the window across the room. "Alexis!" She slumped sideways, but in an instant, she regained her senses. Pauline ran to the window and slapped at Alexis and Servius as they crawled over the windowsill. "Leave them," Ushriya whispered. Her contractions subsided.

"Ushriya!" Alexis leapt to her side and Pauline withdrew. Ushriya felt his warm hand in hers. "I'm here," Alexis cooed.

Eyes closed; she reserved her strength. Servius surveyed the room, concerned for their safety.

Ushriya jolted up from the chair and lunged forward with another contraction. Servius' instincts took over. "Hot water and more cloths," he instructed Pauline, at the same time laying his hand on Ushriya's abdomen. "The baby is coming now." All at once, a contraction sent a sizeable amount of blood shooting from between Ushriya's legs. The baby's head crowned, and one more contraction pushed it into the light. Servius took the newborn, quickly cut the cord of life, and sucked its mouth, spitting the contents on the floor. Staccato newborn cries triggered a faint smile on Ushriya's face. Alexis helped Ushriya to the lectus.

"Boy or girl?" she murmured. Pauline wrapped the baby in soft cloth. Alexis moved in to examine the child.

"A boy," Alexis tenderly answered with a wide smile. Ushriya heard the delight in his voice.

"He is Gaius Antonius," Ushriya uttered. "It is the name of a strong and capable man."

Nodding, Alexis added, "Gaius Antonius. He has my dark hair and your white streak."

Ushriya's eyes opened in alarm. "Our son is in danger, Alexis!" With labored breath, her voice fell to a slow whisper. "You must take him. Now. You must take him to Ruth."

"I will wait for you…" Alexis whispered.

"No time. Can't you see my fate is with God? I'm unable to

move. If you stay, Nero will either take the baby or kill him. Nero is without his senses. Go. Now." The emotion exhausted Ushriya. Servius hovered by her side. "Go with him Servius," she said.

"We have to do as she says. We will take him to Ruth. Pauline will be with Ushriya," Servius said. Alexis handed the child to Pauline who washed blood from the squalling baby.

Ushriya struggled to sit up. "Thank you, Servius. If I survive, I will find my way to Pompeii. Go!" She fell back.

"I will bring goats' milk, enough for two days." With closed eyes, Ushriya heard the plan and nodded. Pauline slipped out the door between the villa guards.

Tears ran down Alexis' face as he studied the child. "We could color the streak with burnt ashes or umber paint," he said.

With a cough and a deep groan, Ushriya spoke softly, "The streak does not matter now. Nero knows I am of his blood, and now he thinks I am his dead wife returned, so he might claim our baby as his own. There really is no time. Go as soon as Pauline brings the milk. But for now, please bring him to my breast, Alexis, that I may give my blessing to you, to Ruth and Servius." Alexis carried the child to Ushriya and supported his little body on her breast; his tiny mouth opened like a baby bird. Quickly finding her nipple, sweet suckling sounds contented Ushriya. Alexis fell to his knees beside her.

"He is beautiful," he said.

"I need to say something." Ushriya's breath slowed. She turned toward Alexis. "I love you. Please raise our child with Ruth, Servius, and your mother. Fall in love again, our son will need a mother. You and Melita will own the Lupanare and know that I wish its doors to be open for gatherings. Phoebe is in Pompeii now and I know Ruth has kept her promise. Give her my everlasting gratitude and love." She smiled at her son. "Grow to be an honest man. Be faithful, love with all your heart and have compassion for others...and learn to dance." Ushriya closed her eyes with a heavy sigh.

Pauline came rushing through the door, bottles of milk clanking in a basket. "They are coming! Nero's guards! They saw the cart by the hedges! Go! Go at once!"

Eyes closed, Ushriya weakly turned to Alexis. "Go, my love. You have the best part of me."

The clinking metallic sound of the guards drew closer. Just in time, Alexis grabbed the milk, Servius held the baby, and they bounded out the window as the guards came crashing through the door.

"Who owns that cart? they demanded.

Pauline shook her head. "I don't know."

Noticing the open window, the guards charged out. As soon as they had left the room, Servius, the baby in one arm, came springing back through the window. Servius clamped his hand over the infant's mouth as he began to cry and took him to Ushriya. She opened her breast and the baby hushed.

"Leave me! I mean you no harm!" Pauline and Ushriya heard Alexis' frantic voice booming through the window. "Let me go!" Then there was a deafening silence.

Servius peeked outside the window just in time to see Nero's soldiers dragging Alexis' lifeless body away. He waited until he couldn't see them anymore, then turned to Ushriya.

"He is gone," Servius said.

With the limited strength she had, Ushriya sobbed within

herself, knowing she could not make any noise or Antonius could be in grave danger. Her sobs pulsed the baby up and down on her belly. Great tears of grief welled inside Servius as well and he, too, sobbed quietly.

Pauline stepped forward. "Domina, I'm sorry, but we must protect you and the baby. I have a plan. I know the emperor is leaving for Rome tomorrow. I will send the villa guards to tell him that you both died. His madness might let him believe that once again Poppaea has died with his child. His moods are so unpredictable that he might even believe the reality that it was his sister who died with a royal child. Nonetheless, he will leave you alone and you will both be safe."

Servius paced thoughtfully around the room. "I think this is a good plan. Please tell me your name."

"I am Pauline, the famulus of the Villa."

"Pauline. Thank you for your care of Ushriya and thank you for your willingness to carry out this plan."

Ushriya nodded weakly.

Servius added, "There are many people in Pompeii who will be worried. I must return to reassure everyone. It will also fall to me to tell Alexis' mother what has happened to him, and that she is a grandmother. Pauline, will this be suitable?"

With a slight bow, Pauline nodded.

"Will it be safe if I take the cart and donkeys, or do you think the soldiers have them? I want to leave," Servius said.

"It will take them some time to take Alexis…" Ushriya began to cry softly. Pauline sighed, then continued. "You should be able to leave now, but please hurry. I will tell the villa guards to allow your passage."

Servius left at once. Following him, Pauline opened the doors, stepped out and spoke with the guards, "Domina Ushriya has left this earth along with her newborn child. Please pass this message on to Emperor Nero. I will take care of their bodies."

Without dispute, both villa guards nodded and left.

CHAPTER 40

JUNE 5, AD 68

The breeze from the ocean is soothing, Ushriya thought. She gazed lovingly down at her sleeping son and curled her finger around his white hair.

Pauline backed through the door carrying a tray of food. "You are looking well today, domina." She sat the tray of bread, grapes and moratum, the cheese sauce Ushriya loved, on the marble table beside the reclining lectus.

"Oh, thank you, but I've been here much too long--has it been four suns? I want to take my leave...soon."

"How is dominus Antonius?" Pauline asked.

"He was somewhat restless during the night but suckles like a gladiator!" Antonius grabbed her finger as she wiggled it in front of his brown eyes.

"The white spot beams from his dark hair like the full moon," Pauline smiled.

"He has the best of his father, accented with a bit of me," Ushriya cooed.

Pauline poured red wine into a clear glass decanter. "Emperor Nero left for Rome at last sun rise. He took his soldiers and all his attendants. It's quiet once more."

"What will happen when he finds out I am still alive?"

"What the Emperor thinks doesn't matter now. He is gone, and you and Antonius are safe; take the time to enjoy your new son. I have no loyalty to the emperor, so it will never be I who will divulge the truth. There was a time when he was quite pleasant, but that time has passed," Pauline declared.

"My heart aches at the loss of my Alexis. I wish he could witness his son grow to be a man. I'm missing his touch, his smile, his..." Ushriya said mournfully, allowing tears. "When I return to Pompeii, Antonius will have many people who will love and protect him. Antonius' grandmother, Augusta, will have but one grandchild, so she will be the most eager."

"Would you like me to take dominus Antonius to his cradle, so that you may rest, domina? He is asleep," Pauline asked.

"Thank you." Pauline took the baby to the cradle.

"This cradle was made for Empress Poppaea's baby," Pauline said as she laid Antonius down softly on the blankets, covered him, and quietly left the room.

While Antonius slept, Ushriya inspected her surroundings. There were frescoes on every wall, each framed with a different shape. Some were painted to look like windows; the walls below were painted in brilliant reds and oranges. Vivid shades of blue in the frescoes evolved into teal, sapphire, and cobalt contrasting against the ruby reds. Overwhelming the room were illustrations of white columns framing an azure peacock with its tail drooping down the side of a windowsill. Regal portraits of people Ushriya supposed were ancestors of the empress lined the walls on each side of the gigantic door. On the opposite side of the room was a window; the window where she had last seen Alexis. Sitting with that moment, the tears came once again. She had lost her love and was ashamed of her cavalier comment of never marrying him. She glanced to the potted lemon trees sitting beside the window soaking up the coastal sun and sighed.

Ushriya knew since Nero had returned to Rome there could be villa guards outside, but the irresistible urge to explore forced her toward the doors. Leaning her ear against one of the massive wooden doors, she couldn't hear a sound. She looked over her shoulder to make sure Antonius was still sleeping, then gradually used her weight to push the door open and peek outside. No guards. Pressing further, she slid into the corridor. No one. She went onto the corridor surrounding a small garden filled with apple trees, oleander, and laurel trees. The cool ocean breeze rejuvenated her. The first entrance to a room on the right was the lararium; a room she knew was there for the protection of guardian spirits of the household gods. Ushriya recalled domina Ruth visiting her lararium in Rome daily to perform rites assuring the safety of the domus. Making her way to another long corridor where benches lined the walls, it led to a much smaller passageway. She kept following the hallway until it turned left into yet another garden facing the ocean. Following the sounds of waves crashing against the rocks and the fishy smell from the sea, she stumbled upon a great room with immense columns that opened into a garden with a path which led between two manicured gardens. *This was the room where I met Nero*, Ushriya thought. She tiptoed into the room.

"Halt!" A guard stopped short and asked, "Is it you, the domina who had the baby?"

Startled, Ushriya turned to recognize the villa guard outside her room, "I-I-I..do you work with Pauline?"

"Yes, she told me you had left this world with your baby," he said.

"Pauline wanted to protect us from Nero, so she sent word that we had died. I needed some air and decided to walk a bit," She spoke faster. "It is quite exquisite; this whole villa is something I have never witnessed. When I was a famulus in Rome…"

"You live! Is the baby…and you were a slave? We were told you were the royal sister of Emperor Nero," the guard was perplexed.

"I am, indeed, alive and so is my son. Will you betray our secret?"

"No, the emperor is gone with his soldiers, and since we are the villa guards, we protect the villa and all who inhabit it," he smiled

"I thank you. It is becoming more apparent that I am Emperor Nero's sister. I'm still getting used to the idea that my mother was Agrippina." She pointed to the white streak in her hair. "And my father was Claudius. Agrippina conceived me before they were married, and when I was born, I was left to exposure and picked up by the bakers of the emperor's favorite spelt bread when they came to deliver to the palace. I didn't ever know my parents, nor they me. At least that is the story that makes the most sense."

"Domina, I appreciate you sharing your story. Will you be staying here at the villa?" the guard asked.

Ushriya laughed. "No, as you have heard, I have just had a son whose father was killed by Nero's soldiers. Anger is a mild description of what I think of Nero. I have no intention of ever seeing him again. Pauline…"

"Yes, we will hold to the belief that you both are not alive when he arrives back to the villa again as we have no loyalty to him anymore. I have been a guard since the villa was built. The emperor has become mad and more perverted as the years have passed. He murdered his mother, wife, unborn child and…and…" The guard stammered.

"And?" Ushriya wanted to know.

"The followers."

"Are you a follower?" Ushriya's eyebrows arched.

The guard hesitated. "I…no."

"I am." Ushriya bowed to the guard. "Allow me to introduce myself. I am Ushriya." The guard gasped and stepped back.

"I know who you are. You do not have to bow to me, domina. I am at your service. And now there are two reasons you are in danger of the emperor."

"I suppose, but he will have to find me first. What are you called?" Ushriya asked.

"I am called Dominicus."

"Dominicus. I am leaving soon. Since Emperor Nero's attendants and soldiers have left, would you arrange a cart with a driver for my son and I, so we may return to Pompeii?"

"I take orders from Pauline for the villa, but I'm sure she would want me to be of service to you."

"Thank you. Now would you be so kind as to show me how to get back to my room? Although the long way would be appreciated, so I may see more of this magnificent villa!"

"We will walk to the back exit of this room and around to the baths," Dominicus said, bowing. "As you know, this is Emperor Nero's favorite room. It is the largest in the villa and he has been known to say it is not even good enough for slaves." He led Ushriya to the garden just out the back entrance.

"There are gardens everywhere. Such beauty! How does the villa support the care of such opulence?"

"Wine is produced inland, and the ocean provides a source for garum. There are slaves producing both. Garum is made all year around, and wine is harvested when the weather turns cooler."

"Who supervises the slaves?" Ushriya wondered.

"Our overseer is Emericus. He knows the work and plans the day. Gustavus drives the slaves to finish the work."

"How many slaves are there?"

"There are many, domina. This is a large villa with different areas in need of labor. I don't know the number of slaves, but I do know Emericus goes to slave auctions in Rome frequently. Is there a reason you are interested?"

"Since I have been a slave, I understand how a soul may be reduced to one goal in their life: that of the servitude of another, just so that person may be a wealthy elite. The irony is both become reduced. The slave, because she has no charge over her own life, and the elite, because she accomplishes nothing. How entirely monotonous to weave and bear children one's whole life," Ushriya said.

"You speak of women? Of course, it is men who make and accomplish the important decisions," Dominicus said.

"Because they are more intelligent? Because they are physically stronger? Because it's said God made us from a rib of another?" Ushriya asked.

"I've offended you, domina."

"No, it's not you who has offended me. I have always known that I have the same intelligence as a man. It is Mary, who walked with the one they call Jesus, which has made me aware there is no difference in men and women. Spiritually, we are all the same, yet, have our earthly differences. I can't provide the seed of life, but you can't bear a child. Is one more necessary than the other?"

"Empress Agrippina was a woman of ambition. I have heard she was frugal, surveying slaves and household items with accountability. If you are the daughter of Empress Agrippina, has it ever occurred to you that her best attributes have fallen to you?" Dominicus asked.

"You are indeed clever, Dominicus. I wonder every day why I seem to need to take chances; risk doesn't frighten me. If rumors are true, she was determined, and I am as stubborn as a donkey." Ushriya crossed her arms. "As a slave, I was busy from sunrise to sunset and, although a slave, I was blessed with a kind domina. When I became a merchant and had the responsibility of making decisions to help others, I was more content. It filled part of my soul. I would like to see slaves become like flowers and bloom to their abilities." She sighed. "I now have two establishments in Pompeii where I have allowed the slaves to become freedmen. They are paid. They may stay or they may go after they are able to buy their freedom."

"Although I have known you for such a short time, I can see there is an ember deep within you, ready to ignite."

"I've heard similar before," Ushriya said.

Dominicus guided Ushriya through a corridor, around some living rooms.

"These are for his Emperor's guests," Dominicus gestured. They passed the baths, one steaming, one not, and continued around the villa passing gardens lined with box hedges on one side and more palatial guest rooms on the other. Ivy climbed around the columns and accented the sculptures. "I would tell you more about the statues, but there are so many, they all begin to look the same, although I know they are either the emperor's family or people he admires, or gods." They rounded a small garden with mostly olive trees and passed the great atrium where Ushriya had arrived for her visit with Nero.

"I don't suppose I will be taking a royal carriage back to Pompeii, will I?" she smiled.

"We will find you a proper cart where you both will be comfortable. Is your son named Gaius Antonius?"

"Yes, that is my son's name." They turned into a passageway where things began to look familiar. Around the largest of gardens, they turned left, then another left and there her room was in sight. A crying baby urged her breasts to leak milk. "My appreciation for the walk and the introduction."

Pauline brought Antonius to Ushriya as she settled into the indigo silk lectus.

CHAPTER 41

JUNE 6, AD 68

Rattling to a halt, the weary donkeys stood still. Servius jumped from the cart and dashed into the Lupanare.

"Ruth! Augusta! Where are you? Servius is here!" Melita emerged from the storage room with an arm full of newly dried clothing.

"Is Iena Ushriya well?" Melita shouted to Servius.

Ruth and Augusta rushed from the culina. With outreached arms, Ruth ran to her husband-to-be and embraced him warmly. "We were so worried."

"Where is Ushriya? Where is Alexis?" Ruth cried.

"Ushriya has had a baby boy. But..." Servius looked at Augusta. Alexis is no longer..."

"No!" Servius and Ruth caught Augusta just as her knees buckled. Lowering her to the floor, she sobbed. "No! That beautiful boy! He can't leave me now, just when he is a father." Alexis' mother wept, as only the mother who has lost a child can weep. "Now they are both gone."

Ruth hugged her tightly and whispered. "You have a grandson." Augusta nodded through her tears.

"A grandson." Augusta rocked in Ruth's arms. "I have lost a son and gained a grandson."

Servius stood up. "When Alexis passed from this earth, he was carrying out the wishes of lena Ushriya. She didn't know if she would survive and couldn't travel, so she asked him to take the baby back to Pompeii where she knew he would be safe. Alexis didn't want to go, but Nero's soldiers were close. Ushriya asked me to go with Alexis. We took the baby, Alexis first; I had the baby in my arms right behind him and was out of the window when Nero's soldiers caught sight of Alexis and killed him. I don't know why they didn't see me. I quickly turned around and went back in with the baby. So, you see, I must travel back to Oplontis to gather lena Ushriya and Gaius Antonius." He gave a quick smile down at Augusta.

"Gaius Antonius! My grandson is called Gaius Antonius! What a strong name," Augusta said.

"He has the black hair of his father and the white streak of his mother," Servius reported.

"How is Ushriya?" Ruth asked. "Did the baby come easily?"

"No, there was nothing easy about the entrance of Gaius Antonius into this world. When I left, she was recovering. She had the famulus of the villa, Pauline, attending her; one who had obviously been at the delivery of many babies. I think Ushriya and Antonius have survived. However, I am worried about that tyrant, Nero. I will leave at sunrise and should be there by mid-to-late morning."

Orange turned to yellow as the sun rose. Servius traded the tired donkeys from the day before with fresh animals and loaded the cart with food and water. He hid the nuts and dried figs Ruth had packed under the seat and threw some hay in the back. Even though the trip to Oplontis wouldn't be long, he tried to think of what Ushriya and the baby would need. Milk! He rushed back into the bakery.

"Ruth!" Servius found Ruth upstairs in the room they shared. "Ushriya is nursing Antonius, but I would like to take some goat's milk in case there is a need."

Ruth sidled up to Servius, eyelashes fluttering. "The travel is short..." She flirted.

"There is nothing I would rather do right now than make love to you, my darling Ruth, but rescuing Ushriya and the baby for our friend Alexis and Augusta has to surpass the yearning in my loins." He winked, encircling her with his powerful arms, then lustfully kissed her. "You are a temptress."

"Yes, I am." She playfully pushed him away. "There is enough fresh goat's milk in the culina. Please be careful." She smiled, cocking her head seductively. Servius swatted her behind and made his way down the stairs.

"Keep your fire burning!" he called over his shoulder.

Pushing at their harnesses, the fresh donkeys trotted as soon as Servius took the reins. As he guided the cart out of Pompeii, merchants waved, calling his name, inviting him to stop and visit.

"I must be on my way! Blessings to you!" By the time he reached the exit, he felt a renewed sense of confidence. Although losing Alexis grieved him, he felt the need to rescue and protect the mother and baby of his friend.

Time alone in the cart aggravated his anxious thoughts. Servius didn't know what he would find upon his return to the villa di Poppaea Sabina. Word from the Senate had spread from

Rome that Nero was an unfit leader; that he was an enemy of the elites. He had become hostis, a stranger to the ruling class. *Had he indeed fiddled as the great fire burned? Had Nero heard the gossip?*

Servius' thoughts turned to his own fortunes, and how they had changed in the past year. He fell in love with a woman who had been the domina of a large domus in Rome. He became a freedman and a partner in an establishment. He became friends with the lena of the biggest brothel in Pompeii, and since learned she was the sister of the Emperor of Rome. His service to others and his love of healing had come from his father, who had served the people of Pompeii before the depravity and immorality of Nero. Reflection of his life up to this moment left Servius missing family no longer of this earth and wanting a family of his own…a family with Ruth.

Arriving at the villa di Poppaea Sabina, Servius guided the donkeys to the place where he and Alexis had left them. From nowhere, all at once there were villa guards surrounding the cart, swords drawn. Servius' hands reached above his head.

"I mean no harm. I'm here to gather domina Ushriya and dominus Gaius Antonius to return to Pompeii. I'm Servius. I've been here previously!"

The guards relaxed their swords. "We were told the domina and baby were…" One of the soldiers said.

"She and the baby are alive," Dominicus smiled and stepped forward, motioning the guards to stand down. "That's all you need to know," he turned to Servius.

"Domina Ushriya is preparing to return to Pompeii, although Pauline has suggested she is not yet ready for travel," he said.

"Will you take me to her? I'm a medicine slave and am called upon by the people of Pompeii when they are ill," Servius stated. "And I am a friend."

"What shall we call you?" Dominicus asked.

"Servius."

"Were you the one that was here when the father of domina Ushriya's baby was killed?"

"Yes, that was me." Servius said.

"The emperor has left the residence, and his staff with him. They left two suns ago, the day after you were here. There is nothing to fear from him now," Dominicus said. "Come with me. I shall take you to domina Ushriya. Maybe you can change her mind about leaving today." Dominicus motioned the other guards to tend to the cart, then guided Servius to Ushriya.

Dominicus pushed the huge door open. Pauline scurried to take Gaius Antonius from Ushriya.

"Servius! It is you." She reached to hug him.

"Lena Ushriya. You are looking well. Better than the last time I saw you a short time ago," he smiled.

"Yes, I am mending well and looking forward to taking my leave. Though Pauline is suggesting I am not yet ready…"

"I think you should take her advice. I have delivered both the good news and the bad news to Ruth and Augusta. They will welcome your return, but only when you are well enough to travel. I will stay for a day or two, to make sure you and dominus Gaius

Antonius…." His voice trailed off as he approached the sleeping baby.

"His hair is black as night! And the silver mark shines through…"

"Like the moon?" Ushriya said.

"I was going to say stars, but the moon suits him, too. He will always know who he is. There will never be any doubt. He is the son of Ushriya, daughter of Emperor Claudius and Empress Agrippina of the Royal Roman Empire." Servius thought for a moment. "I'm just a slave and haven't knowledge of such things, but what will your royal title be? And Antonius'?" Servius asked.

"I know of no titles, nor do I expect one for either of us. Besides, who would bestow them? Nero thinks I'm not alive and we are in hiding from him." Ushriya became thoughtful. "Servius, since Alexis is no longer of this earth, it would be my pleasure if you would pick him up and lift him to let God know he will be raised by his mother."

Servius bent over and gently lifted the gurgling baby above his head. "It is your mother and all who love her that will see you grow to be an honorable man. It is my wish that you bring virtue to your family, that you will someday marry and seed children that will carry the tradition your mother will set forth before you." Beaming, Servius kissed the child and brought him to Ushriya.

"What a special blessing, my friend. It is true. Whatever happens in our lives, we will hold you and Ruth close." Ushriya smiled. "And when are we having a wedding?"

Servius looked to the ceiling. "Soon. Witnessing the birth of Alexis' son has brought an urge to be a father."

"I mourn Alexis every moment. I knew he was happy at

Antonius' birth, and I wish he could be here to watch him grow into a man," Ushriya said.

"He will be." Servius turned towards the window and gazed up at the clouds.

CHAPTER 42

Dominicus had a lectus brought into Ushriya's room so that Servius could care for her and baby Antonius. It gave Pauline a rest and time to spend with her family, whose residence was on site of the villa in the slave quarters. Exhausted, she had not left Ushriya's side since Antonius' birth.

Servius listened outside with Pauline as she gave instructions. "I have cleaned all of the cloth and linens needed for Gaius Antonius. The kitchen slaves know the foods domina Ushriya enjoys," Pauline said. "You may add whatever you like to hers. They will prepare it for you. Dominicus knows the villa well and will assist you. Domina Ushriya usually rests with Antonius after the sun is at its highest. The guards are acquainted with your presence, so they will nod as you pass. Make yourself comfortable in the baths. There are bathing oils and slaves to help you. Outside the villa are the vineyards. Both Emericus and Gustavus know you are here at the villa."

"Pauline, I have been a slave all of my life. I am not accustomed to this. Such grand treatment is not needed," Servius said.

"Domina is well known now. You are Ushriya's friend. No one at the villa knows you have been a slave. They will treat you as they have treated the sister of Emperor Nero…and they will appreciate the way you treat them. Many of them were abused by Emperor Nero's overseers. Sadly, Emericus and Gustavus have taken Nero's example."

"How will I know them? Emericus and Gustavus?" Servius asked.

"Yes, you have said their names correctly. They have been instructed to introduce themselves to you, but I am sure if you are with Dominicus, he will make the introduction," Pauline said. "And now, with your permission, dominus, I would like to be excused to return to my family. I have not seen them for a long while, and…I am eager for the kiss of my husband."

"I have never been called dominus…" Servius hesitated. "Yes, of course. Please, take your leave."

Pauline curtsied and left. Servius peeked inside the doors. Ushriya and Antonius were still resting, so Servius walked softly and stretched out on a lectus. Wondering how many slaves a villa this size required, he began to mentally inventory. Outside the window were well-cared-for plants and trees with manicured hedges, in addition to all the indoor plants. Servius knew there were vineyards and garum production. All needed many hands and strong backs. There were large rooms and a large culina. There were pools, both gigantic and small, as well as baths. There were passageways and porticos, statues, and marble floors, notwithstanding the numerous lamps that needed to be lit. All needed slaves. Servius guessed around two hundred slaves would be necessary to keep the villa in its current state. He slid to the side of the lectus towards the door, thinking he had some free time to roam the villa.

"Hello Servius." Ushriya leaned up on an arm, golden red hair cascading down around her shoulders as she rubbed her sleepy eyes. "Dominicus has brought a lectus for you. I thought it appropriate since you will be tending Antonius and me. Do you mind?"

"No, lena Ushriya. I will be most happy to be at your service." Servius poured some water. "Will dominus Antonius awaken soon?" He handed the water to Ushriya.

"Soon. He is always hungry, and my breasts are ready." She touched her full breasts. Servius cleared his throat.

"I think I will take a stroll around the villa. Dominicus is at the front entrance and said he would escort me when I was ready." Servius headed for the door. "Will either of you be needing anything while I am gone? I should return soon, but I did want to discuss our parting. Will one more day be enough to ready you for travel? Will that be satisfactory?" Servius' words tumbled out.

"Have Augusta and Ruth been told of both the death of Alexis and the birth of Antonius?"

"Yes, and as you would think, they were both grieved and elated."

Ushriya sighed. "I would like one more sunrise before we leave." Antonius was awake and gurgling. Ushriya picked him up.

"I will return soon," Servius muttered and quickly left.

Dominicus was at the front of the villa talking with the other guards when Servius found him. He looked up as Servius approached.

"You feeling well? You look a bit flushed," Dominicus observed.

"I'm well." He cleared his throat again and composed himself. "I would welcome a tour of the villa. I find it interesting how such a large domus maintains itself. Feeding and supporting so many slaves must be quite an effort unto itself."

"The slaves are housed over there." Dominicus pointed down the front of the villa. "On the other side of the pool. "The food they eat is all grown here in the gardens on the border around the pool and on the other side of their area. Would you like to start over there?"

"Please." Servius followed Dominicus down the walk past the immense pool. "What is the pool for? Bathing, exercising? It's the most impressive pool I've ever laid witness to."

"It is for ambience, but once when the emperor was not in residence, it became a bath for the slaves. Oh, what a time it was! It was in the heat of the summer and..." Dominicus winked at Servius. "...many babies were born in the ides!"

Walking in between the luxurious pool and the slave quarters, rows of fruit trees and grape vines lined the border.

"These are the slaves' to tend, harvest and eat," Dominicus motioned.

"The slaves are well cared for, I see," Servius probed.

"Our overseer and driver are harsh on the field slaves. They mimic Nero's cruelty."

"Can anything be changed?" Servius looked up to see two men in tunics approaching.

"Servius, this is Emericus and Gustavus. They oversee and drive the field slaves. Men, this is Servius, who is here at the villa with domina Ushriya."

The men nodded, eyeing Servius from head to toe. Both scowled and walked on. When they were out of hearing distance, Dominicus warned Servius.

"Be careful around them. They have been Nero's soldiers, have been in battle and themselves have taken Greeks to slave auctions for the emperor, therefore have become hardened. Human life is expendable to them."

"I can see that, but I am capable. What about the house slaves?" Servius asked.

"Pauline oversees the kitchen and house. I oversee the guards. We treat our slaves differently than Emericus and Gustavus. Pauline and I want the slaves at the villa to learn their jobs, to live and work here for a long time. We protect them from the emperor when he is here, which is less and less. Emericus and Gustavus see the slaves as muscle and backs. When they break, they are replaced. The field slaves and the villa slaves have separate quarters and don't mingle with each other," Dominicus said.

"I have been both," Servius said. "But I have been treated well. My father was a medicine slave for the same people I was, until the great fire in Rome."

"No one has told me you were a slave, but your manner was apparent. Fates change, as I see they have for you. I lived in Rome as a child. I have been here since the villa was built."

"Have you married?" Servius asked.

"Yes. But my wife died in the birth of our child and I've never since wanted to marry," Dominicus said.

"I was not sure domina Ushriya would survive when I arrived," Servius replied.

"Was Alexis her husband?" Dominicus wondered.

"No, but he would have been, had…"

"Nero's soldiers not killed him? They are ruthless; kill first, ask questions later. And Nero praises them for their undying loyalty. Will you take his place and marry domina?" Dominicus asked.

Servius stuttered, "Uh, no. I am betrothed to another."

"How unfortunate. She is quite a beauty." Dominicus kept walking and pointed to the formal gardens. "These are well kept for the emperor's view from his favorite room. This path leads straight past the columns into the room." They continued walking around the garden and turned left until they reached the baths. "If you're interested, the tepidarium is kept warm and the frigidarium is kept quite cold. Inform one of the kitchen slaves when you want a bath, and they will help with grooming," Dominicus said.

"Yes, Pauline told me. But as I said, I am not accustomed to such leisure or luxury. Where do the slaves bathe?"

"There are two baths in their quarters. One for the house slaves and one for the field slaves. When it is warm enough, they go into the ocean for a swim instead."

As they approached Ushriya's room, Dominicus said. "Please don't hesitate to ask if you have any further questions. Have you decided when you and domina will be leaving?"

"She would like to see one more sunrise," Servius replied.

"I will see you tomorrow then." Dominicus turned and took his leave.

Servius took a deep breath and opened the door. Ushriya giggled as she held Antonius, smoothing his dark hair, and cooing softly.

"Hello, Ushriya. Am I disturbing you?"

"Of course, not. Don't be so formal. Come. Sit." She patted her lectus. "See how strong this baby is!" Antonius grabbed her finger.

Servius walked to the lectus but did not sit down.

"Why aren't you…" Ushriya glanced up quickly. Their eyes locked; Ushriya's gaze followed him as he slowly sat down on the lectus. He leaned in to kiss her, then quickly stood up.

CHAPTER 43

Ushriya gathered Antonius, slowly laid him in his crib and snuggled soft bedding around him. Then abruptly, red faced, she spun around, charged towards Servius, and soundly slapped him across the face.

Stunned, Servius stood motionless.

"How DARE you think of betraying Ruth and Alexis! How dare you! What kind of a man are you? Certainly not the kind I have known. What did you think I would do? Fall into your arms and betray Antonius' father and my dear Ruth, who I might remind you is your betrothed?" Ushriya inhaled deeply. "Leave. You cannot sleep here tonight." Crossing her arms, she turned her back to him. "I am no longer the meretrix of your dreams. I will be addressed as domina by you and all men in my presence from this day forward."

"Domina, for a moment..."

"For a moment, I saw betrayal in your eyes," Ushriya cried, pointing toward the door.

"Forgive me, domina," Servius said softly.

"Get out. I can't look at you right now. If you leave immediately, you'll be back to the bakery and in Ruth's arms by sunset. I'll stay here until I feel well enough to travel with Antonius. I'm sure Dominicus will see me safely to Pompeii."

"Pauline…" Servius muttered.

"I can manage without her tonight. When I return to Pompeii, I will say nothing of this to Ruth and neither will you. You will tell her I insisted you return to help at the bakery, that I am fine and will return soon. I will take this to my end as will you. Now go!" Ushriya commanded.

Servius turned slowly and left.

With long sighs, Ushriya sat down on the lectus and shed long over-due tears. So many tears. Tears for Alexis. Tears for Ruth. Tears of betrayal. Tears of uncertainty. What did fate hold for her and her new baby son? One thing was certain; her future was no longer about her. Tears dried, she sat up straight, feeling a sudden surge of inner strength.

Mind beginning to race, she organized her thoughts. The ownership of the Lupanare and the bakery would provide enough income to buy a small place to live, but what would happen after that? Her contemplations drifted to the building of Eumachia in Pompeii. Eumachia was a priestess who had sponsored her own building; she was the patronus of the guild of fullers that provided the services of tanners, dyers, and clothing makers. It was an impressive building near the Forum. Ushriya remembered admiring the statue of Eumachia as she walked by and wondered how a woman had managed to rise to prominence in a male dominated world. From the first time she walked past the statue of Eumachia with Priscilla after arriving in Pompeii, she was curious what this woman must have encountered along her path to success. As the years went by, Ushriya learned the story of

Eumachia. She had donated to the community, raising her to a beloved benefactor in Pompeii, one so cherished that the fullers themselves commissioned the statue with an inscription that read: To Eumachia, daughter of Lucius, public priestess of Pompeian Venus, from the fullers. *Couldn't it have been inscribed without "daughter of Lucius"?* Ushriya thought.

A soft knock at the door jolted Ushriya from her thoughts. She used her toga to wipe her eyes.

"Domina. Are you well? Did you know Servius left in a rush?" Dominicus asked as he opened the door.

"I'm well. I have sent Servius back to Pompeii because I know he is needed at the bakery. I am not feeling well enough to travel with Antonius yet. However, I do expect I will leave tomorrow or the next day. Would you see me safely to Pompeii?"

"Yes, domina. It would be my pleasure. I know that Pauline is with family tonight. Will you be needing anything from the culina?" Dominicus replied.

"Please have one of the kitchen slaves bring a plate of food. I am quite famished, so anything will be fine. Antonius has quite an appetite and I can't eat enough to keep him content." Ushriya shook her head and smiled. "I would like to take Antonius for his first foray out of this room. Please inform the servi privati that we will be wandering the villa and not be alarmed. We will not be gone long."

"Mostly all know you now, domina." Dominicus bowed walking backwards out of the door.

Ushriya swaddled Antonius, straightened her toga and carried her baby son out into the world. Ushriya mused. *Antonius was born in Emperor Nero's villa. I was born in the palace of Emperor Claudius and Empress Agrippina. Welcome to the world, my son.*

By the time they had strolled around the large garden closest to their room, Antonius was asleep. A quiet baby and the warm sea breeze lulled Ushriya. Benches along the passageway invited her to sit and allow recent events to sink in. She clung to change and re-creation, but even for her, this all happened like the lightning in humid afternoons. It would be necessary to adjust quickly because the bakery and the Lupanare depended on her. Antonius squirmed, a gentle reminder that he was the most important change in her life, so she began the instinctive maternal rocking. Silently surveying the brilliance of the red frescoes behind the ornate benches, she felt content. *I miss you, Alexis. But I feel you. I know you will watch over us.* Tears once again spilled down her cheeks.

"Domina?" Pauline approached Ushriya.

"Pauline." she quickly dried her tears. "I thought you were with your family tonight."

"When one of the guards returned to the slave quarters, he told us Servius had left. I wanted to make sure you were well," Pauline reassured.

"Yes, I'm well. Please don't worry about me. I'm sitting with Antonius and thinking," Ushriya smiled.

"I will leave you, then," Pauline turned to leave.

"Please sit with me," Ushriya patted the bench.

"May I hold dominus Antonius?" Pauline asked.

Antonius awoke and Ushriya passed the squirming baby to Pauline. "Do you have children?"

"No. Once I was with child, but the child passed from this world and I almost died with her. When you were having such problems birthing, I was praying while Antonius fought for life. I've never been able to conceive since," Pauline saddened.

"I'm so sorry. Are you wed?"

"Yes, my husband has had children with other women in the slave quarters. He is one of the field slaves. His children look like him, so others know."

"Why do you stay married to him? Is he kind?" Ushriya asked.

"It is he who stays married to me. He says he still wants me. He does have a temper and occasionally beats me, but not often."

"Oh Pauline, 'not often' is too much. You said you missed his kiss. Did you go to be with him?"

"No, he has another woman right now. I say that so…oh, I don't know why I say that. Hope? I went to be with my aged mother who has served the villa since it was built. Before coming to the villa, she served the palace in Rome. She needs care and has lived far longer than expected. Empress Poppaea told my mother she could live out her days here. She was the Empress' famulus and favorite slave. Mother knows the villa so well; she is still able to teach the youngest slaves how to find what they need, and how to care for each room."

"What a gift to have such a mother. But it sounds like you, too, constantly nurture others. Now you have taken your time to see that I am well. You are a kind and generous woman, Pauline."

"No one has ever said that to me." Pauline smiled broadly.

Ushriya scooted across the bench and gently wrapped her arms around Pauline's shoulders. "I have seen nothing but righteousness from you." She leaned her head against Pauline's.

"If the people around you are as honorable as the slave, Servius, who came with Antonius' father, you must be a righteous woman and are indeed blessed," Pauline observed. Ushriya bristled at the mention of Servius. "He saved your life and the life of this beautiful child," she looked down at Antonius. "He knew what to do when you were losing so much blood. He is praiseworthy. Such a godsend."

Ushriya looked into Pauline's eyes. She hesitated thoughtfully, "Hmmm, you are so right. You have enlightened me and reminded me that we are all not without sin."

"How have I enlightened you?"

"Oh, I forget sometimes that we all sin, that forgiveness is freedom."

"Where did you get such wisdom?" Pauline asked.

Ushriya sighed. "It's not wisdom. It's listening with both ears to a teacher that taught of peace," Ushriya said.

"What a great teacher," Pauline answered naively.

Ushriya changed the subject, "Do you know I own the Lupanare, one of the biggest brothels in Pompeii?

"No domina." Pauline looked confused.

"I do. Over the time I have spent as a meretrix, I have become quite good at pleasing men, yet I grew increasingly angry at their lust. It drives everything they do, which caused a lack of sense to the exclusion of a woman's needs. Antonius' father, Alexis, was a male meretrix when I met him. He used women for profit, but somehow, he knew-and I learned-that this was not his character, but his fate. He taught me to trust and love him. I have lain with many men for profit. I understand there are men who allow lust to control their lives and then there are those who learn to control it. But occasionally, mortals, both men and women, who think they can control their lust, who aren't vigilant, succumb to temptation. I forgot that lesson."

CHAPTER 44

JUNE 8, AD 68

"Are you sure you feel well enough to travel, domina?" Pauline asked. "Has Antonius had time to nurse?"

"I feel fine. My son is temporarily satisfied and should sleep most of the way. I'm anxious to return to Pompeii." Ushriya passed her cloth bag to Pauline and swaddled Gaius Antonius from the cradle, then quickly scanned the room for any leftover belongings. "Seeing my friends will bring great joy, but we'll long for this luxury!" Ushriya followed Pauline out toward the entrance.

"Domina, would you mind taking one last stroll around to the culina? The slaves would like to bid you farewell," Pauline said.

"That is kind, but I am…"

"Just for a moment, domina. It won't take long," Pauline said.

When they reached the culina, the slaves lined up, each bowing to Ushriya, giving their blessings, along with wishes for safe travels.

"I, too, leave my blessings to each of you and your families and hope to see you again." When they left, Ushriya was moved. "How very kind," she said.

Pauline guided Ushriya back to the entrance where a carriage was waiting. Gold with red flowers and peacocks all along the ornamental rims at the top, it was similar, but not as splendid as the previous royal carriage. There were cushions to sit on, both front and back.

Dominicus jumped down from the carriage to collect their belongings. "The emperor will not use this carriage. He says it is not fit for a slave!" He quipped. Ushriya passed Antonius to Pauline as Dominicus helped her up the step. When she had settled in beside Dominicus, Pauline passed Antonius up to his mother.

"Well, it *is* fit for this slave." Ushriya gazed down at Pauline. "Thank you for all you have done for us. I will never forget you, or the place of my son's birth." She bowed her head. "Maybe when we know a time Nero is not in residence, we shall return to visit."

"What great joy that day will be, and to see how Gaius Antonius has grown!" Pauline gently touched Ushriya's toga and bowed. "Safe travels, my domina."

Dominicus shook the reins and turned the horses around. They trotted to the exit toward Pompeii.

The arms of Pompeii opened as the carriage made its way through the entrance. Dominicus was not aware there was an unwritten rule that carts could travel only one way until dark so as not to cause accidents and kept going. Ushriya smiled to herself. This was her grand return, and she wanted to enjoy it. Patrons gawked and bowed at the lavish carriage. Dogs and children scampered, allowing the carriage to pass. Ushriya knew how gossip traveled in Pompeii. Since Servius' return, the town had certainly heard that she was the sister of the emperor, that Alexis had passed from this earth, and that she was returning in a royal carriage with a baby whose blood came from the House of Augustus. The people greeted her as royalty.

"Such grandeur!" Dominicus commented, as the carriage rolled past the opulent houses of the elite.

"Yes, and just ahead is the Arch of Caligula, which has new meaning to me now that I know he is my avunculus." Ushriya shook her head. "It is hard to believe that the blood of so many tyrants flow within me."

They proceeded on past the Forum Baths to the new Central Baths. "A new bath for the elites. It was built after the earthquake," Ushriya said. "Just up ahead is the bakery. Please take us there."

When they reached the bakery, the slaves spilled out onto the street, along with Servius and Ruth. A raucous cheer went up. Dominicus recognized Servius and jumped down from the carriage to greet him.

"It is good to see you in your home, my friend!" Dominicus quickly turned to take Gaius Antonius from Ushriya. Ruth rushed to gather him into her arms.

"He's beautiful!" she cried.

Ushriya stepped down from the carriage and hugged Ruth as she held her son. "Isn't he? He looks just like his father."

"The streak of his mother shines through," Ruth said. "It is wonderful to see you. Come, let us get you inside. Will you make your home here, or at the Lupanare?"

"Oh, here at the bakery until I can buy a small home for Antonius and myself. I will need to visit the Lupanare tomorrow, so Antonius may meet his grandmother. She's lost Priscilla, and now Alexis. I know she is in mourning, so knowing her grandson will bring joy," Ushriya said, turning to Dominicus.

"Domina. It has been a pleasure. I hope to see you and dominus soon. If I leave now, I will arrive at the villa before the moon." He tipped his head and mounted the carriage.

"Safe travels!" Ushriya called and followed Ruth into the bakery. Servius stayed behind to make sure the horses had water and hay.

Ruth guided Ushriya up the stairs to a room she had prepared for her and the baby. Heavy steps came up behind them.

"Domina." It was Servius.

"Oh, were you were taking care of the horses?" Ushriya asked.

"Pauline asked Dominicus to put this in the back of the carriage as a gift from the servi privati of the villa." Servius placed the ornate cradle Gaius Antonius had slept in at the villa before her.

"Truly? Such a gift!" Ushriya exclaimed.

"Where would you like me to place it?" Servius asked.

"Beside my lectus, of course!"

"It stands out against the meager furniture of such a modest room. It is fit for royalty," Ruth declared. "Shall we build a domus to surround it?" she laughed.

"I have it on good word that it was made for a royal. For the baby Empress Poppaea lost at the hand of her abusive husband. But Antonius will bless it and pass it on to his son, who will be as honorable as he," Ushriya smiled. "What is in this bag?" she asked.

"Dominicus said it was the bedding made for the cradle and that you should have it as well," Servius replied.

Ushriya opened the bag, dumping purple silk bedding into the cradle along with a golden silk pillow. She gasped.

"Gaius Antonius is as royal as you," Servius said. Then, grasping Ruth's hand, "Shall we get back to work and let them settle in?"

"Servius, may I have a word with you?" Ushriya asked. "Ruth, please come back upstairs when you see Servius come down." They nodded. "And please close the door." Ruth nodded, closed the door behind her. When her footsteps could not be heard, Ushriya, still holding Antonius, sat down on the lectus. "Servius, I no longer hold anger in my heart for you."

"I'm so sorry...." Servius offered.

"I know and I also know you love Ruth, that you are a mortal, and you are one of the most honorable men I know. It was Pauline who reminded me you saved my life and that of Antonius. I will never forget that, ever. Now I am in a new position. I am a mother. I am a domina, an owner of establishments. I need honorable people around me. People I can trust. You are just that kind of person. Marry my dear Ruth. Have babies of your own, live here at the bakery."

"Thank you, domina." His eyes misted as he bowed his head.

"Now, go! Send Ruth up here before she thinks the worst!" Ushriya laughed.

When Ruth came into the room, Ushriya handed Antonius to her. "Please hold him while I make up his cradle." Ruth cuddled the baby and rocked him. "Soon you will have another baby. No one can replace dear David, but I see it in your soul, and I see it in Servius' eyes."

"You always were quite the visionary." Ruth kept rocking the baby.

Ushriya turned to Ruth. "Are you..." Ruth smiled.

"Yes. I suspected before you and Servius left for the villa, but now I am certain," Ruth said.

Ushriya ran to Ruth, encircled both her and Antonius, hugging them tightly. "Does Servius know?"

"Yes. I told him as soon as he got back. He is overcome with happiness."

"I was talking with Servius about taking more responsibility here at the bakery and that was what I wanted to talk to you about also. Since you are with child, I will look to you to oversee the bakery, to schedule and see to the slaves' needs. Are you feeling well enough?" Ushriya asked.

"Yes. I am. It seems my David's birth was easier than Antonius.' Servius told me how difficult it was for you; that you almost left us," Ruth said.

"Yes, it was, and if Servius hadn't been there, I might not be here. I'm feeling better every day. It's evident Antonius will be my only child. But you. You my dear, will have another easy birth and many children."

Ushriya took Antonius to the lectus and began nursing him. Ruth sat in a nearby chair. "I feel a need to get to the Lupanare. Were you able to see Melita while I was away?"

"Don't worry. She's doing quite well-once the order of things was put into place by none other than Augusta," Ruth stated.

Ushriya smiled, looking down at Antonius. "Your grandmother is a strong one. You have inherited *virtus*, my son!"

"Melita and the girls cleaned the entire building. There are schedules now and when they are unclean, the girls prepare food and go for walks in the sun. Keeping rosy cheeks and laughter among the girls is important to Melita. I think you will be pleased at what she has done. The girls are happy, and even though they still are at the mercy of men, they know they are earning their way to freedom. Melita also has a plan for young girls who come to the Lupanare in the future."

"How wonderful. I look forward to seeing them soon. And dear Ruth…" Ushriya smiled at her friend.

"Yes?" Ruth answered.

"We need to plan a wedding." Ushriya winked.

CHAPTER 45

JUNE 9, AD 68

With a loud clang, Augusta dropped the copper pot she had just reached from the shelf. "Ushriya! It is you!!" She rushed to gather Antonius, looking up at Ushriya through her tears. "My grandson! Ruth told me he is called Antonius?"

"Yes, Gaius Antonius. Alexis and I had agreed upon a name, should we have a boy," Ushriya smiled.

"Alexis," Augusta said with the recognition of a mother. "He has your streak, but I have held this same tiny face in my arms so many years ago. You have given me such a gift," Augusta sat down in the nearest chair, rocking her grandson, shedding tears of joy and sorrow. Ushriya crossed her arms watching Augusta's happiness.

Augusta, never being one to waiver, asserted, "I want to help you raise him. There is no reason for me to stay here at the Lupanare, now that Melita has embraced the responsibility of overseeing the daily tasks, even the marketing and cooking. It would give me great pleasure to help raise my grandson."

At once the door opened and Melita entered. "Lena!" She hugged Ushriya. "I am so glad to see you....and dominus Antonius!" She rushed to Augusta and sighed. "How precious."

"Thank you, Melita. It is nice to see you, too. I know Grandmother Augusta would not mind sitting with her grandson while you and I go for a stroll?" Ushriya glanced over at Augusta. Nodding, she didn't take her eyes from her grandson.

"Ushriya looped her arm through Melita's and guided her from the culina out the back door into the warm sun.

"You look wonderful, my friend," Ushriya said. As they left the Lupanare, Pompeii bustled alongside them.

"I am, lena. Because of you, I have life. I have purpose. And I have love," Melita beamed.

"Love?" Ushriya asked. "Tell me."

"Yes, a man who is a tanner at the building of Eumachia became my acquaintance on my walks past his mercantile. He is kind and required nothing of me other than friendship. As we grew to know each other, he joined me on my walks. He even brought flowers." Melita smiled broadly. "We have never lain together. He knows I am the overseer of the Lupanare, and he knows what occupies my days, yet he still desires my company. That is why he has grown in my favor so much," Melita glowed.

"My heart warms for you. Will you marry?" Ushriya asked.

"I don't know. For now, I'm enjoying knowing a man without laying with him because for the first time in my life, I know it is my choice. I have never known desire; it is new to me. But I desire him. He has not been forceful. He is gentle. And lena, he tells me of another way to live; that he has heard new teachings."

"Ah, yes, that warms my heart. The man you are acquainted with is a follower. I would like to meet him."

"His name is Timeus. His family has owned the tannery for generations; they have made protective clothing for the Roman army," Melita proclaimed.

"Please invite him to meet me," Ushriya said.

"Thank you, Iena. Now what was it you wanted to talk about?"

"Ruth shared with me the notable work you have accomplished while I was away; it pleases me very much. Having been a mistreated slave gives insight to the needs and dreams of the girls who have no other chance in life but to lay with men. It occurs to me you have begun to guide and teach young women to know that they, too, have inner strength and purpose as you have learned. It also occurs to me that since women have no value other than slavery, bearing children or weaving, we can build an undercurrent of power," Ushriya explained.

"What do you mean, 'power'?" Melita asked.

"Nurturing young women adds to their potential and thus, their power. When I feel nurtured and taught, I walk with confidence; now I'm seeing it in you. I have even seen it in Ruth, who had once been an elite, but was never given an opportunity to flourish," Ushriya said.

"Every day since you rescued us from the cages, I am stronger. Simple things such as food, exercise and sun do help," Melita laughed

"They are the foundations of health. I slept little last night dreaming of the potential of you and all the young women we have known. This is the beginning of your life and theirs. Have you heard of the ancient slave, Spartacus?" Ushriya asked.

"No."

"He was a gladiator who escaped slavery and began leading slaves to an uprising. Legend has it that he was angry at the treatment of slaves. Of course, his followers were men, but now I have a calling to apply this to women, in my own small way. As women, we have neither the physical strength nor the reputation to rise and create such chaos, but we can adapt. We can use our unique intelligence." Ushriya explained.

"Lena, are you suggesting we are more intelligent than men?" Melita asked.

Ushriya laughed. "We are not controlled by physical lust as much as men are. You see that here at the Lupanare. While consumed with their lust, that's all they think about. We can use the time, because we are not controlled, to become independent. I have listened to the wisdoms of Mary, a teacher of the lessons of Jesus of Nazareth, who was the one they call the Wonder Maker. She taught that men and women are equal spiritually; that their differences are temporary, solely while they are on this earth."

"Men and women, equal? What foolishness is that? They have physical strength. We do not. How can we overcome that?" Melita was confused.

"Slowly, carefully with thought, dignity and honesty. Mary said by following that which is good, the soul will follow its true spiritual nature and will not have to worry about the physical body. Do you understand what I am saying? We need to respect our true spiritual nature, then we will find the right path. By staying moral and just, we will *think* our way through any problem. I have an example. Remember a time you could not lift a heavy burden into the cart." Melita nodded. "If there was no man around, what did you do? You propped a piece of wood from the cart to the street and dragged it up into the cart. Without physical strength, we must think our way out of situations. Do you understand?"

"Yes. I do. It is a bit overwhelming. Lena, I have been a prostitute for as long as I can remember. What you are saying is above anything I have ever known, but I trust you, so call on me to do whatever is in your heart," Melita said.

"Persist in what you are doing. I will be here, but you have already shown such mercy and love to the girls of the Lupanare that you need little guidance. Follow what is in your own heart." Ushriya's arm tightened through Melita's as they walked. Both were silent, allowing the heaviness of the moment to sink in. Ushriya knew this was significant for Melita, but she also knew her nature. Melita would be diligent in spurring young women who could only see themselves as prostitutes, to become whatever they could dream.

"Would you like to see what the girls and I have done?" Melita asked as they entered the Lupanare.

Ushriya nodded. Turning into the front door, she heard the gruff voices of men who had already drunk too much wine by the time the sun was high. The side door un-bolted, and a large man sprang from nowhere and hurled one of the drunkards into the street.

Melita giggled. "Since Emperor Nero…" Melita paused, "…your brother, closed the gladiator school and they are no longer able to train, I asked some of them if they would help keep order here when those that decide to abuse our girls can't restrain themselves…either from lust or wine. Word is spreading that our girls are clean, not bruised, and not mistreated by our patrons. The gladiators can enjoy themselves with one girl every time the sun comes up and that is their pay, but they must be respectful. It is good for the Lupanare, and good for the gladiators."

"Quite a brilliant idea. Where did you get such a notion?" Ushriya asked.

"I thought about strength versus strength. Turning lust back on itself for protection, came to me when one of the gladiators beat a drunken man who was attacking one of the girls. I thought about how the attacked girl, appreciated the gladiator's actions. When next I saw him, I asked if he and some fellow gladiators would be willing to help protect the girls in exchange for services," Melita said confidently.

"And he agreed. What a splendid example of what I was explaining to you. Do you see what you did? You thought of a solution when you didn't have the physical strength yourself. You are more clever than you think," Ushriya said .

"Now I have at least one gladiator here at all times, and the girls feel safe," Melita added.

"How wonderful. I especially like that word is spreading the Lupanare is clean and safe." Ushriya sighed. "One more thing before I must leave. My breasts are bursting!" she laughed. "Augusta had just told me she would like to help with Antonius when you came into the culina. I could use the help. Would she be missed?"

"Of course she would be, but we have divided work and schedules. Augusta has taught them well."

Returning to the Lupanare, they found Augusta still rocking Antonius as he suckled her finger.

"He's missed you, but I put a bit of goat's milk on my finger to calm him," she said when she saw the door open. "I should be cooking, but I can't put my grandson down." Augusta smiled.

Ushriya laughed. "I want you to know I heard what you said

when we arrived. There is nothing I-nor your son-would love more than to have Antonius' grandmother never lay him down!" Augusta's face beamed and tears again tumbled down her cheeks. Ushriya scooped Antonius from her and Augusta followed. "I am assuming we are in agreement?" She nodded. "You will live with us at the bakery until we find a suitable domus."

"May I have some time to make sure the girls are well?" Augusta said, drying her tears.

Melita stepped forward. "You have trained them well. We will all miss you, but your grandson needs you. Take some time to put your things together, and Servius can escort you to the bakery at next sunrise." Ushriya was impressed at Melita's poised tone.

"Very well. Sweet Augusta, we'll see you after sunrise," Ushriya turned with Antonius to Melita. "Thank you. And please know that I am proud of you. We have come a long way, my friend." Antonius began fussing. "We will take our leave. This little man is hungry once again." Ushriya hugged Melita and headed back to the bakery.

CHAPTER 46

JUNE 13, AD 68

"Domina Ushriya!" Servius took two stairs at a time. Out of breath, he gasped, "Nero is dead!"

"What? Where did you hear this?" Ushriya went to lay Antonius down.

"A farmer who delivers spelt from Rome told us. He said the gossip in Rome is that Nero committed suicide. He heard it from a soldier who was traveling from Rome."

Ushriya heaved a sigh. "He didn't seem like he was planning to take his life when I saw him but ten suns ago. He was, however, quite mad."

"Word has spread that he rode on horseback to his freedman's country house, to gather his wits."

"Why did he need to gather his wits? And why would he go on horseback rather than using the royal carriage?" Ushriya was perplexed.

"The farmer said he had asked some tribunes and centurions to accompany him, but they declined. He must have known there was a growing hatred for him. We have seen it. You have seen it. Gossip says he asked for anyone to go with him to the country house, but none did. They asked Nero if it was such a sad thing for him to die; he must have taken heed to the message. The farmer said the Senate could no longer tolerate Nero's debauchery and declared him a public enemy."

"How did he end his life?" Ushriya asked.

"With a dagger, they say. It's certain he is dead because those that detested Nero in Rome are celebrating with great joy."

"Shall I go to Rome? Am I known by the elites? Who is to succeed Nero?" Ushriya's thoughts spilled.

"No, you shouldn't go to Rome because the farmer also said there is also chaos among Nero's supporters. You, of all people, would be in great danger. Since there is no heir, the Senate pronounced someone who is called, Galba, as the successor. Do you recognize the name?"

"I do. Ruth and Marcus might have known him; obviously, he survived the fire," Ushriya replied, cattily. "I've heard the name while passing through the Forum in Rome. Intentional eavesdropping on the elites was something I enjoyed immensely when I wandered through crowds of huddled togas. They paid no attention to me; I was a slave. But I do remember hearing the name. He was a consul, not of noble heritage, but of wealth. He must have been selected temporarily." She thought further. "I agree there's no need to travel to Rome."

Antonius' piercing cries sent Ushriya to the cradle. "The arrival of Augusta can't come soon enough." With a deep sigh, she raised the baby to her shoulder patting his back as she lightly bounced across the room.

"How often are you feeding him?" Servius asked.

"It truly feels like he is hungry all the time, and he is still not content," Ushriya frowned.

Servius laughed. "It may be that he needs heartier food. Soft grain would soothe him for longer periods. You do look tired. I will get some finely milled grain, mix it in goat's milk." He turned to go.

"Before you go, Servius."

"Yes."

"I know you are going to be a father." Ushriya smiled. "You had said that having a family was in your heart."

"Yes, I'm so pleased, I feel I might burst!" Servius exclaimed.

"I told Ruth we had better plan a wedding."

"Ruth and I have discussed our betrothal. A small wedding with our bakery and Lupanare family would be perfect."

"A grand celebration it would be!" Ushriya declared.

A loud slam from the door at the bottom of the stairs echoed through the bakery.

"Where may I find Ushriya?" a man asked. Servius and Ushriya both recognized Dominicus' deep voice. He did not wait for an answer. Someone must have pointed up the stairs.

"Dominicus!" Servius and Ushriya yelled simultaneously.

"What are you doing here, my friend?" Servius said.

"It is domina Ushriya I've come to see." He stared intently at Ushriya.

"So good to see you..."

"Nero's soldiers have come to the villa," Dominicus was serious.

"We know that Nero is dead," Ushriya added.

"The soldiers came to the villa to see you. They know there are many servi privati, and the soldiers that were with Nero the last time he was in residence at the villa know of you. They are worried Galba will overtake the villa," Dominicus stated.

"Why didn't *they* come to Pompeii?" Ushriya asked.

"They don't know you live in Pompeii but knew that Pauline or I would know where to find you."

Ushriya ran her fingers through the silvery lock on her forehead. "This doesn't make sense."

"They told me to send word you must return to the villa."

"I have Antonius…" she began. "Who are the orders coming from?"

Dominicus did not answer. "I have the royal carriage with enough room for Antonius and Servius if he is to come. We can leave as soon as you are ready. Hopefully, we will arrive at the villa long before the sun sets," Dominicus spoke rapidly.

"Let me think. This is happening so fast." Ushriya quickly sorted it out, glanced at Servius, and began giving orders. "Please go to the Lupanare and fetch Augusta. Tell her what has happened, and that I would like her to travel with Antonius and me. Servius, you will stay here with Ruth. I am confident Dominicus will take care of us."

"What has happened?" Ruth asked halfway up the stairs. Servius started down the stairs explaining, talking past her.

Ushriya called after him, "Servius, will you take the cradle and put it back in the carriage? Ruth, will you help me gather my things? Oh, and Servius, some of the soft grain to mix with milk you told me about would be greatly appreciated." She began stuffing clothing in one bag and Antonius' things in another. "Ruth, I am so sorry to leave these soiled cloths. I will begin teaching Antonius to use a latrine pot as soon as he can walk!"

"Ushriya, don't worry about anything here. Returning to the villa under the orders of the soldiers must frighten you." Ruth supposed.

"Dear Ruth, I went to meet my mad brother when I was big with child. I pushed a baby out, almost died and recovered. What could possibly be worse than that?" Ushriya softly hugged her friend. "You don't worry either. Dominicus will take care of us. You have not met Pauline, but she is the famulus of the villa and a strong woman. She will also take care of us," Ushriya assured her. Having you here to oversee the bakery and keep the patrons' content will calm my concerns. Please go to the Lupanare next sunrise and tell Melita what has happened, and why I have gone. She will have some idea after Servius fetches Augusta, but she should hear it from you; let her know she has my utmost confidence, as do you. Please support each other, and I will be back as soon as I know why I am needed at the villa," Ushriya said.

Ruth nodded as she collected the bags. Ushriya swaddled Antonius while Servius came back into the room to gather the cradle.

"I am thinking we may not need the cradle if I am at the villa for only a short while." Ushriya situated Antonius up on her shoulder.

"Dominicus has said there is room. Loading it into the carriage is an easy chore for me." Servius said.

Ushriya nodded. "Where is Augusta?"

"She is waiting at the carriage with Dominicus. He loaded her bag; I heard them laughing, so I think they have become acquainted." Servius smiled, lifted the cradle onto his shoulder and easily carried it down the stairs. Ruth took the bags, Ushriya following with Antonius.

Augusta clutched her grandson as they reached the carriage,

while Dominicus helped Ushriya up into the seat next to him. He sensed that she would want to sit in the front. Servius handed a small bag up to Ushriya: the soft grain.

"Thank you, my friend," Ushriya said.

Ruth held Antonius as Servius assisted Augusta into the back, then Ruth handed the baby to his grandmother. With only eyes for Antonius, she paid no attention to her luxurious surroundings.

Ruth whispered to Servius, "Ushriya glows with happiness."

"As do you my dear." Servius smiled, putting his arm around her shoulders.

"We'll be back as soon as possible," Ushriya shouted as Dominicus expertly took the reins and turned the horses. Ruth and Servius waved.

Although the travel was short to the villa, Ushriya felt anxious. Nero was unpredictable, and even though he was dead, she wondered what problem he had left that required her attention so quickly? Word was spreading about Nero's long-lost sister, and she knew that her one true claim to his legacy was the white streak that had haunted her all her life. She tossed her head, fortuitously freeing the silver lock of hair.

"Do you have any idea why I have been called to the villa?" Ushriya asked Dominicus.

"I have some idea." Dominicus stared straight ahead.

CHAPTER 47

JUNE 13 AD 68

Dominicus guided the horses to the front of the villa just as the house slaves lit the lamps before any sign of dark. The villa offered a spectacle of luxury at night with all the lamps lit to highlight each fresco and accent the paths around the gardens. Nightfall here was truly Ushriya's favorite time. The lights were enjoyed by all who walked the grounds, even if they were lit for one man.

Dominicus motioned to the slaves waiting at the entrance to help with the carriage. The horses calmed when they recognized the men who took hold of their bridles. Dominicus released the reins and immediately helped Ushriya down. Pauline rushed over to meet them.

"Domina, Antonius!" Her head swiveled.

Ushriya was out of the carriage. She hugged Pauline and motioned up to Augusta. "Pauline, this is Augusta, Antonius' grandmother."

"Alexis' mother. Ah yes, such fortune to have this grandson. How nice to meet you," Pauline nodded.

"You as well," Augusta said.

"She has graciously offered to help me with this young man! And I will tell you now, just on the carriage ride, how wonderful that is!"

Augusta handed Antonius to Pauline, then Dominicus helped her down.

"It's only been a few days, but I have missed you both!" Pauline exclaimed. Dominicus signaled to the slaves to unload the carriage.

In the distance, Ushriya could see two of Nero's soldiers emerging in the twilight from around the corner by the far garden. Their tunics were red, without helmets or metal armor.

"Here they come," Ushriya said under her breath. Dominicus placed himself in front of her.

"We will follow you to the first waiting room." Dominicus addressed the soldiers in a commanding voice. "There you may address domina Ushriya."

Ushriya stepped forward. "Thank you, Dominicus." She spoke to the soldiers, "I am Ushriya. I will listen to your message." Then turning to Augusta, "Please follow Pauline with Antonius. She will show you to the room we used while last here." Dominicus submitted, following Ushriya.

Turning to the left, the soldiers seemed to know where they were going. They turned, following a path around the small garden to one the largest of rooms in the villa. Immaculately decorated, it boasted frescoes of trees and foliage, of men and women dressed and undressed, of animals, both winged and wild. Ushriya realized she had become a bit used to the opulence.

Having explored this room with Antonius on their first walk after he entered this world, she went to the chair she coveted. Stationing herself, Ushriya sat on a tyrian purple silk cushion. Dominicus stepped behind her. The soldiers remained standing.

Ushriya did not wait. "I realize it is now known I am the

sister of Nero. I'm here to meet with you because of my brother's death, am I not? What dilemma am I to hear? I have no power. I am aware Galba is the new emperor and I fear he is quite busy calming the Roman Empire. I hope you are not wasting your time. He will need your service."

Both soldiers approached Ushriya and bowed deeply. The soldier with the most prominent regalia stepped forward.

"We are not here at the behest of the emperor, domina. We are here at the directive of Emperor Nero's most trusted confidant, his freedman, Phaon. Before his death, the emperor disclosed to Phaon that he had a sister and that she was the last blood of the line of Caesars. Nero thought she was no longer of this world. Phaon has known of this villa for many years, that Empress Poppaea loved it and had prepared to have her baby here. Phaon said Emperor Nero would want it to fall to his bloodline, and since you are, indeed, alive, the villa should fall to you, as his only blood. We have been sent here to inform you that as of this day, you own this villa and all rights and privileges shall fall to you, as well as all debt and service."

Ushriya gasped and turned to Dominicus. He nodded with a smile.

"How did you know I was alive?" Ushriya asked.

"Deliveries to the villa from Roman merchants spread rumors that you were alive," the soldier answered.

"I see. And what proof have you that this message is authorized?" Ushriya was dazed.

"Phaon said he thought you may doubt our message. Do you read?"

"Yes, of course."

"We brought a message from Phaon with explicit writings from the Senate that will be recorded by a quastor and housed in the tabularium adjacent to the Temple of Jupiter upon your agreement. He has invited you to come to Rome to speak with him if you have further doubts." The soldier handed the papyrus to Ushriya. She opened it and slowly read it.

"Can you understand why I would be doubtful?" Ushriya asked.

"Yes. Phaon knew the villa needed someone to oversee and maintain it, and the most logical person is the sister of the deceased owner. He has said that if you are unable to come to Rome, he will visit the villa, as soon as it quiets, to reassure you that this is what Nero would have wanted. In the meantime, he would like your assurance that you will preside over the villa. It is yours. It is just a matter of you agreeing, at which time a parchment will be transferred to the tabularium." The soldier stepped back. "What message would you like us to relay to Phaon?"

"Please tell him I am honored and will preside over the villa. I know the slaves here need reassurance and direction. I would appreciate Phaon's visit at his convenience, to reassure me that what you are saying is true. I will hold the message on the papyrus as my witness until his arrival." Ushriya sat taller in the chair.

Both soldiers bowed. "It is our pleasure. We will stay by our horses and leave at sunrise."

After they had left the room, Ushriya's shoulders dropped. "I am in disbelief." Long shadows stretched through the windows.

"Domina, I thought this might be what they were going to say. They had some idea that I had a notion, so they swore me to secrecy. I am delighted, as the other slaves will be, that the villa has fallen to you."

"Where do I start? I have never in my life overseen…or owned such a…a…"

"Large villa? Everyone knows their place. They have been working long enough that they know their tasks. I would recommend beginning with gathering all the slaves together and telling them the news. Pauline had the notion also, so there will be no surprise there. But Augusta might be a bit overtaken," Dominicus laughed.

Ushriya rose and walked to the window. "Dominicus, would you mind if I had a few moments alone?"

"Not at all, domina. Is there something you would like me to do now?"

"Yes, send word to the slaves that I would like to meet in the large garden at sunrise."

"My pleasure." He bowed, leaving Ushriya to reflect on what had just happened.

Gazing into the twilight, she thought of the family she embraced; not blood, but family just the same; Justine and Hanoch, her brothers; Cyrus and Julius; then Marcus, Ruth, and David, then Priscilla, Augusta, the slaves at the Lupanare and her love, Alexis; then Servius and all the bakery slaves; and the most precious of all, Antonius. And now, the villa servi privati. The house slave servants: they would become family. She hadn't prayed for a while but dropped to her knees. *Lord, please help me find the strength to guide and provide for all these people who are your children, just I am. Help me lead them to find better lives and help me lead them to find you. In your name.*

Ushriya rose and took three deep breaths. Wandering through the lit passages without losing her way, she found Augusta,

Antonius, and Pauline in the room where Antonius was born. She slipped in the door.

"This baby boy is so hungry. He is going to eat my finger!" Augusta laughed.

"Are you well, domina? You look worried." Pauline rushed to Ushriya's side.

"I am worried, and you might have a notion of why."

"So, it's true. I'm pleased," Pauline said.

Ushriya smiled.

"What is my daughter worried about?" Augusta asked.

With a deep sigh, Ushriya said, "How would you feel about living here at the villa with Antonius and me?"

Augusta jumped up, placed Antonius in the cradle and marched to Ushriya. "What are you saying?"

"The villa has been left to me, as the sister of Emperor Nero. It seems we are needed and will live here."

"You don't look pleased about this. Come sit. Tell me." Augusta guided her to a lectus.

"You know my life. I've been a slave, a prostitute, a merchant, now a mother. I don't know how to oversee a villa of this size." Ushriya let her defenses down and the tears fell. Augusta's maternal arms comforted her. "I need Alexis," she cried.

"Let me tell you something," Augusta was firm. "Of all the people around you, he was most impressed by your strength. Don't forget you entered this earth with the blood of the Caesars. One thing is for certain. I have never seen you not be able to do what is set before you. When you came to the Lupanare, you were a waif: dirty, lost, and hungry. I gave you a bath and a tunic and you have never looked back. All those things you were, you still are. Where you have come from and what you have learned has prepared you for what is before you. You will make sense of the task at hand and become stronger. And my dear, you have returned to who you truly are: royal." Ushriya fell into Augusta's arms, sobbing.

CHAPTER 48

Antonius was restless. Augusta snored all night, so sleep was elusive. At last, Ushriya fell into a deep slumber until bright sunlight shone through the window. Bounding from the lectus, Ushriya recalled the importance of this day. Her heart raced.

"Augusta," she whispered. "Please use the goat's milk Pauline brought last night for Antonius. Mix it with a bit of fine grain in the bag by the washing bowl. Changes of cloth are in the other bag beside it. I am going to meet with the servi privati of the villa. Since my breasts will be aching, I will return soon." She scooped on her sandals, ran a brush through her hair, pulled it back and tied it with string.

Augusta raised from the lectus and rubbed her eyes. "Don't worry! Pauline showed me the way to the culina, and I have been introduced to the kitchen slaves. Go. Become the domina of the villa." She motioned toward the door.

Ushriya laughed. "Yet I have no time to make myself look like a domina." She quickly went to the cradle, kissed Antonius, blew a kiss to Augusta, and slipped out the door.

Several hundred slaves gathered in the magnificent garden facing the ocean. Most had never been this close to the villa; Ushriya could sense their awkwardness. They fidgeted, arms crossed, looking from one to another. Staying in groups separated by their labor, they did not mingle. Frightened by what might be coming, they were quiet and anxious. Dominicus had fashioned a platform so Ushriya could speak over the crowd.

"Please," Ushriya said to Dominicus. "I want to stand and speak in the middle." She walked into the crowd slowly, each slave stepping aside with reverence. "Sit everyone. Sit where you are." All looked to Dominicus and Pauline for permission. They both sat and the entire crowd began to follow their example, settling where they were. Ushriya stood. "I am Ushriya. I know word has spread that my brother, Nero, has died." The crowd stayed silent. "The villa has fallen to me, and I choose to oversee it in a different manner. I want this villa to be a place where you may all work and raise your families, but there will be one big change. You will be paid." A murmur went over the crowd. "You will all have the ability to buy your freedom if you so desire, and once you have achieved your freedom, you may stay at the villa or leave to lead your life wherever you choose." Dominicus and Pauline both stood, clapping. The entire crowd stood with uncertainty and clapped without feeling.

"May I, domina?" Dominicus asked. Ushriya nodded as he turned to the crowd of confused slaves and asked them to be seated once more as he explained, "Domina Ushriya has given you all a great gift; you will be given coins as you work. As you receive them, you may save them and choose to exchange your coins for your freedom," he said in his deepest booming voice.

"What are coins?" a field slave shouted. "We have never been given 'coins'."

Dominicus took a coin from the bag around his belt and held it up to the sun. It glistened. "This is a coin. It has value. Your work has value. Now you will be given coins of value when you work, so that you may exchange them for something you want, like your freedom. Many of you have taken coins to the market to give to the merchants, and they have given you things such as bread, meat or fruit."

Finally understanding Dominicus' simple version, the slaves rose to their feet and began clapping, laughing, and cheering. Dominicus nodded to Ushriya. She smiled and raised her hands for silence.

"I have another change. Kindness, from Emericus and Gustavus." She side glanced over at the two and they turned away. The crowd cheered again, then quickly settled. "Both Dominicus and Pauline know this and will carry out my wishes. I expect everyone to stay with their work as it is for now. Since you are deciding your own destiny, either staying here at the villa or leaving once you have enough coins, I expect your work to be done as it has been-with one exception. Discipline will not mean a receiving a beating, but it will mean you will not receive your coins." Ushriya smiled. "Working well assures your pay." Another cheer went up. "My infant son Gaius Antonius, his grandmother, Augusta, and I will be living here at the villa; if you hear the cries of a baby through the passageways, you will know...." Ushriya laughed and the slaves relaxed. "It will also be my pleasure to know you one-by-one. Please introduce yourselves when we meet in the corridor, and on occasion, I will follow Dominicus out to the fields and the slave quarters. That is all I have for now. Be well, my friends." A thunderous applause followed as Ushriya made her way back through the crowd followed by Dominicus and Pauline.

"Very well done, domina," Pauline said.

Dominicus paused. "Domina, a moment?"

"Of course."

"Before the soldiers left, they said they met an old woman on the road to the villa. They asked her why she was traveling alone, as there are bandits on the roads. Then they asked her destination. She said she was not afraid, that she was walking from Rome to the villa di Poppaea Sabina in Oplontis. They left some bread and water with her and she continued on to the villa."

"I wonder who she is and why she is walking the long distance. Should we send a cart to meet her?" Ushriya thought aloud.

"She didn't give them any other information. The soldiers said she should be here by sunset, but since she is a very old woman, she must be exhausted; I will send a cart," Dominicus said.

"Very well. I am going to go feed a hungry baby," Ushriya said. "Please tell me when the woman arrives."

Pauline said, "It is not necessary for you to bother, domina. We will take care of the woman."

"I should like to meet her. She has walked a long way," Ushriya said.

"Pauline, this is the woman who walked from Rome." Dominicus escorted the elderly woman into the side room from the front of the villa.

"You have walked such a distance. You must be hungry. I will prepare a plate of fruit and bread," Pauline said.

"Thank you for your kindness, but I would like to see domina. I have traveled to meet her," the old lady whispered, softly smiling.

Dominicus stepped forward, glancing at Pauline. "I will announce your arrival." He turned and left.

Augusta heard a soft knock at the door and went to gather Antonius from nursing. Ushriya covered herself, passing the sleeping baby to his grandmother.

"Dominicus." Ushriya motioned him in.

"The lady from Rome is here and would like to meet you. She says it is you she has come to see."

"How did she know I was here? And how does she know who I am?" Ushriya wondered aloud.

"She doesn't say, only that it is you she is here to see."

"Please bring her to me. I am curious to meet her"

Dominicus returned with the small, elderly woman who had walked all the way from Rome.

When her warm brown eyes met Ushriya's, a gentle smile emerged as she walked slowly toward her. Ushriya rose.

"It is you. You are the one with the mark of the blessing of God; the one with the white streak in your golden red hair I have heard of who has gathered the followers and allowed your slaves to become freedmen and women if they so choose." The old woman's thoughtful eyes locked on Ushriya.

"Yes, I have done those things," Ushriya said as the woman reached to touch her hair.

"And word of your inspiration has spread, even to Rome. I have heard of a bakery and a brothel, and now the villa, I see." The old woman reached for Ushriya's hand. "You are a woman, yet, in all things, your heart does not stop showing strength and compassion to others."

"I appreciate your praise, but I believe my life has been planned by God. It is He who..." Ushriya stammered.

"Yes, that is most certainly true...but you have also listened to the Great Teacher. The One who taught the ways of righteousness and truth."

"Do you speak of the one they call the Wonder Maker, Jesus of Nazareth?" Ushriya asked.

"Yes. The One I have followed all my life; the One I have loved. The One I have known."

Ushriya grasped her delicate hand tenderly. "I am Ushriya."

In a soft whisper, the old woman said, "And I am Mary. Mary of Magdala."